PRA

KENNETH MARK HOOVER

"The Old West wasn't all darkness and murder, unless your name is John Marwood, a man, by his own assessment, 'with a demon coiled like a watch spring in his marrow.' Simply put—He is a killer. Yet that isn't the half of him, and his true nature and his destiny alike remain a secret even to himself. Kenneth Mark Hoover tells the story of an immortal champion in an American West that never was, and so is all the truer for it."

—**Richard Parks**, author of *Yamada Monogatari: To Break the Demon Gate*

"With *Quaternity*, Hoover paints a sparse and unflinching landscape, taking the reader down the dark trail his protagonist John Marwood rides while seeking what is lost and unremembered. As the gnawing hunger in his soul drives Marwood toward his ultimate destiny, the west as it was unfurls before the reader under Hoover's steady hand. If you love realistic westerns and dark fantasy, this is the book for you!"

—**Michael Merriam**, author of *Last Car to Annwn Station* and *The Horror at Cold Springs*

"With a voice both sparse and poetic, Hoover takes on the hoary cliches of Western fiction and dismantles them one by one. In *Quaternity*, Hoover's unflinching look at evil will challenge everything you know about yourself and the world we live in."

—**Melissa Lenhardt**, author of *Stillwater*

"Hoover does it again. *Quaternity* starts with a bang and doesn't quit until a satisfying conclusion. This is my kind of weird west. Love it!"

—**Jennifer Brozek**, author of *Apocalypse Girl Dreaming* and *Never Let Me Sleep*

"In *Quaternity*, his second outing in the richly evocative Haxan series, Kenneth Mark Hoover once again plunges us headlong into the bloody-minded fury of the Old West, mixing the raw violence of time and place with the eerie tenderness of a fantastical fever dream to gripping, visceral effect."

—**Melia McClure**, author of *The Delphi Room*

"Kenneth Mark Hoover's vivid prose delivers an unflinching look at the violent horrors and the stark beauty of the Old West."

—**Amy Raby**, author of *Assassin's Gambit* and *The Fire Seer*

"Twice as vicious as its predecessor, *Quaternity* is operatically mythological, a poetic, doom-laden Western soaked in blood and frenzy. This Cormac McCarthyesque terror fantasia of a prequel both frames and outstrips Hoover's *Haxan*, lending it the perfect amount of context, as Hoover's literally eternal protagonist Marshall John Marwood excavates his past in order to accept his future. Driven by philosophical musings both monstrous and humane, Marwood tracks an interlocking chain of massacres towards a lost city founded on "the long blood of violence," the same dark current underlying almost everything in Hoover's lawless, ultra-violent frontier . . . yet certain spots of brightness still occur here and there, inevitable collisions between fate and free will, love and justice. This is a hard book to read, but you'll savour its bitter aftertaste."

—**Gemma Files**, author of the Hexslinger series, and *We Will All Go Down Together: Stories of the Five-Family Coven*

QUATERNITY

KENNETH MARK HOOVER

ChiZine Publications

FIRST EDITION

This book is a work of fiction. Names, characters, places, and incidents are either a product of the author's imagination or are used fictitiously. Any resemblance to actual events, locales, or persons, living or dead, is entirely coincidental.

Distributed in Canada by
Publishers Group Canada
76 Stafford Street, Unit 300
Toronto, Ontario
M6J 2S1 Canada
Toll Free: 800-747-8147
e-mail: info@pgcbooks.ca

Distributed in the U.S. by
Diamond Comic Distributors, Inc.
10150 York Road, Suite 300
Hunt Valley, MD 21030
Phone: (443) 318-8500
e-mail: books@diamondbookdistributors.com

Library and Archives Canada Cataloguing in Publication

Hoover, Kenneth Mark, 1959-, author

Quaternity / Kenneth Mark Hoover.

Issued in print and electronic formats.

ISBN 978-1-77148-361-2 (pbk.) -- ISBN 978-1-77148-362-9 (ebook)

I. Title.

PS3608.O625Q38 2015   813'.6   C2015-900096-3
C2015-900097-1

CLEARLY PRINT YOUR NAME ABOVE IN UPPER CASE

Instructions to claim your free eBook edition:
1. Download the BitLit app for Android or iOS
2. Write your name in **UPPER CASE** on the line
3. Use the BitLit app to submit a photo
4. Download your eBook to any device

Edited by Andrew Wilmot
Proofread by Michael Matheson

CHIZINE PUBLICATIONS
Toronto, Canada
www.chizinepub.com
info@chizinepub.com

Canada Council for the Arts   Conseil des Arts du Canada

We acknowledge the support of the Canada Council for the Arts which last year invested $20.1 million in writing and publishing throughout Canada.

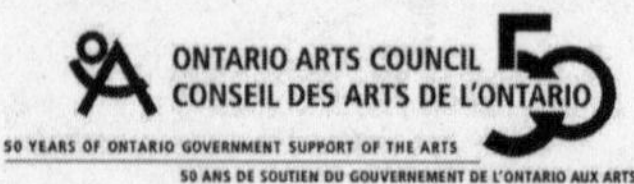

Published with the generous assistance of the Ontario Arts Council.

Printed in Canada

For John Kenneth Arbour

QUATERNITY

The Sunset of Destruction, the Ashes of the West

"I do not point to the evil and pain of existence with the finger of reproach, but rather entertain the hope that life may one day become more evil and more full of suffering than it has ever been." —Friedrich Nietzsche

"I foresee that man will resign himself each day to new abominations, and soon that only bandits and soldiers will be left." —Jorge Luis Borges

"Hell is truth seen too late." —Thomas Hobbes

PART I

The Long Red Light of the West

CHAPTER 1

The killer summered in Camp Eagle Pass, digging irrigation ditches for a plate of beans a day and found. In Galveston he rode guard for a mule train shipping dry freight back up through Texas. After falling out with the owner, he quit the salt sea thunder for life in the interior.

The following months were ones of gnawing hunger and wanton theft for John Marwood. He walked into a Waco bank with his gun drawn. For five days he fought a running battle along the winding Brazos River and scattered oak mottes. Shotgun empty. Two cartridges left in his single-action .44 calibre Colt Dragoon. He lost the posse in the thick live oak and crumbling hill country of central Texas.

On the first of November 1868, he rode into Neu-Braunfels. Raw sleet pelted his head and piled like torn rags in the road ruts. At an Indian trading post he upgraded his outfit. He purchased gunpowder, beans, coffee, salt, and lead enough to run pistol balls.

He pulled for Laredo and rented a hotel room overlooking a convent. And there he thought about the men he must kill.

From his second-floor window Marwood watched the solemn black robes walk between garden rows and marble statuary. He was alone in the world. A professional hunter, this did not trouble him. Throughout his life, what parts he remembered, he often lived alone, apart from other men.

When he did seek out their company it was as much to kill them for bounty as anything else.

After cleaning his gun he got into bed. The bronze church bell pealed matins, vespers, evensong. The bells were ringing when he fell asleep. When he woke, they were ringing still.

He took supper in a dirt-floor cantina and bought an hour with a sloe-eyed Mexican girl. She sat at his table, dressed in long green velvet with the top half of her breasts exposed. Her blue-black hair fell to her waist. She was emaciated, barefoot, filthy.

"I never go outside." When she smiled he saw her lower teeth were broken. "My feet, they are always blue with cold."

Marwood followed her upstairs. She undressed and told him her name was Adoración. Marwood asked her if she had family. He did not think she did—he recognized a kindred spirit.

"My father is a poor dirt farmer," she said. "After the drought we had to slaughter stock and he sold me to a whiskey drummer, who then sold me to this cantina. Jorge Maypearl owns this building. He is a most cruel man. He beats us so the bruises, they do not show."

She laid her dress on the back of a wooden chair. Marwood hung his gun on a bedpost and took off his pants.

"My mother was a schoolteacher," she went on. "She taught me English. She drank and met a Negro gambler from Baltimore. That is why my father hates me. I remind him of the wife who left."

"Have you no one at all?"

"I had a baby last year, but it died before I had it baptized. Every night before I go to bed I say a prayer for its wicked soul."

Adoración turned down the embroidered counterpane and slipped into bed. She wore a frayed ivory chemise with a rounded neckline. There were stains down the front. She put her arms around his neck.

Afterward, she watched from the rumpled bed with dark and wounded eyes while he dressed. There was no sound in the room other than her sobbing, the filtered traffic from the thoroughfare, and the bronze church bells ringing.

Marwood put on his hat and descended the stairs. Maypearl stacked glasses behind the bar. He had a thick black moustache, a clipped beard with thinning hair, and mud-brown eyes. There was a fresh knife wound under his left ear. The scar was badly sutured with Yucca fibre, the puckered flesh proud and inflamed where it met the jaw.

"You enjoyed Adoración?" Maypearl asked in a thick voice. He was dressed in a bright blue guayabera and black pants. The collar, cuffs, and seams of his clothes were frayed and ragged, and the elbows patched.

"Coffee."

Maypearl poured a cup. "She is *la amada de uno*, yes? The cowboys like her very much."

Marwood drank the coffee black. There were four Mexican men in the cantina playing monte at a back table, and two girls watching with disinterest. He studied the men in the fly blown mirror behind the bar. The sour sawdust on the floor stank. On a deer antler hung a distended pig bladder filled with *pulque*.

"You are needing work, señor?" Maypearl asked.

"Maybe. Why?"

"You have a gun. You fight with the *pistola*?"

Marwood met his eyes. "Who wants to know?"

"I had a man to protect my girls." Maypearl shrugged. "He got drunk one night and tried to kick a goat. He fell into the del Norte and drowned. I need a man who is not a *bufón*."

"I'm not interested."

"*Por favor*, señor."

"How much does it pay?"

"Nothing, but you can *chingar* the girls all you want."

Marwood pushed his empty cup forward. Maypearl refilled it from a blue enamel coffee pot.

"I have no money, señor." Maypearl blew his nose and wiped the bar with the dirty rag. "I pay sin tax. The doctor comes twice a month to inspect the whores for pox. Whiskey and clothes and broken furniture erase my profit. I will tell you a thing, señor. There is no money in whores. This is Texas. There is money in religion and politics and cattle. But never whores."

Adoración came downstairs and sat beside the rough adobe wall. The batwing doors to the cantina were latched open. Lighted carriages and wobbling, squeaking *carretas* rolled past. She watched them go by.

"Adoración likes you," Maypearl said.

"Is that right."

Maypearl placed a hand over his heart. "On the blood of the Christ, señor."

Marwood paid for his coffee. "I'm not interested."

But Maypearl was not one to give up easily. "Señor," he urged, "I am desperate. Where can I find you if you change your mind?"

"I took a room at La Posada."

Maypearl smiled. "That is a fine hotel."

"Yes. You can hear the church bells."

Marwood pushed through the doors of the bar and looked up and down the thoroughfare, then checked the windows of the buildings opposite him. He crossed the wide street and walked to the livery stable to see about his horse, a narrow-chested grey mare with a round back and long legs. He returned to La Posada, retrieved his room key from the desk clerk, and mounted the stairs.

On the first landing two men emerged from rooms on either side. Both had their hands inside their coats and were coming straight for him. Marwood pulled his gun and shot the first man point blank in the face. The noise from the Colt was terrific; the reverberation shook loose dust from the *vigas* and rattled a glass lamp in the wall.

The back of the man's head disintegrated. The wall splattered with brains and bone and blood in an upward spray that reached the *vigas* and ceiling lathes. His knees bowed and his feet skittered out from under him. As his boot heels rapped down the wooden stairs with staccato thumps, Marwood turned to the second man, who had drawn a small, single-shot derringer from his black Mackinaw.

Marwood couldn't turn his heavy gun in line to shoot fast enough. He clubbed the derringer aside and drove an elbow into the man's chest. The assassin rebounded off the wall, gun hand wavering. Marwood kicked his knee with the sharp edge of his boot heel, tearing cloth and skin. The assassin brought his gun to bear and snap fired. Searing flame and heat ripped Marwood's forearm.

Something inside Marwood thundered. All he saw was red heat and hate and this man standing between him and the gates of death. There was nothing Marwood could do to save his life if he wanted to, and he did not. He was under control of the blind thing.

Marwood whipped the octagonal barrel of his gun across the man's cheekbone. The assassin reeled back and grabbed the blood-slicked bannister. Marwood came down the stairs after him. The assassin tried to get his legs under him, but Marwood kicked him in the jaw and stomped his face until the bones were broken fragile reeds under pulped skin. A patch of skull glistened red under a flap of hair.

He rammed the gun barrel against the man's head. "Are you working for John Chivington?"

The man's face and eyes were webbed with blood strings. His hair was in disarray.

"Were you at Sand Creek?" Marwood asked. "You're going to die anyway."

The assassin tried to speak, choked on the loose teeth in his throat.

Marwood rolled the hammer back and fired. He shoved the body away with his boot, watched it roll down the last few steps and come to rest on a cochineal carpet in the lobby.

"Stop there, you bastard." A county sheriff rose from behind the front desk, pointing a double-barrelled shotgun at Marwood. Grey hairs dusted the tips of his thick red whiskers and upswept eyebrows.

"Drop your gun and face that wall," the sheriff ordered.

The gun in Marwood's hand dripped blood. "I am not going to die with my back turned."

"I'm keeping you alive long enough to watch you hang." The twin barrels jerked a notch. "I will not repeat myself, mister."

Marwood set the hammer on half cock and placed the Colt on the bottom step. He had learned long ago never drop a loaded gun. Didn't think much of anyone who thought it was a good idea.

"Those men tried to assassinate me," he said, straightening.

"Well, you sure as hell did for them," the sheriff replied. Three deputies rushed the hotel lobby with their own guns drawn and flanked the sheriff.

"All right, boys," the sheriff said. "But watch out. This mad wolf bites."

They manacled his hands in front with Pittsburgh steel. The sheriff walked up, beaming. He was all high hat and collar. Marwood let him get closer. He pulled a buck knife from under his belt and flipped it open. It was a long slender blade that would not close upon his fingers when he struck bone.

The sheriff saw the knife and slammed the barrel of the shotgun across Marwood's shoulders, and he fell.

"Motherless bastard." The sheriff kicked the knife from his hand. It skittered across the hardwood floor.

"Goddamn if you ain't right, sheriff," one of the deputies wheezed. "He's a mean sumbitch."

"He's a dead sumbitch now," the older lawman said.

The sheriff lifted and pile drived the gunstock down. There was a long sheer of horrible light, followed by black, and the ancient thing inside Marwood ceased to roar.

CHAPTER 2

Marwood awoke in a holding cell, half-buried in freezing mud. The walls were uncured adobe, many yards thick and rotting out. The floor was deep red clay with no bottom.

His throat burned with unimaginable thirst. He wasn't manacled, but he could not climb out of the pit. The walls were slick with mud and there was a heavy iron grate three feet above his head. His hooked his trembling fingers through the mesh, but was unable to lift himself from the sucking mud.

He fell back, exhausted. The muck and mire oozed over his body. Light spilled from a tall window in the hallway outside the sunken cell. It was high morning, but he had lost track of the passing days.

His flesh was striped with red welts. They covered his back and arms and legs. He could not remember how he got them. He tried to move around in the pit, a creature born of mud and pain, like some ancient thing birthed from a Celtic bog.

The back of his head was matted and crusted with dried blood. He probed with his fingers and lay gasping when the pain rippled along his spine.

The pain subsided in hammering waves, his blurred vision returned to normal. Marwood scraped muck from the walls and fashioned a poultice of sorts. He trowelled the cold mud into the wound, gritting his teeth. He could not stop shivering though his skin was hot to the touch. It was as if he had a fever.

Marwood scraped mud off his chest. By degrees he examined the long worm-like welts covering his body; he was webbed with them. He could not stand because of the deep mud and low iron grating, which he was fine with because he didn't trust his legs to carry his weight. They were coated to the knees. His feet were numb and his boots were gone. He shivered in the darkness, stocking feet poking red mud.

He knew he would die here.

"Sheriff Brookstone whomped you with a yoke chain." The rough voice came from a dark cell across the central passage. "He near beat you to death with it."

Marwood made out a vague outline of pale arms hooked through cell bars. The man's face was covered in warts and boils. His nose was a shapeless mass. Blue and yellow bruising circled his eyes like elaborate South Seas tattooing.

"Lucky that mud froze near solid before you woke," the man said. "Come spring, when the water table rises, a man can sink plumb under. My name is Spaw. Lewis Spaw."

Marwood made a gesture to show he understood. He dropped his hand, exhausted by this modest exercise.

Spaw pressed his ravaged face against the bars of his cell. "The deputies wanted for you to run so they could shoot you in the back. But you kept coming straight at the bastards. Brookstone, he wore out his arm on you."

"My name is Mar—" His voice rasped, his head ached.

"Brookstone don' stick a man in the Pit without thinking on killing him, Mar. You ain't his first. Prod that mud, you'll pull up a rib cage." The ravaged face withdrew from the bars like an animal retreating into its grotto.

Days and nights passed. Marwood rubbed his hands and feet to keep the blood circulating. When his fever broke a deputy pushed food scraps through the iron grating. For drinking water Marwood pressed a hand into the muck and the water slowly filled the depression. There was no slop bucket. He slept but little. Once, upon awakening, he saw the cell occupied by Spaw stood empty.

Early the next morning three deputies came for Marwood. They unlocked the heavy grate and hoisted him out by his armpits.

Another deputy stood down the hall with a .10 gauge Stevens shotgun. He carried a separate gun, a Colt Navy pistol, thrust through his belt. He had the gate open so the gun would not slip through his trousers.

They handcuffed Marwood and half-dragged him down the hallway. Clots of mud fell from his body. He was too weak to stand. They brought him outside and dumped him beside a water trough.

"Gotta wash before you see Judge Creighton," the man with the shotgun said.

Marwood looked at him and turned away. He drank deep draughts to cleanse his guts from the foul water in the cell. He splashed through the freezing water, used handfuls of sand to scrub himself clean, and threw water over himself again.

One of the ancillary deputies threw him a rough horse blanket. Marwood dried himself off and dressed in his clothes, boots, and deerskin jacket.

"Where is my gun?" he asked.

The man with the shotgun turned his head and spat. He looked at Marwood and shook his head. "Don't be stupid, mister."

They allowed him to visit the jakes. When he came out they brought him back inside the jailhouse. It was much warmer. Marwood felt something akin to human again. He decided he would not kill the entire town of Laredo. Just these sons of bitches would be enough.

Sheriff Rex Brookstone met them in a well-appointed office fitted with an iron stove and pine walls pasted with county and state maps. He wore a white shirt, pinstriped vest, dark trousers, and polished boots with Spanish heels and gold-inlaid rowels. His long mustache was combed and waxed. His right hand rested on the butt of an 1858 Remington-Beals. It was a good gun. Marwood figured he would enjoy killing the man with it.

Brookstone addressed the deputy holding the shotgun. "Was he ever out of your sight, Charlie?"

Charlie looked at the other deputies, shook his head. "He went to the shitter by himself. I didn't allow as I had to wipe his ass for him."

"Search him. Someone may have left a weapon for him in there."

"He ain't got nothing on him, Sheriff," one of the other deputies said.

"Do like I say, Charlie."

Marwood was searched. The deputies gave way. Charlie eyed Marwood, fingering the trigger of his shotgun. Marwood knew what the deputy was thinking, and he would have done the same, sheriff or no.

Brookstone approached him. The two men traded hostile stares. Marwood wondered if Brookstone had family and how long it would take to rip that poisonous seed from the earth.

"I am going to send you through that door to see Judge Creighton." When Brookstone talked his bottom lip pulled away from his pink gums, revealing tobacco-stained teeth. "He will ask you many questions. You will answer them, and you will listen to what he has to say."

"Where is my gun?"

"When the judge is finished you will be remanded to my custody. What happens then will depend on what transpires inside that room."

Brookstone jerked his whiskered chin at an oak door set in frogged brick. "Go on. The Judge is waiting, and he is not a patient man."

The black door was polished from stile to rail. A brass-gyred handle gleamed. It did not look inviting. Marwood entered and closed the door behind him. He was in another office, smaller, south facing, with bright windows with mullioned panes of glass. Beyond the windows was a big water fountain in a ramada roofed by withy branches, and the winter Laredo sky, crisp blue. The walls of the office were lined with law books. A separate shelf contained Melville, Defoe, Cooper.

A ribbed cast-iron stove smoked in one corner. Black soot flaked from the crooked flue pipe. A sideboard held the remains of breakfast: boiled eggs, pork chops, and fried potatoes. The air smelled musty and warm and dangerous, with a hint of cigar smoke and sharp creosote from burning too much green wood.

A writing desk beside the door was snowed with loose paper and open law journals full of dog-eared pages. Its larger brother was placed in front of the main window with a Morris chair behind it. In the chair sat an older man with the bearing of a statesman, and the watery blue eyes of a stone killer.

Judge Creighton had on a coal-grey business suit, black string tie, and gold watch chain. He had snow-white hair and a thinning crown, with dark muttonchops and thin eyebrows. His fat chin had a spot of razor burn between the folds. The nails on his red meaty hands were clipped.

"Sit down," he said.

There was a split-pine bench in front of the desk. Marwood sat and was glad to do so. He didn't think his shaky legs could hold up for a lengthy interview.

"Those men you killed were ex-Pinkerton agents," Judge Creighton said without preamble. "Their names were Frank Darling and William Treat."

It was not lost upon Marwood that he used the word "killed" instead of "murdered."

"Those men were out of San Francisco. They were carrying paper on you. Did you know them?"

"No."

Judge Creighton did not take his eyes off Marwood. "What makes you believe they worked for John Chivington?"

"Who says that I did?" Marwood asked.

"Witnesses say you said it before you killed Darling."

Marwood didn't remember. He might have. There was a lot of noise that night. He shrugged. "Colonel Chivington and his political machine didn't like what I had done. Especially after."

"You mean after Sand Creek," Creighton said.

Marwood didn't answer.

Judge Creighton shuffled the papers on his desk, held one at arm's length. "You know what this is? It's a report telegraphed to me from the War Department in Washington, D.C. It states you received an honourable discharge, though you refused a lawful order from your commanding officer on the battlefield."

Creighton raised his watery blue eyes. "Most men are shot for less in the United States Army."

"I wasn't alone," Marwood said. "Captain Silas Soule also refused to fire on that Cheyenne village."

"True. But Soule did not spirit Black Kettle out of harm's way. Nor was Soule charged with desertion when the killing was over."

The chair creaked. Judge Creighton leaned back and crossed his long legs. "Do you know the date today?"

Marwood squinted. "It's on to December. I lost track in that mud pit."

"Today is December fourth," Creighton said. "A week ago George Armstrong Custer killed Black Kettle on the Washita River. Shot him in the back, which is what Custer does best when he's murdering aborigines. Whatever you hoped to gain by helping Black Kettle seven years ago was for naught."

"I didn't hope to gain anything," Marwood said. "It needed doing, so I done it."

Creighton didn't speak for a long minute. He cleared his throat. "You served as a lieutenant under John Chivington in Glorieta Pass. Is that not correct?"

"During the war."

"Yet you refused his direct order at Sand Creek and testified against him during his court martial. Did you think a proud man like Chivington would forget how you disparaged his honour?"

"Judge, I don't give a damn what Chivington thought," Marwood said, "then or now."

"Even after what happened to Soule in Denver?"

"The men who kiss Chivington's ring killed Soule, or had it hired out. But they won't kill me. Bet on that."

The morning sun poured through the window and crept slow across the carpet while they talked.

Marwood leaned forward, his hands together. "We put four howitzers up on that hill. We fired fragmenting shells down on the village before we rode in. I saw drunk soldiers bayonet babies and blow the brains out of squalling children. Women bared their breasts to show they were not warriors, and were raped and disemboweled. There was an American flag draped over Black Kettle's tipi. He thought this country would protect him. I saw that flag burned. I saw Chivington and his men take scalps and cut the breasts off women while they were still alive. One sergeant carried a girl's private parts around on a forked stick. Another officer had the heads of babies stuck like plums on his cavalry sword."

Marwood stared at the older man across the desk. "Don't lecture me on propriety, Judge. I know the world for what it is. I was at Sand Creek. You were not."

"Yet it remains your contention Chivington hired those two Pinks out of California to assassinate you?"

"If it was not him it was one of his political ass lickers." Marwood frowned. "Of which he has many."

Creighton searched his desk for another sheet of paper, found it. "You are a marked man in more ways than one, it seems. Have you ever been to Waco?"

"No."

"A bank was held up there, and two men killed in the posse."

"I don't know anything about that."

Judge Creighton studied him. He removed a Cuban cigar from a cedar humidor and rolled it between his fingers. The overleaf crisped. He lighted one end with a lucifer and smoked as he came to his decision.

"Look," Marwood said, "what do you want with me?"

"I have a proposition of employment to put to you," said the judge.

A hollow pit formed in Marwood's stomach. "I'm listening."

"Simply put," Creighton removed and examined his burning cigar, "I have need of a man like yourself. I want someone as hard as the spoilers who kill and rape their way across the *frontera*. I want another murdering son of a bitch who will meet these killers on their own terms, and take them down."

Marwood breathed slowly. "I am not a lawman."

"You were a range detective in Kansas after the war. That's on the record as well."

"That is not being a lawman and you know it."

Their eyes met. "Look, son," Creighton said, "I need a U.S. Marshal under my employ with your credentials and reputation. I want a hard killer I can send after other killers who keep this country from being tamed and civilized."

Marwood stared down at his hands. "I am not a lawman."

"I am trying to help you."

"I know that."

"You keep going and you will wind up on my gallows. You may end up there anyway, even if you take the job. But you will be killing men what need killing."

Marwood met Judge Creighton's gaze. "I am not the man you're looking for."

"How do you know?"

"I am not the man."

"Will you think about it?"

"I done thought about it."

"All right. You can go." Then, as if he thought the point deserved elaboration, "I will not hang a man who killed assassins that drew on him first. But you must leave Laredo. We catch you here again, you will be put back in Sheriff Brookstone's mud pit. And you will never get out."

"Yes. Yes, sir."

"You don't call many men 'sir' do you, son?"

"Most men don't deserve it called."

"All right, then. I guess we understand one another after all. One more thing: I know you are wondering why I want you on my staff. It's because of Sand Creek. It's because, despite the man you are, there are lines you won't cross."

Marwood rose from the bench and quit the office, closing the door behind him. Brookstone met him on the other side.

"You riding out today?" the sheriff asked.

"That's right."

"Gun's over there."

Marwood found a corner table beneath a large Webb County map. He picked up his gun, knife, and a Mexican holster.

"Where is my horse?"

"She's at the livery stable. The Judge paid full board out of his own pocket."

Marwood glanced back at the door. No sound came from

the other side. "He did that?" He buckled his holster and made to leave.

"Be out of town by sundown." Brookstone leaned his hip against his desk, arms crossed. "I'll be watching."

Marwood put on his hat. "Sheriff, you won't see me coming. Not you, nor any of your deputies. I am never going to forget that pit."

"Take the San Augustin road," Brookstone said. "It's the quickest way out of town. You'll come to a place where you can water your horse."

Marwood walked out of the jailhouse and down the steps into cold sunshine. People drew water from the plaza and sold food and wares. He followed a rackety ocotillo fence to the stable and got his mare. He rode down Zaragoza Street past La Posada and hitched outside the cantina. Sunlight flared off the river. Marwood checked the loads in his gun and went inside, let his eyes adjust to the darkness.

Maypearl served tumblers of mescal from a five-gallon carboy behind the bar. Marwood shouldered through the morning patrons. When the barman saw him his face went white as sacking flour.

"Señor." Maypearl tried to say more, but he could not put the words together.

"I want to ask you something." Marwood spaced each word. "I want you to think long and hard before you answer."

"Señor."

"Did you send those Pinks after me?"

Maypearl licked his lips. "I do not know what you are speaking of, señor."

Marwood drew his gun and pointed it at Maypearl's face. He rolled the hammer back. The men beside him finished their drinks and slid out of the bar by ones and twos.

They were alone.

"Remember, I work with the *pistola*," Marwood said. "You

are the only person who asked me which hotel I was staying at. Tell me about the two men."

"Señor, I am a poor bartender, and I know nothing of these serious matters."

"You are about to be a dead bartender. And you are correct. These are very serious matters."

Maypearl was visibly shaken. "Yes. Two men. Looking for someone of your description." His voice was high with fright. "They said they would cut off my hands if I did not tell them where you were." He touched the inflamed knife wound under his ear. "They gave me this. They said they would cut up my girls. I did not know they wanted to assassinate you, señor. I swear I did not know this. They said you owed them a gambling debt. I did not know they wanted to accomplish murder. You must believe me."

Marwood let the hammer down and holstered the gun. Maypearl found a bottle under the bar and poured a shot of rye whiskey. The bottle clinked against the glass. He pushed the drink forward.

Marwood drained it.

"Thank you for believing me, señor."

"I don't believe you." Marwood put the shot glass down. "I am going to do something I have never done before."

"What is that?" Maypearl poured again. His face was drained of colour.

"I am going to let you live."

"Señor?" Maypearl took a step away from the bar, holding the bottle by its neck.

"Another man did me a favour earlier today. He didn't have to, but he did, and I am paying it back."

Marwood drank the second shot. He turned the glass over on the bar. "But I owe no one any favours this day forward. I want that made clear."

"Señor, *por favor*, I do not understand these reasons."

"It doesn't matter. All that matters is I understand them." Marwood glanced around the cantina. "Where is Adoración?"

Maypearl raised his hands in abject surrender. "She ran away. I opened up one morning and she did not come downstairs to work. These whores, they cannot be trusted, señor. They are like all women, except they are whores."

Marwood left the cantina. He sat on his horse, thinking. He rode out of town following the dirt road north. That evening the Pleiades glittered high in the east. He came upon a dugout at the bottom of a high bluff scoured by wind. The place was in a wooded draw and had a water pump. The ground was littered with dung, both animal and human, and clumps of wiregrass. There was an empty cow pen. A handful of scrawny chickens roosted on the top rail like gargoyles.

Marwood reined in. A man dressed in filthy rags emerged from the dugout. Marwood asked the owner if he could take on water.

"Pay a nickel," the hermit said. His rotting clothes blew about his naked legs. "I can't make my meat giving it away."

"I will pay." Marwood stepped out of leather and watered his mare. A man walked out of the brakes leading a dun gelding with a charro saddle. He gripped a brass-framed Henry rifle in his other hand.

"Brookstone post you out of town?" Spaw asked.

The smashed nose and bruised face had partially healed, but Spaw's face remained swarthed with warts and boils. Under the light of the winter stars he bore the countenance of a savage grendel-like creature. He wore a black Kossuth hat with a white ostrich feather. His clothes were white with fine road dust.

"I got pushed out," Marwood said.

"Where you headed, Mar?"

Marwood peered down the dark trail. "Figured I'd see how the string played out on this here road."

"I'm riding for Piedras Negras myself."

Marwood adjusted the bridle on his mare. "I don't know."

Spaw paid for and watered his horse. The hermit returned to his deep, dark hole in the ground. Spaw mounted up and Marwood did the same.

"Sure glad I run into you again."

"What are you doing out here, Spaw?"

The man glanced back at the glittering lights of Laredo on the desert floor. "I finished something that needed finishing. Now I'm able to ride on." He smiled at Marwood. "Somebody did me a hurt once. I don't like leaving my enemies behind." He pulled the plaited leather reins through his hands.

Spaw pursed his lips. "You don't have to go with me," he said.

"I know."

"I got someone I'm meeting in Mexico. Man with the kind of temperament to suit our blood."

"That so."

Spaw sat his dun horse a spell. The night air was dry and bitter cold. An owl called across the flat.

"There's liable to be killing involved," Spaw said.

"That's everywhere in the world," Marwood replied. "One more place won't make any difference."

They reined their horses around and rode side by side out of the draw, into the dark arms of the night.

CHAPTER 3

Riding upriver, they crossed a glistening mudflat bordered with seep willows. They rode between the boles like phantoms released upon the world. They splashed into a shallow ford, up and over a sandbar, back through deep river water.

The water sprayed from the legs and breasts of their horses like white diamonds. They spurred up a steep bank and reined in while the horses steamed and stomped and snorted in the gathering cold.

Spaw looked across the border into Texas. "Well." He reined his horse around. Marwood followed.

That night they fixed camp. Marwood gathered firewood and cow chips harder than anthracite along the sandy bank. Spaw dug a pit and built an outlaw's fire while Marwood lashed together a windbreak in case the weather turned. They untied their bedrolls and shared cold pinto beans and charred tortillas as a bank of clouds pushed in from the north and blanketed the stars.

Spaw shook out his makings and rolled a cigarette. While he smoked he found a square of pale leather in his possibles and rubbed it between his fingers. The campfire lighted his face as if he were staring into the kilns of Hell.

"I never saw nothing like it," he said as he smoked the cigarette. "The way you kept coming at Brookstone that way."

"Man should die standing if he's going to die at all," Marwood said. "Who is this person you're meeting in Piedras Negras?"

"That's what I wanted to talk to you about." Spaw poked the fire and brought it back up.

Marwood pulled a wool blanket over his legs. He had used blades of aloe vera to medicine the welts and gunpowder burn on his forearm. The ride, and other events of the long day, had all but exhausted him.

"We got a private contract to blow Mexican farmers and squatters off so the big ranches can take their land." Spaw stopped. He flicked the ash from his cigarette into the fire and continued. "The man I work for is Captain Abram Botis."

"Botis," Marwood said. Then, softer, "Botis."

"You know the name?"

"I heard it somewhere before." It wasn't as much the man's name as it was something old, and yet familiar to him.

Spaw caressed the leather square with the pad of his thumb. "Botis was a Franciscan monk or friar or whatever them Papists have. He got into trouble in the Old Country and was excommunicated for an apostate. All I know is he ain't for religion anymore, but he damn sure don't mind killing. He has taken to that with single-minded purpose."

"What else can you tell me about this job?" Marwood asked.

Spaw crushed out his cigarette. "The big Texas ranches along the border have piled into what you might call a combine. They don't want to wait for the scales of justice to tilt their way. Empires don't have much patience, I guess."

"You say this work is back in Texas?"

Spaw made a sweeping motion with his free hand. "Up and down the border. New Mexican Territory. Wherever we ride and break ground. It's an open contract. I was on my way there when I got sidelined in Laredo. There're a lot of people to run off, and it won't be accomplished in a single season. Pay looks to be right promising."

"What's the wages?"

"Take and carry, plus a share of the original contract."

Marwood watched the campfire dance. "A big enterprise of ranches, and what they have to protect, is not going to let us ride clear when the work is finished." He looked up at Spaw. "Does this Captain Botis know that?"

Spaw grinned broadly. "I think the captain knows it better than they do."

The following morning they saddled the horses and led them to the river. The dawn was cold and grey. A thin frost covered the ground; there were sheets of skim ice in the shallows under which small fish moved.

Marwood filled his canteen in the murky water while the horses drank and spluttered. Spaw splashed his monstrous face and scratched the back of his neck. He squatted on the bank, arms lank, black Kossuth hat between his hands as if he were begging for alms on a street corner. He peered across the wild expanse like a primeval god. He stood, clapped the hat on his head, and mounted up.

"Let's go," he said.

They kept to the Mexican side of the border, riding through candelilla shrub and avoiding an ox-drawn *carreta* led by a man and a boy with one eye and a withered arm. There was no other road traffic. Later in the day they stopped at a stone water tank outside a wooden *tienda* and ate huevos rancheros and refried beans, and drank cups of mescal. They rose from the table and purchased five pounds of cured side meat, a bag of Spanish grind, and grain for the horses. It was enough food to see them through the next four days.

As Marwood fed his mare a handful of oats he looked at Spaw's horse, with its charro saddle and plaited leather reins fashioned from human skin. He had seen the smooth pliable leather after Sand Creek, and recognized it again now. He remembered Spaw rubbing the cured bit of leather with its champered edges between his fingers, and again on today's longish ride to water. It was as if the tactile property of man leather quieted something deep and turbulent inside his soul.

Marwood knew what that was like, having a dry and silent power inside waiting to give terrible voice. He found himself wondering which way Spaw would have jumped at Sand Creek.

They rode off and made another early camp. It rained that night, thin and freezing. The next day dawned clear, with a south wind bending the tops of trees. As Spaw broke camp Marwood recharged his gun with powder, ball, and percussion cap.

Spaw watched him clean the revolver. "You change them loads ever' morning?"

Marwood closed the cylinder and put the gun back in its holster. "Got some rain last night. I don't want a misfire."

"Five new loads everyday," Spaw said, contemplating the logistics. "That gets downright expensive."

"So is dying."

Spaw swung into his saddle and repeatedly pulled the reins through his hands. The man was always fiddling. "Yes, sir," he laughed. "Captain Botis will like you just fine."

They hit Piedras Negras four days later and drank raw *pulque* in an empty *taqueria* with a low ceiling and a smoking coal oil lamp that stung their eyes. The day burned itself out with a final blaze. They took supper in a restaurant off the main plaza. After filling up on tortillas fried on a clay comal, and strips of goat meat smothered in chili peppers and onions, they walked up a deserted street through one of the mud *barrials*. They reached a dilapidated bodega overlooking the slow brown river.

There were horses tied to the outside rail. A light shone through loose door slats, cast corrugated stripes on the uneven ground at their feet.

Spaw hammered the door with a gloved fist. Someone on the other side unlocked it and Spaw pushed through the low doorway. Marwood followed.

Men were crowded around a central table playing cards. Some had half-dressed girls on their laps, or standing at their shoulders to refill an empty glass or light a cigar.

Spaw grabbed the arm of one of the women and pulled her out of the way. He walked to the edge of the main gaming table. "Hey, Dan," he said, "where is the captain at?"

A wide-faced Dutchman with gapped front teeth looked briefly at Spaw then back to his cards. "Where you think?"

Spaw found a glass of whiskey and drank it down. "Bring me a bottle from somewheres, Lovich," he told the man. "We come off the trail."

Dan Lovich possessed long blond hair braided with flint arrowheads and silver beads. His eyes were the colour of dark molasses. His barbarous beard ruffed over his collar. His clothes were filthy and he wore more animal skins than anything store bought.

"Does it look like we done come down from church?" he growled. He discarded two cards into the deadwood pile and drew like. "Get one of these here doxies to comb your cock for you. I ain't your goddamn mother."

Spaw faced Marwood. "We won't see the captain tonight. I'll show where you can stable your horse and bunk down."

Someone called across the room. "Spaw, that the new man?"

The man who spoke was bald. His sharp features were squinched together in the middle of pallid flesh and heavy jowls.

"That's up for the captain to decide," Spaw told him. He explained to Marwood, "That's Amos Choteau, the Cajun. Crazier than a shithouse rat. But I ain't never seen no man better to break horses. The greybeard sharpening his harpoon is Old Bill Rota. He used to sail them Boston whalers out of

Nantucket. He's older'n any of us by a few years, but he'll come off the wall and back your play. That tall nigger eating piñole is Pat Spooner. Got him a family in Bexar. You'll meet the others come later. Jubal Stone ain't here tonight. He's watching our break camp across the river. Got us a camp slut, too, name of Rachel. She's always ripe and ready. Also got two Tonkawa scouts working for us, but we don't never let them sleep with us in town."

"Where do they sleep?"

Spaw shrugged. "Wherever Indians sleep. We will all meet together once we cross into Texas. There's near a dozen of us all told."

"When do we ride?"

"When the captain decides, Mar, and not before. I've seen the time he took a fortnight before he made a move. You play chess?"

"No."

"Captain does."

They stabled their horses and returned to the main house. Around midnight Marwood rolled the straw mattress down on his cot and crawled onto it. Another man or three drifted to bed an hour later while the rest stayed up drinking whiskey and hazing the whores.

Come morning, after a plate of sofkee and spicy chorizo, he was brought before Botis. Spaw had met with the captain for ten minutes before calling Marwood inside.

It was a storeroom off the *cocina* where an arthritic beldam dipped clay breakfast bowls in dishwater and wiped them with her dirty apron. The room was arranged in an impromptu office with a nail barrel for a desk, bags of feed corn in one corner, and an open window in the eastern wall.

Marwood could see the brown glint of river water through the reeds and rushes. Down in Piedras Negras proper a donkey brayed, welcoming the dawn.

Dan Lovich was standing in the room with a cut down double-barrelled shotgun cradled in his arms. Marwood got the impression Lovich was the unacknowledged lieutenant of this outfit. In as much as military rank or class had any bearing among these rough and wild men.

It was the first time in a long time he felt at home.

Marwood stood before the nail barrel. Abram Botis was a long, slab-sided man with a black, broad-brimmed galero atop his round head. His sun-browned face was heavily bearded, the hair on his forearms thick and matted. He was dressed in black and brown. His muddy leather boots stopped below his knees with drooping mule tugs on either side.

Botis plucked a pair of tortoise-shell glasses with ivory plaquettes from his pocket. He perched them on the end of his nose and inspected Marwood. The other men in the tiny room remained in one place and did not speak.

"Lewis informs me you are a man who can ride the river," Botis said. His deep voice emanated from some black crack in the centre of his chest and boomed from his throat. "Well, that's what I want to know. Can you?"

Marwood shrugged. "I wasn't born on my knees. I don't figure going out that way."

"Would you ride with a man who would?"

"No," Marwood answered, "I would not."

Botis watched him close. "Neither would I." He leaned forward in his chair and tapped the top of the nail barrel with his forefinger. "Nor would any man in my employ. Do you have a horse?"

"I have a good mare, but she can't go all day."

"We will get more horses," Botis assured him. "You can add your mare to the remuda and cut out any horse you want, except Acheron. That stallion is mine. He won't let another man ride him, anyway. I take it you have your own saddle?"

"Yes."

"Well, that's something." Botis nodded at his gun. "I see you carry a Colt Dragoon. That's heavy iron for six shots."

"Five."

"Indeed?" This answer pleased Botis. "You are a careful man. I take it you know how to use that gun to its fullest capacity?"

"I do."

"Ever kill a man outright?"

"Yes."

"In cold blood?"

"I have done."

"He did for two Pinkerton detectives in Laredo," Spaw put in. "The whole town was buzzing about it when I got out of the jug."

"May I examine your gun?" Botis held his hand out without waiting for an answer.

Marwood put the hammer on half cock and handed it over, butt first.

Botis turned the Colt in his hands, running a broken thumbnail over the square-backed trigger guard. He stopped and stared at the yellow bone handle. He went on to check the loads, springs, and action of the gun, his long fingers moving with delicate expertise. Then he re-examined the bone handle in some detail.

He handed the gun back to Marwood. "You carve that handle yourself?"

Marwood holstered the weapon. "Yes."

No one spoke. Spaw looked at his boots and rocked slightly on his heels.

"You know what we are about here?" Botis asked Marwood.

"Spaw said something about blowing poor Mexican farmers off their land."

"You say that like you don't believe we can do it."

"I say that like I expect lawyers and judges will have something to say about it."

"Maybe," Botis conceded. "But in this country, as in all countries, land belongs to the man strong enough to take it, and hold it. We are operating at the behest of an important combine, which has hired us to act as lawful agents on their behalf." Botis looked out the window. "Land came at a premium along the border after the war. These big spreads will not wait for some mealy-mouthed judge to decide what plat belongs to them, and what does not."

He turned his attention back to Marwood. "These Texas ranchers have a Calvinistic hatred of Mexicans, Indians, and anyone else who steps in their way. It is always thus with the world. Those with power and money shape history, and the chaff and duff are blown aside. Do you understand these principles?"

"I believe so."

"There will be killing. There will be a lot of killing if it comes to it. And it's going to come to it."

"I don't have a problem with that."

"I ask nothing but a man keep his gun clean and follow my orders. First sign of treachery I will put a ball in the back of your head and ride on. Payment will be on a percentage basis of the total contract, plus whatever you pick up along the way. Does this arrangement suit you?"

"I've worked for found before. What's the contract worth?"

"One hundred thousand dollars. These people have it to burn."

"I guess that's all right."

Botis spoke quickly, perhaps to challenge Marwood, or expose him. "You're not a man who cares about gold, are you?" he asked.

"I don't care about it at all."

"I prefer to be called 'Captain' among the men in my company."

"All right."

"Neither do I," Botis admitted after brief reflection. "Gold that is. I am after something bigger. But I guess you may have cottoned to the fact an outfit like ours would not be interested in shaking down Mexican farmers for shits and giggles." He gave a minute nod to Lovich. "I am satisfied with this man. Hire him on with full pay."

"I guess he will stick," Lovich said, eyeing Marwood.

Botis stared at Marwood again. "He'll stick for himself. Whether he will stick for us is another matter altogether. But that is any man, and I cannot fault him for that."

That same morning Marwood and Pat Spooner were charged to go into Piedras Negras to buy supplies for the expedition. As Marwood tied heavy packs to his horse outside a chandlery he noticed a Mandan Indian sitting cross-legged on the far side of the street.

"He's looking like you stole his watch," Spooner said.

"I never saw him before."

Spooner bent his lanky frame and lifted the provisions onto his horse. "Well, he's watching you mighty hard like you done him dirt."

Marwood tied a sack of salt bacon to his saddle and strode across to the old man. "Why do you keep watching me?" he asked.

The ancient did not deign to acknowledge he was being addressed. He was garbed in leather breeches, his upper torso bare. Long muscles moved under his skin. His grey hair was as knotted as sheep scut.

"Look," Marwood said, "I don't want any trouble."

"*Numank maxana*," the ancient said.

"How's that?"

The man pointed north, insistent. "*Numank maxana*."

Marwood returned to Spooner holding the reins of their horses.

"What did he say?" asked Spooner.

"I don't know. He doesn't speak American. He's crazy." Marwood lifted himself onto his saddle and fussed with the reins in an uncharacteristic way. "I told him I didn't want trouble. That's all."

"Well, you acting like he put a bug in your ear."

They rode the supplies back to the bodega. That night the men stood outside and watched the heavens open up. Someone passed a bottle. Marwood watched stars rain from the empyrean black, leaving cold trails of vaporous fire.

Bill Rota shook his head. "This is a bad sign to start off with, boys," he said. "I knowed a three-masted ship that went down off the Japans on a night like this one."

"Well, we ain't the Japans, old man," the Cajun said. He was sweating, and his bald head glistened like a white stone. "This here's Mexico."

"That doesn't mean we won't go under, boy, when the time comes," Rota intoned. "You'd best remember that."

The Cajun squinched his pallid features into a fierce mask and spat into the river. "Hell," he said.

Botis watched the display from the same veranda, his thoughts unreadable. Marwood was standing directly behind the man. Botis was stripped to the waist and there was a brand across his back—a word or sigil scrawled between his shoulders with a hot running iron. Marwood could not make out the sign or read the brand mark. It was as if the hot iron had slipped, or the person branding Botis had been careless. Aside from the brand, however, there were no other marks on the man's body.

The men did not speak much. They went to bed early once the star shower had ended.

The morning following they packed their gear and cleaned their guns and rifles. Powder horns and pouches were filled. The Cajun and Bill Rota ran lead balls.

When evening drew down two women came to the bodega and cooked a large meal. The men devoured mounds of corn tortillas, charro beans, and fried beefsteaks. Following supper the women were sent away again, and the men gathered their last supplies and individual bedrolls. They saddled their horses and together crossed the river into Texas.

They spoke little and nothing was heard other than the creak of leather and the metal clink of caparisoned horses.

Botis pulled rein. Marwood checked his mare and the other men followed. The desert night was soft. Beside Marwood, the Cajun scanned the night sky. The stars did not threaten to fall again.

Botis sat a blue roan seventeen hands high, with a broad chest and dark mane. The stallion's nostrils smoked like fumaroles in the cold air, and its eyes reflected the starlight.

"A great charge is upon us," Botis told them. "We have but one loyalty, and that is to the gun. From this day on we sup on the devil's leavings."

He turned his horse around. They rode over dark ground and met the Tonkawa spies, and the other members of the gang, in the red glimmer of dawn. The girl, Rachel, her face and hands smudged with dirt and sleep, rode behind Botis on the wooden cantle. She was a strange creature who followed them whenever they moved camp. Elfin and wild, she rarely spoke, but went from man to man as Botis beckoned around the fire. She normally did not accompany the men on any night actions, or other depredations, unless they were riding fast. Usually she waited for their return with one of the Tonkawas along some deep creek rimmed with broken salt cedar and deadfalls, or in an earthen cave.

They rode south into Texas, staying off the main road, passing unnoticed through heavy brush and clumps of purple nopal. The morning rose over Marwood's right shoulder, like a column of gold fire. Rising above the morning sun stood a luminous pillar of light. The men sat and watched in awe from the backs of their saddles.

Still they did not speak. They rode toward the pillar of light like men called to an ancient destiny. As the day brightened, and the miles passed under them, the pillar disappeared, and the empty sky lay blue.

“I told you it weren’t nothing to worry about,” the Cajun said. No one answered.

Following Botis’s lead, they turned north.

PART II

Cibola

CHAPTER 4

They hit a string of wagon carts that had the bad fortune to pull out of a stone coulee the same moment they were passing by. They left burning wrecks, stunned men, weeping women, and bawling children. They shot all the oxen.

Marwood watched as Botis gathered the dazed victims in a circle and addressed them from the back of his tall horse. "You know why we are here," he said. Then he spoke to them in Spanish and pointed to a bare patch on the ground.

Three men from the victims were chosen by Lovich and Stone at random, pulled aside, and shot in the back of the head. Their bodies pitched forward. Women threw themselves upon their dead husbands and brothers. They wept and tore their clothes and begged for mercy.

Botis, however, was after much bigger game than wagon trains. They rode on, and two days later entered a quiet *domicilio* of mud homes and stone corrals ten miles south of Carrizo Springs.

They rode through the central street, shouting and shooting and burning single-room houses, which were nothing more than hovels and *jacals*. People ran from the conflagration. One of the men ran in front of Marwood, aflame, beating at himself like a madman. A naked man stood in the doorway of a kiva, bleary-eyed. He had been awakened by the sudden noise and gunshots. He held an unlit tallow candle in one hand. Sporadic gunfire chunked him apart in sections. A frightened farmer ran across an empty cornfield, his round hat flying off his head. Rota spun his horse and rode him down, flung his harpoon through the farmer's back. The barb struck bone. Rota dallied the rope around his saddle horn and the ex-whaler dragged the poor soul screaming and bouncing across the prairie, thereupon he died.

By the end of the day fifty surviving members of the extended family of squatters had packed their things and were moving out. As Botis rode away into Zavala County, the farmers straggled in single file along the road, carrying what meagre possessions they had rescued from the fire, or had not been broken or stolen outright by the company.

The harassment and killing did not stop there. Botis knew which *estancias* and *rancherias* to hit. They cut a bloody swath through south Texas. One morning Marwood looked back from a towering hilltop and saw rising smoke columns from three days prior.

At first he could not figure out Botis's plan. It was as if their captain followed some secret known only to himself.

On Christmas Day they burned an *estancia* on the del Norte and stole twenty horses. They killed a beef and cooked it over hot coals, and ate and packed meat for the ride ahead.

That night Rachel went around the camp giving the men water. She was thin and pale and already used up despite her years. She handed Marwood a wooden ladle and he drank.

"You want me anytime," she said, "you just need to ask."

Marwood finished his drink and handed her the ladle. "I thank you," he said. "But I don't expect I will need you for that."

"Well, you need to know how we do things here," she said, and went off to tend the fire.

They rode on and dipped back into Mexico through Ciudad Acuña. Riding single-file, they cut across blind, hard country. There, Apaches fell upon them, and they fought a running battle for their lives across fifty miles of brutal desert and xeric valleys.

"I thought all these sons of bitches were dead," Jubal Stone said. He was a small, wiry man with wide set eyes and black hair straggling over his ears. "Or on reservation in New Mexico Territory, or up down Chihuahua way, starving and grovelling for handouts."

"They seem sprightly enough for starving people." The Cajun had a gash across one cheek and powder burns on his guayabera. "Belike someone pushed them off their land like we're doing these here Mexers."

They fought through the ambush, and were worn out and half dead from starvation and crushing thirst by the time they reached La Linda. Their torn clothes and hard faces were blacked with gunpowder. There was only powder and ball enough for a handful of rounds among the thirteen of them.

Botis was angry.

"We have lost time dealing with these godless aborigines," he said. "But I will not forget their wicked impressions upon our design." He stalked off to find a telegraph office and relay the news of the delay to the heads of the commercial combine that he served.

Come the New Year they crossed back into Texas and hit farms and settlements located south of Fort Davis. They remained close enough to the border not to garner too much attention from the United States Army.

Nevertheless, some people in Texas were beginning to take notice, even if the only ones rousted from their homes and futures were poor Mexicans. One day, Botis led his party back through a *domicilio* they had burned out a month prior. Marwood saw whites raising raw lumber where other families had once lived. A Baptist preacher stood among them reading a passage from his Bible.

"God must surely love Texas," Lovich said.

They turned up country and rode the sun down and the moon up until they reached Del Rio; they needed powder and shot, beans and bacon and salt. In the remote border town of clapboard shacks and sunbaked roads, the Cajun gutted a Cherokee mule skinner in a cantina. The Indian had stepped on the Cajun's foot whilst coming away from the bar with a demijohn of *pulque*.

The Cajun withdrew his Green River knife from the man's thin belly. Red ropey guts spilled in a hot mass onto the sawdust floor. The Cajun was arrested by the town marshal for aggravated murder and locked away.

That night Botis looked at the faces of his men gathered around the campfire. Grasshoppers and insects clicked and chirped in the black brush that surrounded them.

"We have to go get him," Botis said.

"That marshal in Del Rio is a hard ass," Lovich said. The flint arrowheads in his beard caught the firelight. "I heard talk about him long before he turned a key on Amos."

"He's alone," Botis said. "His deputies are riding a handful of prisoners out to the state penitentiary for hanging. We will have to go get him."

"Like you say, Captain."

The following morning Botis visited the jailhouse with a deputation of three armed men: Marwood, Jubal Stone, and another black man in their ranks named Ed Gratton. In a cultured and reasoned tone Botis informed the marshal the Cajun was doing important work for an empire of ranches who would not look kindly upon their progress being impeded by law enforcement.

The town marshal, an illiterate Hoosier who had deserted during the war, garnered meaning enough to realize his life was in no little danger.

Nevertheless, he was a man of the law, and he maintained he had received no word from Austin on this putative expedition, of which Botis purported to be a member. Botis assured the marshal this was so, inasmuch as he was not important enough to be made aware of decisions propertied men made, since their stations in life were much elevated above his own.

"Furthermore," Botis pressed on, "there is no law against killing a drunk Indian who stepped on a white man."

"I have a moral duty to uphold the spirit of the law, if not the actual letter," the marshal argued. "The law," he maintained, "has to be interpreted in various ways upon the frontier to propitiate the safety of all men, be they Indian or white."

Such was the marshal's stance, and he felt he was on firm legal ground. He was willing to telegraph Austin to inquire upon the finer points of the law, if Botis so desired.

"I do not require it," Botis said. He pulled a loaded .32 calibre pepperbox gun from his skins and rammed the barrel against the marshal's head. He told the lawman to name a fair price for the life of one Indian who would never amount to a white man, even if he lived a dozen lifetimes.

Without hesitation the marshal named a price, which amounted to a simple fine of disturbing the peace. After the money changed hands—ten dollars in silver coin—and a receipt signed, the Cajun was freed. The marshal was dragged into one of the back cells, pistol-whipped, and his gun hand was broken with a framing hammer.

They rode out of Del Rio with the Cajun seated on a fresh horse.

That evening they camped in Seminole canyon and sat around the fires and smoked their pipes. The Tonkawas watched the horses. Rachel sat beside the main fire stitching leather with a sewing awl. Her long red hair hung over her face.

"That marshal sure did squawk when we put the pressure on," Gratton remarked. His stubbled beard was shot through with pepper and salt, and his hands were wide and calloused from working with horses all his life. "Yes, sir," he said, "the world sure is made for dying."

Botis thought this over. Then he began to speak. It was not the first time Marwood had heard him elaborate on the way of the world, but it was the first time he started to see the world as it must be seen through another man's eyes.

"The unadulterated clay of man is his extremity, nay, his very love of violence," Botis said slowly. "I tell you, Edward, agony is the art of all things human. Man is born of blood. His entrance into the world is one of agony and violence. So must be his exit, come when it may."

The men nodded and smoked.

"Our marshal today learned this important lesson," Botis said. "He is better off, for most men never learn this simple truth. Yes, Edward, man is but a creature of terrible measure borne, and born."

"I don't know, Captain," Spaw said, standing next to Marwood. "Life can't be all killing."

"Why not, Lewis?"

"Well, the Good Book says love is important, too. Like the love of a man for a woman. Or a brother for a brother. I go by that some, I guess."

"Ah," Botis leaned toward the fire until his features were illuminated. "What of love? I tell you, Lewis, the only pure love is the love of violence. Any other is man's false attempt at immortality. To embrace primitive ferocity is his single birthright. To accept the Hegelian view as the driving engine of history, that is man's reality. It is real, Lewis, because it recognizes opposite polarities are the true reflection of human society. It is real because men see the world unencumbered, and without shadow, and operate freely therein."

Marwood thought about this. He had not heard words spoken like this before in his life. He didn't know if he believed them, but they tugged at something deep within him.

"But God loves man," Spaw said. "All men are loved by God."

"Including the people we have killed?" Botis asked. "And the ones we will kill tomorrow?"

Spaw broke a stick and threw it on the fire. "Yes," he said with firmness. "God doesn't make distinctions among them poor sons of bitches like we do."

Botis leaned back, draped a heavy arm over one knee. "Yes, Lewis, you are correct. God does love all men. Which is why he has apportioned certain men this great work, killing upon the surface of the earth he created."

The men looked at one another. They looked at the captain.

"For in the process of killing," Botis explained, "man may, or may not, learn incisive truths about himself and the world around him. For the apostate like myself, all paths are open, like skin flayed from a slaughtered bull. All avenues are unchecked for the apostate." His eyes found Marwood's and moved away. "Others must find their own path, as they will."

"You can't kill everything there is, Captain," the Cajun said. He was lying on his back with his feet crossed. His eyes were dark with thought. "That ain't nowhere possible."

"No, Amos," Botis agreed. "Which is why man is all failure and will prove it out as years, and futures not yet imagined, unfold."

They retired to their bedrolls. One of the men called Rachel over, and she put down the awl and went to him. Come morning they packed the camp and rode for Uvalde. Marwood accompanied Botis and Lovich into town. The day was cold and the sun high. It had rained the night before; sunlight shimmered off the puddles in the middle of the street.

They passed a sheriff's office in plain sight and made for the telegraph agency. Botis filled out several blanks in a dead language and sent them off. They waited out most of the day for replies. When the wires came—also written in Latin—Botis read them each in turn and burned them. They rode past the sheriff's office and out of town, and back to camp without molestation.

Botis dismounted and addressed the Tonakawas. The Tonks immediately left to scout ahead for water while the men hid in a stand of greasewood along a dry creek bed. When the scouts returned two days later, they pressed on.

They rode a two-week arc across empty shattered land that mirrored the bend in the del Norte, sixty miles away. They were at the southern limit of Texas Hill Country, entering the bleak desolation of South Texas. Nothing but cactus, horned toads, and mad dogs survived here. From Uvalde to St. Gall they saw neither beast nor willful man.

During a four-day waterless ride, twenty-eight miles out of St. Gall, one of the company of fifteen winters, Calvin Zapata, had his horse spooked by falling rock. Marwood's mare reared up and flicked her tail. Jubal Stone's horse took this as a sign she wanted to be mounted and tried to do so with Marwood in saddle.

Marwood kicked the other horse while he got his own animal under control. He put all his weight into the right stirrup to keep the saddle from rolling out under him.

"Keep your damn horse away from mine," he barked. Stone hauled on his reins, trying to back his horse away. He pulled so hard the leather parted from the cheek of the snaffle bit. His horse tossed its head when the bit left its mouth with a pop.

Meanwhile, Zapata was having his own brand of trouble. His three-point bay reared, broke a cannon bone on the loose talus and scree, and collapsed, shrieking. Zapata was slammed against the hard wall of the narrow arroyo they had been moving through. He fell from the saddle, half-dazed, bleeding copious amounts from his mouth.

"Oh, my god," Rachel said. "He's been killed dead."

"Belike he got something bad broke inside," the Cajun said,

watching Zapata spew blood on his leather chaps and boots. The boy could not catch his breath. The Cajun rose in his saddle and looked down quarter. "Hey, Tunk, we got a man down here."

"Goddamn, you keep that *gringo cabrón* away from me," Zapata cried. He continued to spit blood, doubled over in pain. "Oh, my, I think I'm done for."

Tunk Quillen, an ex-surgeon drummed out of the Confederate Army for practising resurrection and other nameless arts on patients who had not slipped into God's Glory, rode up and dismounted. He was Botis's trail doctor, of arcane sorts; he sewed gaping wounds with boiled horsehair and bled a man for God's measure.

Zapata watched with fearful eyes as the scarecrow figure approached with an air of martyred patience. Quillen carried a black medical bag in his left hand.

"Oh, *Dios*," the boy said, tears welling. He could not take his eyes off the bag. No man in the company knew what horrors were contained therein, and few dared to guess.

Quillen grabbed a handful of the boy's sweaty lank hair and pulled his head back.

"Open yer mout'," the ex-Confederate ordered. "Open it, damn you to all hell."

The boy did so; he was afraid of what the ex-surgeon might do if he did not follow these instructions. The surgeon pressed his fingers on either side of the boy's bony jaw, activating nerve points so the mouth remained open. He poked around with a stick. Zapata's eyes rolled helplessly. Silent tears streaked his face. Quillen released the patient and wiped his hands on his pants.

"Bit your tongue in two," he pronounced. "You won't be licking cunt for a month." And with that diagnosis he proceeded back to his horse, and whatever demons he wrestled in his mind.

"Oh, *Dios*," Zapata burbled. "Now I got to shoot my own horse."

"Such is our great work upon the surface of the earth," Bill Rota intoned.

The men looked up column to make sure Botis was out of earshot, then reeled to and fro in their saddles like drunken hoot owls.

CHAPTER 5

They rode the day out and halted when they spied a file of cavalry picking its way across the hazy landscape—a thin line of black riders escaping into a westering sun.

"Negro Cavalry," said Rota, who, despite his advanced age, had the best eyes among them. "I expect they're out of Fort Stockton. We're close enough."

"You figure them to be after us?" Lovich asked.

"Best hope not," Doc Quillen said, coming up. "I've been to Stockton and those soldiers play for keeps."

"What about it, Bill?" Lovich asked. "Are they after us?"

Rota leaned off his saddle and spat. He wiped his mouth with a gloved hand. "Can't rightly say without going up and asking one of them."

Botis watched the silhouetted figures disappear into the long evening light. "I would not think they are searching for us," he said. "It is too soon to be onto us, and they are headed the wrong direction. Daniel?"

"If they are headed west," Lovich said, "they are headed into Comancheria. Punitive expedition. Assuming any of those mothers' sons make it out of there alive. Which they won't."

"We will keep to their southern quarter," Botis suggested. "I prefer not to fight my way to the Mexican border if it comes to that. I want a clear line of escape. If we must, we will muffle the hooves of our horses when we cut their trail later tonight. Mount up."

They nooned and watered the next day at Comanche Springs. "Patrick," Botis said, dismounting, "you and Mar ride to St.

Gall and fetch new supplies." He turned to attend another matter in camp. Rachel had found an old hackberry stump for firewood and she needed help dragging it to the fire.

Pat Spooner grumbled at this delegation of work. "Captain," he groused, "why I always got to ride for victuals?" He picked up his saddle and bedroll, threw them down in frustration. "I ain't no new man. Why not send Charley Broadwell or Sam Decker out with Mar? They're both of them newer 'n me."

Dan Lovich led a yellow gelding past the central campfire Spaw was building.

"Spooner," Lovich threw over his shoulder, "Lincoln may have freed the slaves, but your soul belongs to Captain Botis. You do like he says."

Marwood and Spooner readied their horses. "Take the long way around," Jubal Stone came up and told them. His long greasy hair curled over his ears. "We don't want them Buffalo Soldiers backbearing up our asses."

"I guess I know how to ride for bacon, Jubal," Spooner shot back.

"Well see you don't lead them Negro soldiers back here, that's all I am saying."

They rode off and camped the night in a low spread of mesquite brush and sacahuista. The moon was a cotton ball in the sky. Spooner appeared in better humour now that he was away from the main company.

Spooner carried a lightweight Colt .44 revolving rifle as his main weapon. He cleaned the rifle bore with an oily rag. "There's a burr under the captain's saddle," he murmured. He wiped the bore down one last time and loaded the weapon. "Ever since I knowed him."

Marwood fed small branches into the fire lengthwise, Indian fashion. They caught and burned. "What burr? Is he looking for something?"

Spooner charged the chambers with ball and powder, placed percussion caps over the vent nipples at the rear of the cylinder. He propped the rifle beside him and looked at Marwood in all earnestness, eyebrows cocked.

"Man, don't you know who you're riding with?" he asked. "The captain, he don't like being proved wrong 'bout nothing. Especially somebody just joined the outfit."

"I am not out to prove anyone wrong," Marwood said. "I don't know what you're talking about."

Spooner kicked one leg out. He settled down and watched the fire. "Captain says he can remember every day of his life, and I believe it." Spooner looked up. "One night we threw date and time at Botis and damn if he didn't have all the facts at his fingertips. Naturally, we couldn't prove he was in Germany or France on such and such a date, or what the weather was like in Belgium in March of '52. But, I don't think no man could make it up so quick on the fly. What convinced me was when I gave the date I married my old gal, Sarah Anne. That was in San Antone, years ago. Damn if Botis didn't have the weather down to the temperature, plus the fact a freight-wagon had overturned in the *alameda* and crushed a little girl's legs. A doctor had to amputate on the spot. The captain was there at the time, you see, and he remembered everything that happened about the day."

Neither of them spoke. The fire snapped.

"I don't know where he gets that power," Spooner said. "If it was something he found or was born with. But I can't deny he has it."

Marwood said nothing.

Spooner coughed into his hand. He looked at the yellow sputum and flung it into the brush then wiped his thin hand on his shirt. "But you asked about something else and I'm going to tell you. If you ride with us you best know. The captain says he saw something somewheres up in high prairie country. He rode toward it, but it disappeared. Every time he sees it and rides for it, it disappears on him. He knows it's there, and one day he will find it." Spooner noticed Marwood's growing doubt. "That's what the captain says."

"You mean like that sun pillar we saw the first day?" Marwood asked. "I've seen those before, too."

"No," Spooner said. "This is something else."

"What did he see?"

"Why don't you ask Spaw," Spooner hedged. "Or Old Doc Quillen, maybe. He's been with the captain longest. They both of them know more than I do."

A coyote called in the dark. The moon did not answer back.

"You believe this vision story, whatever it is?" Marwood asked.

"It don't matter a damn what I believe," Spooner said, listening to the coyote with his head cocked. "All that matters is what the captain, him, believes."

Marwood draped bacon over *palo verde* poles to crisp. When Spooner spoke again his voice was soft and pliant, as if he were kneeling in a confessional, professing past sins.

"You ever seen the captain's horse?" he asked Marwood.

"Yes," Marwood said. "Damn thing's a monster."

Spooner shook his head with a faint grin. "You take a closer look at that horse one day, Mar. You'll see what I mean."

"I told you I've seen his horse."

Spooner kicked his other leg out until his boots were side by side. He tapped the toes together. "Not up close you ain't, or you wouldn't say that you had."

"That logic doesn't scour, Spooner. Is every man in this outfit crazy?"

Spooner laced his hands across his belt, lifted his thumbs. "You free and white. You ain't got to do nothing I say."

The coyote called again. Another answered with short

excited yips, farther away. The men listened to the desert speak around them. They ate in silence.

"What's the matter with you, Spooner? You've been chewing on gristle ever since we left Piedras Negras."

"It don't concern you none, mister."

"That is where I am inclined to disagree." Marwood finished eating and wiped his hands. "If I can't trust you to watch my back it concerns me greatly." He scrubbed the tin dishes with handfuls of sand and packed them away.

"Don't you worry yourself none about me," Spooner said, his eyes brick hard.

Marwood watched him across the low campfire. "I have to worry if a man is preoccupied with himself and not watching his job. It's my life that worries me."

Spooner picked up a pebble. He rolled it around in his hand and let his breath out in a long hiss, like steam from a kettle. "I got me a woman," he said low, "like I done told you. I ain't seen her in a long time." Pause. "Long time."

"I heard something about how you had family up in Bexar."

Spooner nodded. "In the Laredito. There was a boy afore I left. I'm his father and I couldn't tell you if he's alive. Think about that, Mar." He threw the pebble away. "Hell, I couldn't feed them or keep them in clothes, so I lit out. But my woman, Sarah Anne, she's alone up there with the boy, and her sick mother, and an old blind uncle who never did nothing but slouch in a rocker and eat boiled eggs and shit himself. I guess I ain't seen them going on five years now. Near close to six, mebbe."

"You want to see them?"

Spooner shook his head in an incredulous manner. "You got any family, Mar?"

"No."

"Well." Spooner didn't say more. The two men bedded down while the stars wheeled overhead.

"I can't remember my family," Marwood admitted.

"Well," Spooner said again, "only what's remembered is ever worth knowing in the first place. Otherwise, best leave it alone."

They caught up with Botis and company many days later. The excommunicate had moved off from Comanche Springs in search of new targets.

"Them Buffalo Soldiers came back after you and Spooner left," Spaw told Marwood, "so we had to skeer. The captain, he never did have the patience of glass. He's got a tear on something fierce for them now."

They found a Mexican traveller sitting on the side of the road. His *burro* had died and he had no money to eat on. He had pulled his dead animal under a shade tree and was cutting on its hindquarter, eating the meat raw.

Botis asked him where any *estancias* or *rancherias* were in these parts. The traveller said he thought there was a large one to the south, five miles from the border. Mexican squatters, Botis asked. Yes, the man nodded, there were some Mexicans there. They had a church.

"Them's the sons of bitches we're looking for," Lovich said.

"Yes," said Botis, "it appears so."

They gave the old Mexican food and water, and two American paper dollars, before riding away.

They came upon an isolated *estancia* that had been proved up. There were quarter horses stabled in a painted barn, and fifty head of longhorn cattle browsing on prickly pear cactus and haulms of grama. They were settled in the middle of nowhere.

"This ain't them, Captain," Lovich claimed. "We haven't come near south enough like that old Mexican said to."

"No, Daniel," Botis agreed, "it's not them, but they will do."

Botis waited until the family and ranch hands sat supper

before he kicked in the door. He made them kneel outside, their hands crossed on their heads. Rota and Spaw set fire to the furniture inside the house and barn, and shot the screaming livestock. There were eight family members and two work hands. Botis capped each in the head, stopping once to reload. By the time he got to the last victim, a dark-eyed girl of fifteen, Dan Lovich had returned with a grain shovel.

"You want to keep this one alive, Captain?" Lovich asked.

Her head was pushed forward into her slim hands and she sobbed. She wore a white dress with blue ribbons on the shoulders. Botis mounted his blue roan. The horse stood like a rock upon the ground, its long mane and tail blowing in the wind.

"We have a camp slut," Botis said, gathering up the reins.

"I thought we might could use us another one," Lovich explained.

"Can't spare the water." Botis turned his horse away.

Lovich reared back and hit the girl on the back of the head with the blade of the shovel. She fell forward and trembled as her brains leaked from her ears and nose. One of the scouts, Red Thunder, put his foot on her back and scalped her. The long black hair made a wet stripping sound when it came away from her skull. Red Thunder whirled the scalp. Blood dripped on his naked chest and sprayed his face.

There were whoops and gunfire into the air as if something within the company had been released and given voice. Many of the men bent to take trophies—hair, ears, and teeth—stuffing them in their belts or rolling them up in leather *mochilas*.

Jubal Stone and Spooner lassoed the mutilated bodies and dragged them into a row. Lew Spaw and another man, Sam Decker out of Murfreesboro, Tennessee, picked them up head by foot and threw them into a stone cistern used to water livestock.

That same night they hit an outfit trailing cattle up from Brownsville. The cattle were milled down for the night. They shot the trail boss—a man named James W. Slocum out of Dallas—and his two sons, and fired the chuck wagon. The remaining cowboys put up a sporadic fight before they gave way and fled into the gathering darkness.

Marwood found a Sharps rifle and a box of .52-50 shells under a pile of firewood in a separate supply wagon. Carrying torches and waving blankets the company stampeded five hundred head over the lip of a slot canyon. The animals lay five and ten deep, shattered bones and twisted bodies, a heap of broken flesh in the bottom of the canyon. When the sun came up they burned two more settlements, riding into wickiups and shooting bleary-eyed squatters in their beds. They fell upon a Spanish mission in the middle of nowhere. Botis tore down the altar and set fire to the church. People fled before them, hands covering their heads, as they rode through other *colonias*. The next *colonia* they entered the squatters were gone, and the streets and buildings were long deserted.

By week's end they had shot and killed a deputy sheriff out of Fredericksburg delivering government papers to one of the forts, and they stole six horses from a *posada* in Crockett County.

Two days later, they stopped and took stock of themselves.

They pushed south, crossing and re-crossing the border, playing tag with a tatterdemalion group of Texas Rangers that jumped them on a creek bank. They rode the night through and lost the Rangers over hard, rocky ground.

On the Ides of March, with a brisk south wind blowing, Botis removed a pair of range glasses from his saddlebag. Marwood had never seen their like. The tubes were cemented inside the empty shell of a red-eared turtle; they were an ungainly, bulky contraption. He watched as Botis put them to his face, grinning with satisfaction as he swept the country with the lenses to reconnoitre another town half a mile away.

They kept the sun behind them so no light flashed on buckles, *conchos*, or metal bridles. After Botis glassed the town and its mud streets, they backed off and retired to a dry wash enclosed by a stand of trees.

Rachel knelt beside Botis like a supplicant attending a black mass. The riders gathered 'round.

"We have a contract to fulfill," Botis told his command. "I want no misunderstanding or hesitation on this point. Except the contract has become one of our own interpretation. This ride through Texas did not change us. It has liberated us. Now we choose our own path among men, and make our own world."

The men looked at one another and nodded. There was no disagreement on this principle. They had to a man passed beyond routine social constructs like honour and loyalty to their employers. They were one entity, and had but a single purpose. They were a Hydra, multi-headed with a voracious appetite and collective focus.

"We will hit them at sundown," Botis said. "Get your gear."

The men prepared themselves, talking in hushed whispers. Some glanced in the direction of the sleepy town then went back to cleaning their guns.

Spooner sat on the far side of the camp, watching Marwood. When Marwood caught his gaze the tall black man looked away, or looked at the ground under his feet.

Spaw sidled up to Marwood. "We've crossed the border so many times I lost count what side we're on," he said.

"We're in Mexico," Marwood said.

"You sure?"

Marwood finished loading his gun. "Yep."

Spaw turned his head and spat. He looked at Botis across the way, back to Marwood.

"What are we doing here?" he whispered. "These bastards ain't done us nothing wrong."

"Mayhap you can ask the captain that question," Marwood said, eying him quietly. "See what answer he gives. Spaw?"

"Yeah."

"Nothing. But this isn't on our contract."

Spaw shook his head and walked away.

A few men used Rachel to work off their edge, but for the most part each kept himself centred and honed for the upcoming battle.

When the sun's red disk touched the horizon they blacked their faces with lampblack and grease oil, tightened their saddles, and waited to be unleashed.

CHAPTER 6

Marwood watched the Cajun and Bill Rota drive the stolen mules and horses through the cobblestone plaza. As they rode they displaced layered bands of wood and gun smoke that drifted through the streets of the burning town.

Rota carried his harpoon in his right hand, the leather thong curled around his forearm. He and the Cajun disappeared with the running horses into a dry wash. Behind them, the clapboard shacks and trampled crops flamed and charred.

Spaw and Marwood sat their horses at either end of an *alameda*. Spaw covered the terminus of the road where stood a white Spanish mission crowned with flowering nopal. A weathered cross, painted gold, topped the church roof. The wooden shutters were locked tight.

Sheets of fiery ash rained from the sky and obscured the bell tower. Outside the mission, bodies sprawled, mouths and eyes agape in death. Many had run flaming into the night, some of the women with their hair smoking, only to be shot down by murderous crossfire.

Those villagers who remained alive were imprisoned inside the church walls. Marwood heard their plaintive cries behind the thick masonry. They wanted their sons and daughters, they cried. They wanted to live.

Spaw turned in his saddle, lifted in his stirrups. He looked where homes were gutted by fire and swept his eyes along the flat *azoteas*.

"Spooner rode behind this *tienda* not more than ten minutes ago, Mar," he said. "I never did see him ride out the other side."

Marwood unleathered his Colt's Dragoon and opened the gate with his thumb. He checked the percussion caps and loads by feel. He closed the gate, put the gun on half cock, and reholstered it in his usual crossways fashion.

He listened to the screams inside the church.

That's bad if Spooner got himself killed, he thought. Or worse, if he ran.

Spaw turned around, dropped back in his saddle. "Mar, did you see Spooner ride out on your end?"

The red light from the town fires wobbled. The ground was dark. The street and the bodies in it were dark.

All the world was dark.

"No," Marwood answered. "I didn't hear any shots come from that direction, either."

Spaw yanked his brass-framed Henry rifle from a saddle scabbard. He cocked the weapon. "I never thought it possible," he claimed. "I never thought Spooner would light out on us."

"I didn't know him like you did," Marwood said, and fell silent.

Somewhere in the mean dark Lovich fired his shotgun—a reverberating explosion that could only come from a sawed-off, double-barrelled .10-gauge. Killing loads that shredded a man to splintered bone and gobbets.

Marwood wondered if Lovich had caught Spooner trying to slip away from the battle. Better for Spooner if that was so, he thought. Maybe, better for them all.

Enter Botis. Rachel perched on the wooden cantle behind him, her hands on the broad shoulders of the apostate.

Marwood wondered if Botis would kill the people inside the church. Or kill the children under the guns of the two

Tonkawa scouts, Red Thunder and his humpbacked, half-idiot cousin, Little Shreve.

"Captain," Spaw called, "I think these Mexers did for Spooner after we rode in. We can't find him."

Botis rode by without checking his big horse. The jingling traces of the blue roan glinted dull red in the shifting firelight. He dismounted outside the mission, led the roan and Rachel a few more paces before dropping the reins in the dirt. He pulled a Bowie knife with a staghorn handle from his belt. The knife's bolster and guard were polished silver and a fresh scalp hung from the tang. The long blade gleamed like ice.

Captain Botis went down the street from corpse to corpse. Jubal Stone and Dan Lovich cantered up and joined him in the butchery. They worked one end of the street to the other. They took scalps, ears, and noses as it pleased them. Botis added ears and fingers to a wire scapular hanging from Acheron's throatlatch. The remaining scalps were bundled together and tied to saddle gullets.

Once finished Botis remained in the middle of the street. The knife in his hand dripped.

"You believe Spooner lit off on us?" he asked Spaw.

"I do not know, Captain." Spaw drew a shaky breath. "Yes, I think he did so."

"You see him leave, Mar?" Botis asked.

"I did not, Captain."

"Back to Bexar, maybe," Lovich suggested.

"He's got a woman there," Jubal chimed. Lovich nodded in concurrence, and spat as if that put an end to any discussion.

Botis wiped his knife blade on the bottom half of his shirt. "Where is the *alcalde*?" he asked.

The men listened to the staccato pop and snap of burning *vigas* and wood frames. Thus, Spooner's fate was sealed, and no man present would speak up in his defence.

"I'll get him, Cap," Jubal Stone said. He unlocked the *tienda*, the one Spooner was supposed to have guarded. Stone went inside the dark interior and pushed the *alcalde* out. The *alcalde* stumbled toward them in a rising cloud of dust. He was a thinning rail of a man, with shock-white hair and glassy eyes. His arms were tied behind his back with baling wire. Marwood could hear the bones in his shoulders crack under the strain.

Hemp rope was knotted around the *alcalde*'s neck. It hung between his shoulder blades to his bluing hands. He walked with bent, splayed knees, and had to look at his captors sideways. If he tried to straighten his body, the slipknot around his throat would send him kicking throttle-faced to the ground.

Botis shook a paisley handkerchief from his vest and methodically wiped his hands. He cleaned each nail with delicate care. When he finished, he folded the handkerchief and returned it to his vest pocket. He allowed himself a moment to consider the trembling prisoner before him. He plucked the fingerpiece pince-nez and placed it square on his nose.

"*Donde esta Cibola*?" Botis asked, viewing the *alcalde* through the small glass windows.

Marwood straightened when he heard the name of the city. His mouth was dry and his heart thumped.

"*Que*?" The old man gawked in disbelief at the mad creature standing before him.

"*Siete ciudades de Oro*," Botis said.

The *alcalde* stared with growing wonder at the grim faces pressing close. Men of dark light and crackling shadow. As wolves, deeply hungered, or iron kings who drove their enemies before them like leaves before a storm.

The *alcalde* swung his eyes and saw the blue roan with its bridle of human skin, and the wet scalps hanging from the saddle. He thought of his little grandson, and the children in the dry wash waiting for the pale wings of death to clatter over them, and he wept.

"*No hay tal cosa*," he told Botis.

Botis pulled an 1861 Navy Colt with gutta-percha grips and put the barrel against the *alcalde*'s forehead.

"*Somos pobres*," said the old man, quaking. "*No hay oro. No hay oro*."

Botis rolled the hammer back.

"*Una ves mas*." Botis let his words sink in with finality. "*Cibola. Donde esta Cibola*."

The *alcalde* shook his head again. The pistol barrel followed his movement. "*Por favor, Dios*," the *alcalde* said. "*No se lo que estas hablando*."

Botis fired. The man spun and fell. His blood pooled.

"Bring the rest of them out," Botis ordered.

He waited for the captives to file into the central street. Botis opened his gun and with his thumbnail flicked the spent percussion cap away. He used a powder horn to recharge the bore and patched and rammed a new ball.

The central street filled with shrieks and moans. Women clapped their hands over their mouths when they saw the tonsured, grinning skulls of the scalped victims. Botis watched them run back into the church and return. They piled a meagre offering at his feet, what little wealth the church possessed: two clay cruets, a brass chalice with paten, a silver-gilt ciborium. They brought forth a porcelain washing bowl, and linens and vestments from the sacristy. Alms from the offering box were surrendered, amounting to twelve dollars American, plus change.

As the frightened women piled the treasure at the boots of their conquerors, the men of the company whistled and shouted lewd suggestions. Many of the women turned away. One or two stopped to look with dark eyes and tangled hair, perhaps hoping to spare their lives a little longer. The men laughed and called to them.

Lovich kicked the priest from the crowd and shoved him to the fore. The robed man faltered. Lovich grabbed his arm and whirled him around. He whipped the walnut stock of his shotgun behind the man's knees. The priest collapsed to the dirt, his robe flaring out around his bare legs. An older woman in the crowd fainted. No one tried to pick her up.

Botis walked up and, in one movement, levelled his gun and fired into the back of the priest's head. He then picked four more men at random out of the crowd and shot them, one by one, in the back of the head. As he recharged his pistol a woman in a blue *rebozo* broke and ran headlong for the gully. Perhaps she had a child there, or maybe she thought the people in the gully would be the last ones killed. Whatever her reason, Lovich spun on his boot heel and discharged both barrels into her. Lovich broke the barrel of the shotgun open, blew down the tubes, and reloaded.

Marwood watched and thought about Sand Creek.

"*Me paseo con los demonios*," Botis told the frightened peasants. "*Y he venido entre vosotros*."

Women screamed anew. Men turned their faces. Some fell to their knees, weeping, and raised their arms to Botis in supplication.

Botis quieted them with a raised hand. "*Quiero encontrar Cibola. Donde esta?*"

The words whipped from his mouth like a command. The villagers told him they had no gold. They had nothing, only their lives, which he would take from them this night.

They fell to their knees with hands clasped and they pleaded and begged. Women kissed the hem of his bloody shirt, his hand.

"*Por favor*," they said, "*no maten a los niños. No tenemos oro*."

"Let them go," Botis told his men. "I think they're quits, and they don't know anything that can help us."

The villagers did not wait for the translation. They rose and ran, some staggering and retching with relief. Most went after the children, while others began to sift through the blackened wreckage of their homes, turning over cracked plates and shattered furniture.

The killers mounted their horses and filed out of the ruined town.

"What about Spooner?" Spaw asked.

Botis did not answer. He was watching the horned moon, contemplating its barren glow.

Sam Decker's voice growled out of the night. "What happened to Spooner?"

"Ran off like a scalded cat," Charley Broadwell said, a black hat over his eyes.

Decker shook his head back and forth. "No shit, you say. Crazy nigger."

The entered a dark scope of woods west of the border town and the other smoking settlements they had all but destroyed.

"Maybe Spooner followed Rota and the *cabrón* Cajun back to camp," Calvin Zapata suggested, ducking under a low hanging limb. He kicked his horse forward and caught up with Marwood. "Maybe he is there, and the *jefe* won't kill him. What do you think, Mar?"

"I don't know," he answered. "It's bad, either way."

"I hope he's back at camp," Zapata said.

The other men agreed this was a possibility. At the very least, it would be best for Spooner if it were true.

They rode until dawn.

CHAPTER 7

They stopped to breakfast in a wide field of prickly pear; long blades of light stretched over the empty land and surrounding hills. Faces blackened, clothes stinking of wood smoke and blood and gunpowder, the scarecrow band of killers dismounted.

They stalked with collective weariness between the cactus plants, picked the ripe tunas, and ate. Purple juice stained their lips and fingers. Men sucked their fingers and tossed the pulped remains back into the cactus stand while startled doves circled above them, their wings whistling.

There was a large oval clearing in the centre of the cactus patch. Spaw and Jubal gathered enough loose wood to build a fire in this clearing. The rest of the men kicked away rocks and dug shallow holes in the dirt in which to sleep. They lined their wallows with wool blankets and bedrolls and turned in.

Spaw dug up a mano and metate while making his bed. He kept digging and turned up an atlatl. He brought them to Botis for inspection.

"What are they, Cap?" he asked.

"The Alpha and Omega of primitive man." Botis weighed the implements in his hands.

The men drifted off to their separate beds. Marwood awoke in the late afternoon. He tipped his hat to protect his face from the sun, watching as a slim form rose from a rumpled bedroll and stood cameo to the westering sky.

Rachel shook out her long hair. Her thin cotton dress clung to her like second skin. Her legs were white and bare below her knobbed knees.

She glanced in Marwood's direction and approached the smouldering fire. Marwood edged a few sticks into it lengthwise. The flame caught. Rachel sat down beside him, her arms wrapped around her skinny legs.

"Ain't there nothing else to eat on?" she asked. Her pointed chin and fingers were stained purple from the tuna juice. Her face was smudged with traces of lampblack. She looked like some disaffected mummer from a road carnival. Her uncombed hair and hollow eyes were wild, more animal than girl.

"I have charqui," Marwood said.

"What's that?"

"Buffalo jerky."

She wrinkled her nose. "I guess so." He gave her a strip from his rawhide pouch.

She chewed the dry meat and watched the fire with solemn eyes. "My name is Rachel."

"I know that."

She studied his quiet profile. "You don't much want me, do you? The other men do, but you ain't never called on me as yet."

"How old are you?" he asked her.

"I'm old enough to get my monthlies, I guess." She took another bite of jerky and chewed. Her lips were chapped from the dry wind and she kept licking them.

"Well, when I want you, or any woman, I'll let you know," he told her.

She shrugged her bony shoulders. "If you don't, then you don't. You ain't doing me no favours. It's better than a beating is all I'm saying."

"Who beats you?"

"My Pa used to, lots." She finished the meat and sat with her elbows pressed in the pit of her stomach. "Mama died when I was born, so Pa, he strapped me and the other kids some. It don't matter. He'd a done it anyway because he's a man."

"Where is your Pa?"

"Up to Salt Lake City, last I heard." She picked her teeth with a broken fingernail. "He went Mormon and churched a widow and turned deacon. Last I saw of him was in Auraria, the night he kicked me out of the house for good. He told me he had a new family to worry about and I was none of his lookout no more."

"Is that why you ran away?"

Rachel looked at Marwood as if his question were so crackbrained it didn't warrant an answer. She bent her head and played with the hem of her frayed *chalina*. Marwood thought she was crying, but when she looked up her eyes were bright with fury.

"I ain't got no place else to go," she said. "This here camp is as good as anywhere."

Marwood paused, thinking of his own past—what little he remembered. How it all fit together, if it did.

Where he belonged. If he did.

"You may be right," he admitted. "This place is as good as anywhere."

Rachel looked like she was ready to talk about something else. "You think Spooner run off like they said?" she asked.

"I don't know. Looks like he might have done."

"What is he going to do?" she asked.

"Who?"

Rachel pointed to the sleeping form of Abram Botis.

Marwood looked across the rincon where horses cropped grass.

"I think he's already gone and done it," he told the girl.

"How do you mean?"

"The Tonkawa scouts are gone."

Rachel looked around the camp with alarm. She gave a minute shudder. "I hate that one."

"Who?"

"Little Shreve. He's always pawing himself like some scratchy ape. I think there's something wrong in his head. Well, I hate him, that's all." She found Marwood's eyes. "Sometimes I think I should up and quit this place and go back to Auraria."

"Why don't you?"

She shook her head. "I told you I ain't got no place else to go. Besides, them things are easier for a man to do."

They watched the horses graze, side by side.

"What if I did up and leave him," Rachel said out of the blue. "Are you going to take care of me?"

"No."

"Well, stop all your talk of leaving." Her face flushed red. "You don't think much of me, so go to hell."

"I didn't say that."

"You don't have to. All you sons of bitches are the same after you get pussy. You don't think high of me because I stay with him. But a man can leave when he has to in this country. A man can make where he needs to go. A woman can't. Not always, she can't."

She hugged her knees tight and lowered her head. Another man rose from his bedroll and went off to make water. One by one the encampment started to wake and move about.

Rachel watched the men. "We could do it," she said quietly. "We could run. We could go north. So far north they could never track us."

She faced Marwood. "You could kill them." She nodded at his Sharps. "I know you could kill them with that."

"I guess, but I'm not going to do that."

She mulled it over. "So, why don't you leave?" she asked him plain.

"Because I don't have any place else to go, either," he told her truthfully.

She picked at her ragged nails. "I heard them talk about you the other night."

"All right."

"They said you used to be a range detective."

"That's right."

"They're going to kill you some night."

Marwood smiled. "What makes you think that?"

"You think these men are going to let a detective live long? You're as cracked as Little Shreve."

He laughed at her. "Do you know what a range detective is?"

"I know a detective is with the law."

Marwood shook his head. "A range detective works for someone who operates outside the law. I used to ride down rustlers and such. We'd either hang or shoot them. That's all I ever done."

She cocked her head to one side. "Are you for certain you ain't no lawman?"

"I think I would know," he said. He thought about Laredo, Judge Creighton, the men he had killed, and whom he might kill tomorrow.

He thought about lines he didn't want to cross.

Rachel rose to her feet and brushed herself off. She adjusted her *chalina* and stared down at him. "My name ain't Rachel," she told him. "That's what he calls me, but that ain't my real name. The other men, they call me it, too, because they want to do like him. Well, I guess you've noticed that much."

She turned and walked through the camp and went out of sight. Marwood got up and went among the horses. He walked up to Acheron and inspected the animal. The horse had corn marks on its flanks—old scarring from ancient battles. He came closer, talking soft, and stroked the animal's muscled withers. He walked around the horse. From fetlock to withers to quarter, a winding blue-black colouration like a long river with tributaries and rills flowed over the animal, winding a dark and ancient magic throughout. Marwood fancied he could feel a hidden power emanating from the horse. A pulsing connection to his own past, perhaps, and the thing he carried inside. A key that might unlock the unknowable of his life. Like Cibola.

But such a thing, he thought, could not be true. If it was true then he was crazy. Marwood stepped back from the horse. He was breathing hard. "Acheron," he said out loud.

The horse flicked an ear forward.

A single gunshot sounded, toward camp. Marwood walked back. The men were gathered around something lying on the ground.

"I saw it jump and tag her in the neck," Spaw said.

"What was she doing out there?" Rota asked.

Marwood edged between them. Rachel lay on the ground, her face bone-white and her hands composed over her breasts. Her neck was mottled red and swollen to twice the size. There were puncture wounds in her throat with slight bruising around them.

"What happened," the Cajun asked, tucking his loose shirt inside his pants. "Did somebody find Spooner?"

"Naw, it's Rachel."

"Hell happened?"

"She went off yonder to make water and this here bull rattler popped up and bit her in the neck. Killed her stone dead."

"Weren't there nothing you could do?" the Cajun asked.

"Well, shit, I killed the snake," Rota said. "Hell else do you want?"

"Where is that goddamn snake?"

Someone kicked its limp body. "Right here it is."

"Goddamn hell. It's big enough to wrap a wagon wheel. Look. Them rattles are big as a bull's pizzle."

Silence fell upon them like a winter's cloud.

"If Spooner was here he could cut that snake up for stew meat."

"You do it, frogpecker," Rota said. "I got to dig a grave for this whore even though I'm the one who killed the snake. Where's the shovel?"

"Botis has it. Hey, Captain, the camp slut got killed. We need the shovel to bury her."

Botis came forward, stripped down to the waist. "What happened to her?"

"She went to piss and this rattler jumped her. Oh, hell no, Quillen, you stay away from her. Captain, tell that ghoul to stay away from her."

Botis cut the rattles off the viper with his knife. They were longer than his hand.

"Best bury her quick before she spoils," he said. "I will say a few words when you are ready." He left to tie the rattles to the latigo of his saddle.

"Hey, where are the *cabrón* Tonks?" Calvin Zapata asked.

"They lit out last night after Spooner."

"Oh, shit. Poor Spooner. I done forgot about him."

Lovich laughed at their solemn faces. "If this don't beat a crooked stick up the ass," he said.

The men looked at him.

"We should've kept that little Mex gal alive after all," he explained.

They buried Rachel and piled stones atop the earthen mound. Then they gathered around the grave and removed their hats.

Botis presided at the head of the grave. "There are people who travel between clouds of what was, and what should be," he said. "So have we gathered around one fallen to the hunger of the earth. One day, we, too, shall dip into its maw. It is ever thus where the devil strides unopposed, and men fight for recognition." He put his hat back on his head. "May Rachel find her place to rest. Amen."

"Amen," the men said in a ragged chorus. They retired to the campfire. They ate but little. Few had any appetite, including Marwood. Some packed their pipes or rolled paper and smoked, or cleaned their boots with their knives. Marwood repaired a buckle on his saddlebag while Jubal Stone and Lovich ran more lead balls and piled them in a hat.

"Captain," Spaw said, "what are these things? I mean, really." He laid the implements he had discovered earlier around the fire pit.

Botis picked them up one at a time. "They are the tools and descriptors of a primitive man," he said. "First, the plate of life, and the grinding stone that makes bread. Into how many throats did the grain pounded upon this stone find its way? How long did yon stone lie under the earth until stumbled upon by our band?"

He laid them aside and picked up the stone atlatl. He turned it over in his hands.

"But it is this implement of war that acts as the binding mechanism," he said. "Man defined. The mano and metate cannot exist without the atlatl. But the atlatl can, and does, exist separate from all other things. I tell you this weapon is the true measure of man. What's more, it is the measure of him who created man."

The next morning, Red Thunder and Little Shreve returned on their unshod ponies. Their half-naked, tattooed bodies glistened with grease in the broad sunlight.

They led Spooner's empty horse between them by the reins.

When the band broke camp they cantered single-file past the stone grave. A sheet of brown man skin with empty arms and legs hung on long mesquite thorns. It billowed and stirred in the moderate breeze as if invested with the spirit of the man it once contained.

On top of the lone grave were the mano and metate. The atlatl was nowhere seen.

CHAPTER 8

They regrouped and rode back into Texas, ready for war. Fifteen miles outside Las Moras they ran into a pack of surprised Rangers and fought their way clear. It was a fortuitous engagement for both sides: no man was wounded, but Marwood lost a heel on his boot and came away with a bruised calf muscle. Balls whizzed through the air with their peculiar buzz. Toward the end of the day they lost contact with one another in the mingling brush. Both sides took the opportunity to disengage, honour intact.

A week later they rounded up stolen stock and used the money to buy new supplies in Uvalde. Marwood had his boot repaired and sought out a farrier's. He walked into the open shop. The air smelled of strong acid. There were powder kegs in back, and sawdust and shavings covered the wooden floor. A workbench with a vise contained blocks of pecan and walnut wood, waiting to be lathed, along with scattered brass tools, saws, and moulds.

"Yes, sir, help you?" the farrier said.

"I need someone to tighten the stock on this here Sharps."

The farrier took the gun, looked it over, and went to work. The other men in the company scattered throughout town, but kept their helling to a minimum. Spaw found a group of Texicans willing to purchase his scalps so they could bump the price and send them to another buyer in London. Lovich bought himself a new Mexican saddle. Jubal Stone had a knife handle repaired while Calvin Zapata bought a new pair of boots and a tooled leather belt.

They met up later that afternoon and pressed on.

They killed when the mood took them, and it took them often. Their torn clothes soon reeked of blood and powderblack again. As their rancid clothes rotted they dressed in barbaric skins and rank leather sewn with raw thews. Spaw took to wearing a necklace of teeth. Bands of coyotes followed them on the trail, snuffling their collective stink and moving from bush to cactus like liquid smoke.

They were on the deep trail when one day Jubal Stone looked behind them and chucked his tongue at the stalking coyotes, with their yellow eyes and red, lolling tongues. He turned back around.

"When I ran niggers across the Atlantic," he began, "we always had sharks follow the slaver ships. Hundreds of the devils, all kinds and sizes, too. They waited for us to toss the dead overboard, you see, and there were always new dead to cull from the holds. God, you never smelled such a stink in your life. It would permeate the wood. Union ships found us at night from the smell alone. You had to draw a knife to cut your way from taffrail to mainmast."

He rode on, marshalling his thoughts. "Yes, sirrah," he told them all, "ebony gold. All gone now, though. The sea, the sea. You malandered sons of bitches will never understand what that was like." He raised his voice, "What say you, Bill?"

"Aye, scrimshander," the ex-Quaker replied from up-column. "There ain't nothing to make a man feel as alive as a rising sea and a canted deck under his feet. I have never seen the like before, and I fear I never shall again."

Rota clucked his tongue and took in his dry surroundings. "It ain't right men like us who saw the sea should have to die in Texas," he said.

That night they found a lone buffalo in a wallow about to give birth. Her belly was swollen, and she was mired shoulder deep in thick mud. The Cajun thumped her belly.

"She's a ripe melon," he said. He used a mesquite stump to crush her head in. Jubal Stone and Dan Lovich cut her open and pulled a half-formed calf from her gaping belly. It was encased in a thin membranous sheath, its legs jerking. The calf lifted its blind and feeble head, and bawed pitifully. They spitted the calf and hung it on heavy *palo verde* poles to smoke over a fire. As the black skin crisped they pulled it off and ate the succulent flesh beneath. Grease dripped into the fire, flared at Marwood's feet. Spaw gathered the blood-milk from the dam's bursting udders and apportioned it out in bowls.

The men stood about the edge of the fire, drinking the milk laced with hot blood. Marwood drank when the bowl came his way. The milk was warm and had a not unpleasant tang. Sparks from the fire spiralled upward. The stars overhead were thick as sugar.

Before Spooner died, the two black men and the Tonkawas always kept separate fires. Water, ammunition, and food were divided equally in that company, but little else in the way of physical comfort.

But on this night, while the Tonkawas stood apart, silent as shadows, Ed Gratton took his place beside the main fire. Men shuffled aside to make room for him. Nothing was said, in welcome or dismissal.

Lovich watched Red Thunder and Little Shreve strip handfuls of mesquite beans from the stunted trees and chew them.

"Goddamn, they'll eat anything, won't they?" he said.

"They ate Spooner right enough," Jubal Stone put in.

Lovich's face hardened. "Blast your eyes, that ain't funny."

Jubal threw a bone he had been gnawing into the fire. His black hair hung on either side of his face. "Who's funnin'?"

They rode through Zavala County and into Carrizo Springs with Botis in the lead. The town looked deserted until they spied a mass of people assembled in the town square. Some of the townsfolk were holding torches and candles.

Botis dismounted and pressed through the crowded sea of humanity. It seemed every person born was present.

"What are you hammerheads gawking at?" Lovich brawled.

One of the men in the crowd answered back. "There was the most godawful thunderstorm last night. Washed everything out. Fred Glick lost his new barn. The city graveyard collapsed into the creek after it overflowed its banks. Some of the coffins were turned up at all angles like wagon spokes. You never saw such a dreadful sight. They found this here coffin with a girl in it and dug it out."

"You don't say."

"See for yersel', if'n you don't believe me."

"I expect I will," Botis said, and proceeded to do exactly that. He pushed to the head of the crowd and there spied a coffin propped across two barrels. Set into the coffin's lid was a rectangular pane of glass, thick, rimmed with lead. There was a hairline crack in one corner. Reposed inside was a twenty-year-old blonde girl with a white shroud over her face.

"It's like the angel was buried only yesterday," sighed an old woman in the crowd. "But there is not man one in town who can remember the day it happened, or who she ever was."

"The glass is cracked," Botis said. "Air is seeping inside. She is beginning to decompose. You can see it plain."

"We've been watching it happen all day," a bank clerk affirmed. "She's turning to dust before our eyes. Yet she was pure as snow all these long years buried."

"The ways of God are mysterious," another woman stated. She crossed herself and kissed her rosary.

An eighty-year-old man with a beaked nose and close-set ears shuffled forward. "I think that there girl might be my mother," he said.

Everyone turned to see who had spoken such strange and outlandish words. The old man had a long, stubbled jaw and wild hair that stuck out from under his hat like twists of paper. He lurched into the crowd and stood before them, opened his mouth to speak again.

"I remember my Daddy, he said we buried Momma in a coffin with a glass window." The people standing around him started. They leaned forward. "Daddy said when the day of Resurrection came God could look into her eyes and lift her straight into heaven."

The old man touched the corner of the coffin with trembling fingers. "She died of the fever, you see. I was but a baby myself when it happened."

One of the younger men in the crowd threw back his head and laughed. "Oh, hell, Harvey, the only thing you remember is the gutter you slept in last night."

"That, and the vomit he swamped off my floor for a bucket of chock," said another man, owner of one of the saloons in town.

"Mister," a thin reedy cowboy with red hair and a rash of pimples on his neck and forehead addressed Marwood. "Don't you believe a word Harvey Spivey says. He is the lyingest sumbitch in Dimmit County."

"I can prove it," said Harvey, who by this time had become positively emotional, either from the moment or from being called a liar in front of the entire town.

"Well, go on, Harvey," another man called. "Show us your cards."

Harvey swallowed hard. His entire body trembled. "My Daddy, he told me my oldest brother Jim was buried in the same coffin Momma was. Jim was one and a half years old. Daddy did that to save money to the undertaker. That's what my Daddy told to me before he died and it was true."

"He's full of shit."

"Somebody get a crowbar."

"Aw, hell, just bust the glass."

Eventually, a boy was charged to run to the livery and fetch a hammer, pritchel, and maul. Men worked the lid off the coffin with no little trouble; it had been cemented and puttied until every nick and crack was sealed for eternity. Final nails screeching, they at last removed the top and set it aside.

"I will be goddamned," one of the workmen whispered. A soft sigh went up from the crowd. They gave way like a tide as Harvey approached the coffin. Torches spat and guttered. No one spoke a word. There were heavy tears in Harvey's red-rimmed eyes. He reached into the box and drew forth a small, bundled form. He picked the paper wrapping from its tiny, crumpled face.

"He looks like me," Harvey said. His voice cracked. "I am holding my older brother, Jim, dead these seventy-odd years."

He began to bawl outright.

The women pressed around Harvey and spirited him away. Some began to sing and chant psalms. A collection was taken up for transit and reburial of Harvey's mother and older brother in a double grave. The plot was to be kept in perpetuity until the Rapture. Even though it was Sunday, stores opened their doors for business. Drinks and food were sold in the square, and then given away outright. Marwood ate a huge plate of machaca and stewed corn, and drank *colonche* from a ceramic ewer. Some of the men took out their guns, howled, and shot at the moon. There was a general, festive air. Someone found a guitar and an impromptu band formed. Three men carried a piano outside. Not to be outdone, the owner of the local saloon had his employees bring out a player piano. But the scroll jammed and the player piano was scrapped and added to the central bonfire.

People slept and danced and drank in the square, and not a few bastards were conceived that night. Daybreak—women in their underclothes baked buttermilk biscuits, pans of jalapeno cornbread, and boiled gallons of black Arbuckle coffee. When no one was looking they threw in an extra handful of coffee beans until it turned this side of syrup. Marwood drank several hot cups with lots of sugar. Botis and his men stuffed themselves on platters of cornbread and goat cheese, bacon, and fried potatoes.

Botis had been drinking all night long. He lurched into one of the land agents, a man whose dubious claim to fame was in having his father shot by Roy Bean in Sonora.

Botis took the man aside. "We are looking for a ranch," he said.

"There are some good plats up to the Leona River."

"No, this would be a larger place."

"Uncut land larger than for you and your men to work?"

"No. This would be established and proved up."

"You mean a tract of land moved out and prime."

"No. A large ranch owned. I know there's one in this area."

"You must be talking about the Lancaster outfit. That's the only big place I know hereabouts. Run near a million and a half acres. That sound right?"

"Yes. Yes, it does."

"Lancaster joined up with the Stackpoles and bought out Old Man Twillinger," the land agent said. "Bob Lancaster, he runs it now. Well, they say he runs it, but everyone gets a share of that pie. He married into Molly Frierson's family up down Reynosa way. It's her twin brother, August Frierson, who's the real brains of that outfit. He owns the house, anyway. Lives there now."

"Are there any larger?"

"You mean in Texas?"

"Yes."

"Not in Texas."

"Where I can find Mr. Frierson?"

"At his ranch like I said."

"Yes. Do you know where that might be?"

The county clerk sketched a map in the dirt with a hickory cane. "Go out to LaSalle County. This here bend in the Nueces River? Got a real nice place there. Can't miss it. Close your eyes and throw a rock and you'd hit it. The Double-barred V is their brand. When you get there tell them Ol' Victor remembers the time Bob Grat let that skunk loose in the milking room. He'll remember. You just tell him."

"I will tell him," Botis said. He rejoined his men and handed Spaw three separate slips of paper with printing on one side. "Send one telegram in the morning, noon, and at nightfall," he instructed. "Do not wait for a reply. They won't come."

"Where you going, Cap?" Spaw asked.

"To balance the books. I will take two men. Lovich and Mar, get your horses. We will meet up with you other boys later."

Marwood and Spaw went to exercise their horses. When they brought them back to the stable Spaw said, "It ain't going to be easy with Rangers and God all looking for you."

"It's not Rangers I'm worried about," Marwood said.

Spaw rubbed his horse down with a sugar sack. "I guess you noticed the captain is a little touched." Spaw stood with his arms draped over the back of his horse. "I know you ain't happy about that Mexican village, Mar. I ain't saying I liked it, either. But Botis is a good man to ride for. We wouldn't stick if the pay wasn't right."

Marwood watered and curried his mare. "I'm not complaining."

"No, you're not the kind."

Spaw tossed the wet sacking in a corner and took a deep breath. "Look here, it's naught but trail talk, Mar. I don't set store in it. I take it when Botis killed that abbot over to the Old Country he thought they were trying to hide the existence of this city he's looking for. He's had a strong hate on for them ever since."

"How so?"

"Like I said, I think he killed somebody and had to run." Spaw lifted the foreleg of his horse and cleaned out the frog with a paddle knife. "Anyway, he once't saw a vision of a golden city. He says it's somewhere in the west. He wants to find it again, open up its gates and go home. He prays for it daily. Doc Quillen was with him at the time. So was Dan Lovich."

Marwood stopped currying his mare and stared at Spaw. Shafts of sunlight spilled from open chinks in the roof, highlighting ragged spider webs and drifting dust motes.

"The hell," Marwood said.

"That's true. I heard them talk and they weren't spinning." Spaw stared through the open door of the stable. It was as if he were looking thousands of miles away. "They was out there alone and they saw it lift from the desert with towers and spires of spun glass." He shook his head and came back to himself. "I don't think such a thing exists. But if it does, it needs to be stopped. Thing like that, it don't belong in the world of men."

"Well, I don't know," Marwood said.

"Listen, Mar, I want for you to take my dun."

"I couldn't do that."

"No, you listen," said Spaw. "Your mare, she can't go all day, but this dun, he can. You are liable to get yourself in a jackpot out there. If you do, you'll need a fast horse."

"You give me your saddle, too?"

"I ain't giving you my saddle, you son of a bitch."

"How about your blanket?"

"I hope you get shot and skun like Spooner."

"Well," Marwood said. "I thank you, anyway."

"Be careful out there, Mar."

"See you down the trail."

"Yeah. I guess."

"Yeah, I guess so, too."

Marwood led his horse from the stable and met Botis and Lovich already sitting their saddles. Marwood swung into leather and the three rode abreast into the high cane grass.

The men who stayed behind watched them leave with various looks of envy and muted disappointment.

The Cajun hooked his thumbs through his belt and shook his head. "Well, if this ain't the drizzlin' shits on a Sunday afternoon." He looked around at the men. "They done gone and left us high and dry."

CHAPTER 9

They rode out of a roiling cauldron to the east and came upon a lone ranch house. They hid their horses in the bottom of a dry streambed. Botis chewed hardtack, lying on a grassy hummock on one thick elbow. He surveyed the layout with his turtle shell binoculars.

The house was a ten-room, two-storey clapboard affair. It had a wide colonnaded porch and a pair of white stars painted on its slanted red roof.

Groups of mounted and armed men came and went from the structure at varying intervals throughout the day. Botis remarked it was telling enough since pickets had been pulled from their posts. The house and grounds, for all purposes, were unprotected. Eventually, a large group of men gathered on the front porch, checked their guns and rifles, and, with packed saddlebags, rode off to the north. They did not return.

The day wore on. A black-tailed hawk razored through the cobalt sky. Nothing else moved. Marwood held his loaded Sharps rifle at the ready. He could hear naught but the beating of his heart.

"I reckon it's our turn to balance this ledger, like you say, Cap," Lovich said low.

Botis agreed. "Let us go down into Canaan together."

They retrieved their horses and rode through an open Hampshire gate. They paused on the veranda and went inside the closed-up house, guns drawn.

The interior was furnished in dark Spanish style with beaded board and expensive floor rugs. An elderly woman wearing blue spectacles met them at the bottom of the stairs. She carried a wicker basket of dirty wash sheets. She dropped the basket and, with a scream caught in her throat, turned to run. Lovich caught her in a wallpapered dining room furnished with a long table and wood-burning stove. He rapped the stock of his sawed-off .10-gauge on the back of her head and she went down.

They tied her up with clothesline, gagged and threw a horse blanket over her, and folded her into a root closet. She kicked the wall. They dragged her out, tied her feet together, and shoved her back inside. Lovich locked the door and braced a Morris chair underneath the glass knob.

The three killers mounted the stairs. The hickory steps creaked under their combined weight. They found the dying man in the third upstairs room. The windows were thrown open for a breeze. A johnny-pot in the corner was filled to the brim with yellow mucous and brown slime.

August Frierson was in bed with a red silk counterpane up to his shoulders. His skeletal hands lay outside the counterpane, holding two six-guns. He was too weak to lift them.

Gentle as milk, Botis took the guns from August Frierson's hands and placed them on a polished dressing table. He stared at the dying man with something akin to pity, like a man might feel for a dog with a broken back.

"We are just going to kill you a little," he said.

Lovich tore the covers away and hauled the living skeleton out of bed. The sick old man was dressed in soiled bedclothes, and he stank. His arms and legs were thin from the wasting disease that cindered his bones, but his paunch was large as a water keg and wobbled on his frame. His feet were bony with long, spider-like toes. The slack skin on his face hung like loose gutta-percha rubber.

Lovich steadfastly uncoiled a long rope. He slung one end

over a ceiling beam and slipped the noose over the old man's head. Marwood got on the other end and caught up the slack.

"*Grrk.*" It was the first sound Frierson had made. He sat on the floor, thin rooster neck stretched so the cords and muscles bulged; one shiny white leg extended, the other crooked beneath him.

Botis sat on his haunches, beside the old man. He folded his hands and stared Frierson square in the face.

"I am the only friend you have in this room," Botis said. "That man on the other end of the rope will never let out slack once he starts to haul in. Never have I seen a man so taken to killing for the sake of vengeance. He is my Hotspur."

Frierson tried to turn his head and look at Marwood, but he could not find the right angle. His breath sawed in short, choking rasps.

"The other Texas families have abandoned you," Botis continued. His voice turned mellow. "Now that the truth is out, they will not risk public shame and imprisonment to save your hide. They will not risk their worthwhile lives to save your worthless one. You are the dross and dunnage of their existence. To save themselves they have thrown you to the wolves. They have thrown you to me."

"I . . . I," Frierson gargled.

"It is man's right to kill what comes before him," Botis said. He lifted a finger.

Marwood set his legs and hauled on the rope, and the old man rose thrashing into the air. Legs like knobbed sticks kicked with furious impotence; hands flailed at the noose, trying to find purchase.

The struggle lessened. The hands dropped and his body spun as the hemp plies untwisted. Botis lowered his finger and Frierson crashed to the floor so hard the walls shook.

The old man lay beside Botis, weeping like a damaged and humbled child.

"I entered our contract in good faith," Botis said. He loosened the noose around Frierson's throat to let him breathe and smoothed back Frierson's wiry hair. "I did as I was charged. I upheld my end of the bargain. Yet you betrayed my service, and now you find yourself bereft of friends and hope."

"I will give you ten thousand dollars if you let me live."

It was a markedly apparent statement, delivered from this frail creature with such conviction. It was both indication of intent and desperation.

Botis frowned and shook his head slowly. "We are beyond crass monetary weights. We have moved into a dark realm, you and I. Here do we walk together, hand in hand, through a shadowed valley. We are between the rope and the gun. It is ever thus for men like you and me."

"I don't want to die," the man said.

"I do not blame you. A narrow life is a wasted life."

The old man rose into the air. He kicked and spun and gurgled. Face blue, he soiled himself. The pale yellow urine dripped off his toes onto the floor; his movements turned feeble and spasmodic.

"Let him down, Mar. Mar, let him down."

Marwood lowered the man. Botis put his face close to Frierson's. There was very little life left in this thing. Very little air. "A man can afford the luxury to love his enemy only after he kills him," Botis said. "This is the Great Truth. If you cannot understand this, you cannot understand anything about me."

They bundled August Frierson up and carried him outside, arms and legs dangling like limp cordage. Botis went into the barn and came out with a roll of French barbed wire. They tied him up. Lovich straddled the supine body, thumbed back the hammers on his shotgun, and cut loose with both barrels. The sound of the blast echoed between the two-storey house and the cottonwood trees ranked along the riverbank.

They brought the horses around and climbed into saddle and rode away, leaving their offal sacrifice in the road for the turkey buzzards, and the other nameless things that did crawl and slink upon the ground.

CHAPTER 10

They rode into Bexar past the Spanish Governor's Palace, with its Hapsburg coat of arms carved in stone. They hitched their horses on the Plaza de Armas and passed through a dark courtyard with a central water fountain and lush, green foliage.

Marwood followed Botis and Lovich into a public house across the divide. Inside, a huge pecan tree grew out of the hardwood floor at a thirty-degree angle, right through the centre of the saloon and out the rooftop. The huge trunk was half again the circumference of a wagon wheel. Canvas louvers were set in the ceiling, operated by long tipi-like poles. These were used to let smoke out or rain in, or redirect circulating breezes into the stifling miasma of cigar smoke, perfume, sweat, and the general stink of the saloon.

Hanging on the walls were gilded mirrors and fantastic oil paintings from dead Dutchmen in Paris. Tattered Texas flags were prevalent, including relics like the Gonzales Banner, the blood-torn Goliad Flag, and the 1819 First Texas Lone Star Flag from when Texas was nothing more than an outflung province of the Spanish Empire.

Across the length of the room stood a mahogany bar with a tiled countertop, polished brass rail, and ivory-carved corners. Spittoons ringed the bar. Glasses and bottles of every shape and size imaginable filled open shelves from floor to ceiling. Tables, chairs, hard-backed settees, all manner of furniture took up every possible square foot of flooring.

Two sweeping staircases supported by white marble colonnades curled like cattle horns from the second-storey landing. Arrayed along the upper storey walls was door after door of polished oak. Each door had a number, and each number had a brass key assigned to it and protected by an armed man with green leather ledger and black inkwell.

Painted women, with exquisite hair and subtle perfumes, moved through the hall. They dressed in hoops, whalebone, and lace, and sailed to and from the ports of men. There were ladders of every description and colour placed around the giant pecan tree. Laughing women sat atop them with their knees open, smoking machine-rolled cigarettes. They fielded lewd calls and eager hands with obscene sallies of their own.

Adjoining the main room were private alcoves with tightly drawn curtains. Occasionally, here and there through a vertical chink of light, Marwood saw a man riding a wild-haired Creole on a green leather couch. Or a woman unclothed and drinking raw gin from a cut glass tumbler while men warred with cards for her favour.

There was much noise and music and speech, and the saloon proper was a hot press of pink flesh, wanton lust, bribery, greed run riot, and suppressed sexual violence.

Botis walked up to the bar with Marwood and Lovich on either side. He laid his big hands flat. "What do you have that you don't apportion out to the rabble?" he asked.

The bartender, a man with Macassar-oiled hair and red cuffs around his sleeves, replied, "Well, sir, for a man of . . . refined taste and judgement, I always suggest Glenlivet. It's the best single malt whiskey from the Speyside distilleries in Ballindalloch."

"I'll take a gill of that horse piss. And again for these men."

"Yes, sir. Happy to oblige." The bartender's eyes took in their rank clothes and rundown appearance. He hesitated a fraction too long.

"You want to see my colour," Botis said. "Is that it?" He started to open his wallet.

"Well, sir, this is a special shipment we receive only once a year. Few men are as elevated in their palate"—the bartender swallowed painfully—"as you are. Most customers are happy with the more economical purchase of aged busthead, or chock out of a tin pail. It's easier on their wallet."

"I am not happy with busthead or chock," Botis said.

"No, sir," the bartender said in a hurried manner, "I see you are not. I'll pour your drinks right away."

"Make it a bottle so's I don't have to crack it over your fucking head."

"Yes, sir. One bottle of twenty-five-year-old Glenlivet. Our only bottle. Coming up."

The bottle and glasses were produced and Botis laid down the required coin. They drank. Twenty minutes later, a town sheriff with a phalanx of armed deputies came into the bar and addressed Botis.

"Gentlemen, I would ask you to lay down your guns and come peaceably with me."

Marwood moved his hand along his belt and closer to the butt of his gun.

Botis caught his arm and shook his head. He turned slowly around. "How can I help you, Sheriff?"

"I am placing you under arrest for crimes against the State of Texas."

"What crimes have we committed against Texas?"

"Well, you broke the hand of a town marshal in Del Rio with a split maul, for one."

"He probably broke his hand pulling his pud. What is the name of this unfortunate?"

"Marshal Bill Ikard."

"Don't know the man." Botis turned away. He poured the last of the Glenlivet into their three glasses.

"Sir, do you deny you shot and killed a deputy sheriff outside Fredericksburg?"

"Never been to Fredericksburg. Not near a hundred miles of the place." Botis swallowed his drink. "I got no kin there," he said low.

"Do you also deny you burned homes and killed innocent men and women along the Mexican border?"

"Burned homes, you say? By God, I'll deny it. Who levied this calumny against me? I'll shoot the son of a bitch in his sleep." Botis faced the lawman, leaned toward him. "Sounds like you got Comanche trouble on your hands, Sheriff. You goddamn Texas shitheels better get things in order before every man's son, and woman Christian, is done for and devirginized by them savages."

"Now look here," the sheriff blustered. "I am not going to argue the point." He touched the pocket of his coat. "I have a state warrant for your arrest issued from Austin—"

"Sheriff Owen, if I may intrude one moment," commented a man who had emerged from the ringing crowd. He wore an expensive brown cattleman's suit with a silk string tie and a grey Stetson. "I believe I can clear this matter up to everyone's benefit. These gentlemen you are interrogating have been in my staid employ during the entire time in question. I will attest to that in any court of law."

"Why, Mr. Lancaster." Owen was flummoxed. "I don't know what to say. I am surprised at you, sir."

"Well, I do know what to say," Bob Lancaster went on. "I expect another telegram from Austin is waiting on your desk, which will obviate that state warrant mouldering in your pocket. Please, let me explain . . ." He made to pull the sheriff aside.

The lawman was having trouble, however, accepting these events as they transpired. "How long have these men been in your employ, Mr. Lancaster?" he asked.

"Since the Dawn of Creation," Botis boomed from over his shoulder. "Go on, son," he told the sheriff in a low voice, "it's over."

"Sheriff, if I may explain further . . ." Lancaster laid his arm around Owen's shoulders and drew him away.

Botis grinned at Lovich and Marwood. "Once he's done with that sheriff I shall accept his terms of surrender. Our Mr. Lancaster does not want his fine reputation sullied. Nor does he want to end up like the good Mr. Frierson. Ah, here he comes now." He slapped two gold double eagles on the bar.

"You boys have yourself a time," he said. "I'll be back shortly."

"For what is man's mind but a caution of madness? The stars, man. The stars were *wrong*. And I believe then, as I do now, that Botis opened a seal unto a corridor, which does cross worlds. A rift between mountain and moon. Where a man might travel without misstep or tribulation."

Lovich drained the last of the *colonche* from a clay jug. "In truth, Mar, he, too, carries the Nameless One inside—like you—and it pushes him to find its way home."

"Well, boys," Botis said, once he emerged from the Governor's Palace, "we are posted out of town. But do not despair. Father Botis has found a new line of work."

"And what might that be?" Marwood asked.

"We are going to work from sunup to backbreak for the state of Texas. Apaches, gentlemen. It appears they really are having Indian trouble out west. We have been charged with a private contract to see what we can do about it."

It was mid-dawn in the Laredito, cool and clear. They stood on a wooden sidewalk watching sporadic traffic roll past. On the street corner a Mexican woman fried chili peppers on a stone comal. The aromatic smoke drifted through the street.

Lovich had his back propped against one of the wooden sidewalk posts. His head was in both hands. "Oh," he said.

"That is, unless you nimblejacks have other ideas," Botis said, not expecting any.

"Well, Captain," Marwood spoke up, "I have no great love for Texas, but I have been thinking on this a spell."

Botis was clearly taken aback. This man before him was not known to ask for anything.

"All right, Mar," he said with care. "I'll hear what you have to say."

"Captain," Marwood said, "I want to find Cibola. I can't remember my past, but I think I come from there. Just like you, and I think I've got to go back."

Marwood had the sun behind him. Botis narrowed his eyes to look full into his face. Whatever he read there, he kept to himself for the remainder of his days. But it was enough to satisfy his mind and answer any questions he might have raised on the spot.

Botis smiled with no little surprise evident on his broad face. "I guess that's what we shall do, Mar. Daniel? What say you to this idea?"

"My head hurts," Lovich said.

"Then it is unanimous." Botis slipped a black cigar from his vest and lit it with a sulphurous match. He flipped the spent match into the street.

"Boys, get your horses," he ordered. "We are going west, where the dragons live."

PART III

The Mountains of the Moon

CHAPTER 11

The line of shadows from the riders moved in tandem along the broken ground.

The Hydra was complete once more. Spaw and the remainder of the band were picked up in Del Rio. They rode together out of Hill Country onto the blasted wastes of the Edwards Plateau. To the north lay all of Comancheria, where no sane man dared go; to the west, the burning hell of the Chihuahuan desert. The days before them were long, the nights short and freezing.

They nooned in an abandoned fort built by Indian traders. The fort was constructed against a lava mountainside. The *bajada* outside the structure was full of spindly ocotillo and cat's claw. Gnarled stumps of pin oak had been sawn and lumbered to make the walls of the interior rooms.

The main gate had been wrenched off its massive cotter pins and thrown down, as if from some great cataclysm. They rode through. The main walls of the fort were burned, breached by Mescalero Apaches in a night attack long, long ago. Nothing remained in the fort. After its capture, the interior of the fort was gutted and disassembled to feed Apache cooking fires, build travois, and repair tipi poles. The only thing the company found of any monetary worth was a pig of lead and scrap tinware. There was nothing else left to take, and Marwood could see that the hammering spring rains were slowly sloughing the adobe walls into slag.

Deep piles of soot and ash and black coals were in frozen drifts throughout the enclosure. Spaw kicked at the petrified remains of a mule, its scabrous hide sun-dried to iron across a skeletal-ribbed framework. There was other trash here, too. Metal tongues from wagons, oblate wheel rims, flint knappings, and potsherds. Broken clay plates, a knife with no haft. Old clothes so crusted with black blood when Sam Decker pulled them apart they crackled like pine logs snapping in a kitchen hearth.

Jubal Stone rolled a wheel rim out of the way so he could make room to sleep. He let the warped metal fall to one side with a clang. "Well," he said, "these sons of bitches are around here somewheres."

They spent a frozen night in the abandoned fort watching a magenta sunset burn itself out. The Milky Way arced so bright Doc Quillen could read his Bible by it.

Come morning they stirred and coughed, got the horses, and pushed west. On the trail Dan Lovich killed a porcupine. While they rode they ate the meat of the animal raw in their saddles. Over the course of the next few days Lovich used its quills to make a pattern on his gloves and the back of his coat. It was a large starburst of radiating colour, which diffracted light as the quills dried and reflected the sun. Sometimes the pattern changed with the temperature, becoming darker, or lighter, as the mercury fluctuated.

Marwood often rode behind Lovich, and did so now. He could not recognize the design, but he thought it had meaning to him.

While crossing the San Antonio-El Paso Road they held up a mail coach. Marwood shot the lead trace horse. They sent the driver, guard, and three passengers into the desert without their boots. The victims had an eighty-mile walk through Apacheria before them, with no food or water, until they reached the U.S. Army quartermaster's supply station on Cibolo Creek.

Rota lowered the metal strongbox from the coach. The

Cajun could not find the key to the strongbox so he beat the lock with a pin hammer and smashed it open. Inside were mail contracts and letters of credit from Wells Fargo in El Paso. They burned the letters and government correspondence, ripped open mail pouches, and stripped the canvas off the wagon to use as shade during the heat of the day. Doc Quillen cut up the dead horse and laid sheets of red meat to dry on a flat rock. He brushed away swarms of snarling flies with his hat, and cut away the white eggs from those who did manage to lay them.

The other three horses, fairly good stock from the coach, were added to their remuda. One of the older horses in the herd, a tall dapple usually ridden by Calvin Zapata, was seen limping. Botis examined the foreleg. It had a hairline fracture in the sesamoid bone. He studied the rough country and shook his head in despair.

"What do you think, *jefe*?" Zapata asked Botis. Hope lay in the boy's face.

"No," Botis told Zapata. "I'm sorry."

Tears welling in his eyes, Calvin went to Marwood. "I done had to kill one horse," he said. His brown hands were thrust in his pockets and he kicked at the ground in frustration. "I don't want to have to shoot another with my own gun."

Marwood took out his pistol and handed it to the boy. Calvin walked over, stiff-legged, like a man driven to a desperate task. He cocked the hammer and shot the dapple through the heart. He returned Marwood's revolver and sat by himself for a good hour, unfit for company, sulking and snarling curses in Spanish when someone got too close.

Following the robbery of the mail coach, and the increased possibility Mescaleros were buzzing around, Botis made the tactical decision to travel at night for a while. It was his intention they avoid notice until they could find the Apaches and fall upon them with wild vengeance.

They rode past one of the cattle ranches owned by Milton Faver. During the day they holed up in the rugged lava rocks of a hillside, or the steep flank of a mesa. Between catnaps, Marwood watched the open country for movement. Come dusk the exhausted men rode, heads and backs bowed. Sometimes they reeled upright with a sudden jerk or a soft cry. Marwood chewed dry coffee beans to stay awake. In this fashion did they crawl across the level plains of tall yellow grass to Fort Davis, and by a sly southern route through desert scrub and volcanic cliffs, avoided the armed Buffalo Soldiers stationed there.

When night fell once again they crawled from their freezing holes in the lava rocks like nocturnal spiders. As they saddled their horses, Spaw spotted a newly kindled fire on a wind-blasted mesa ten miles away. The riders drew nearer and dismounted when they reached a *bajada*. They led their horses across a black alluvial fan sloping upward in a gentle climb. The Tonkawas pressed ahead to scout. When they returned an hour later Lovich met them to hear their report.

"They say an old *dama* is sitting alone on top of that mesa," he told the men. Lovich shook his head in wonder. He leaned, spat, and wiped his mouth with the back of his hand. "Craziest damn thing I ever heard of."

Botis and company retrieved their horses and rode closer to the signal fire. It was a huge bonfire of everything ignitable in the desert: dried dung, rotten cactus and ocotillo, the occasional mesquite bush chopped and splined for kindling.

A ten-foot square rock house with a shoddy roof of withy lathes stood outside the rim of firelight. The roof and corners were crooked, and the house cocked away from the fire as if it were an animal seeking the comfort of darkness. There was a single low doorway, little more than five feet high, with a stone lintel. Something was engraved on the lintel, but Marwood could not make it out in the shadow, even when he tried to trace it with his fingers. Two small windows, arrow slits at best, adorned one wall. The interior of the house—if house it was and not prison—was pitch black, and no man dared to enter it.

The party walked their horses into the firelight. Marwood's shadow stretched from his boots to meld and become one with the greater darkness.

A venerable Mexican woman looked up from a wooden plate of raw lizard and a piñole of ground mesquite beans. She was dressed in black threadbare clothes and wooden *huaraches*. The ebony *mantilla* she wore, pinned with a bone *peineta*, was more straggled cobweb than elegant Andalusian lace.

"*Que es este lugar?*" Botis asked her. He waited patiently for an answer.

She chewed her mush of mesquite beans, refusing to even acknowledge his presence.

"*Usted está parado en mi casa de duelo,*" she said. She picked a stringy bit of lizard meat with her fingers and nibbled.

"*Quieres hablar conmigo, vieja madre?*" Botis asked.

She put the plate aside, maintaining an air of solemnity. Something between her and Botis had changed. Her dark eyes ranged over him and his roughshod, shadowed men, arranged behind him like petitioners at the gates of hell.

"*Se puede caminar con los demonios,*" she said, looking them over. She turned her gaze to Botis.

"*Sí,*" Botis answered. He watched her carefully. He pointed to the men and to himself. "*Con los demonios.*"

"*Te diré.*" She crossed herself and motioned to a patch of ground between them. "*Sentarse, y te diré de los fantasmas del pasado que frecuentan este lugar.*"

The killers did as she asked and sat around her, resembling wounded acolytes at a roadside shrine. The Tonkawas remained outside the encircling presence of the *bruja*'s electric spirit. They were wary of all strange phenomena in the desert, including the salt ghosts that roamed the howling wastes, and other flickering *fantasmas* that pulled men's spirits through their nostrils. They would have none of it for themselves.

The *bruja* began to speak, and the men listened.

"I will tell you a thing," she said in Spanish, "and you will take it with you to the end of your days."

As she spoke she often looked at Marwood. He leaned close to listen. She told them when she was young and pretty she was engaged to a handsome goatherd. His name was not important, because over the years she had forgotten her own name. But the power of what she had to tell them this night lay not in forgotten names, but in deeds, and a measure of hope undone.

She stopped talking to make sure they understood this. If they did not, there was little reason to go on with her story. The men listened to the night sounds close in around them. They told her they understood and urged her to continue. The old woman went on with her halting story.

When her lover was in the field, tending goats, she said, she would every evening climb a hillside that overlooked the valley and light a fire to let him know she was there. But a fortnight before they were to be married, Mescalero Apaches killed the handsome goatherd, and scalped him.

She found his mutilated body in a dry canyon not far from this place. She buried him there, and also her heart. And for uncounted years, she had built a bonfire every Sunday night, so his grieving spirit would know its warmth, and remember her love.

The *bruja* stopped to gather her thoughts. Now here was the part of the story that must be told, she warned. It was part of her life she sometimes forgot, but she remembered it now because these men had come out of the dark to listen.

Some years after the goatherd died she did marry. For such is the human need to go forward and put the past in a corner where you can understand it. She did not love this man as she loved the goatherd, but she gave him children and there was happiness. They were all dead now, her family. The man had died, as old men do, and the children and their wives and their children's children were all dead from wars or plague or burning famine. Yet she remained on this borderland mesa lighting her signal fire for the one lost soul she had ever truly loved.

Sometimes, she said in a hushed voice, looking at Marwood, she was not sure she was real. Marwood felt his skin crawl. Maybe only her fire was real, she said. For fire was eternal, like man's soul. That was why people sat before a fire and stared into it. They were staring into themselves. No other thing, no mirror, no god, could peer so deep into man's abyss. Fire alone had that unique power.

In other tellings this would be story enough, perhaps. But over the years, when she lit her signal fires, something grew heavy in her heart like a stone. She began to realize she hated the goatherd for leaving her with such a grim responsibility.

It was her fires, you see, that kept him from crossing to the other world. Maybe even into hell. He would see the signal fire and stay in this world, and not go where spirits must to be judged.

It was an act of selfishness on her part to keep him as close to her as she could. To anchor him to this world. She knew that was a sin.

But she had lost, too. She had lost her life and her family. Now all she had left was the fire, and she wasn't sure that was enough.

One night she did not make the signal fire. She knew what would happen next, but she also knew there must be a reckoning between her and the goatherd. She was not surprised when the goatherd came to her through the clouding dark. His ghostly form walked up the slope of this *meseta* and he sat showing his bone-scalped head and his dripping wounds, and asked why she had abandoned him. She told him she, too, had been abandoned, that there was no one to build a fire for her in this world.

The handsome goatherd reached into his chest. When he withdrew his hand there was a small blue flame in his palm. She took the flame and she swallowed it, and the stone melted in her heart like ice on a hot comal. The goatherd rose and turned to walk away.

"Where are you going," she asked him.

"I have given you everything I have," he said. "Now I must leave to be judged by God."

"I will always light the fire for you," she told him.

"That is the nature of fire," he said, and disappeared into the dark never to return again.

No one spoke when she finished the story. Botis watched the flames for a long time. His face was unreadable.

The men got to their feet in ones and twos. They asked the *bruja* if she wanted to go to Presidio with them. They told her they would fight for her and keep her safe. They told her they would come back and keep the fire burning, if she wanted such a sacrifice on their behalf.

The old woman declined the offer. "*Voy a morir aquí,*" she said. She patted the wooden settle she sat upon. "*Aquí.*"

They gave her money, what meat they could spare, and a pouch of salt. Marwood was the last to leave. She brushed his hand with hers.

"*Usted es un hombre solitario.*" She held his hand pressed between both of hers. Her hands were cold and he could feel the bones under her paper-thin skin. "*Tienes que ir al norte.*"

"I don't understand," he said. "I am not who you think I am."

She nodded emphatically. "*El hombre solitario. Norte.*" She pointed to the Great Bear, and the circumpolar stars that blazed with jewelled fire. "*El fuego guema. En la tierra de nieve grande.*"

"That is not my home," he said. He disengaged his hand from hers and went to retrieve his horse.

He did not want to, but as he was riding away he turned and looked back. She was standing in front of the fire. Gifts of food and salt lay at her sandalled feet. The updraft from the bonfire lifted the tattered remains of her *mantilla*, revealing a skeletal face with yellowed flesh, dark eye sockets rimmed with salt, and an open maw that could swallow worlds.

"*La sangre de diez mil làgrimas es sobre tu alma.*" She placed a hand over her bosom and cried, "*Tu alma!*"

Marwood's heart hammered and his throat was dry. He had lingered too long. The rest of the company were riding single-file down the mesa. He reined his horse around and larruped it away.

"*Tu alma.*" Her high-pitched voice followed him through the desert air, swirling and bouncing off rock. "*Tu alma.*"

In Presidio they rode past multi-storeyed *pueblos* of adobe blocks and mud mortar. Wood smoke and wind-driven dust paled the burning air and stung Marwood's eyes.

Jumano Indian women baked bread in *hornos* built from sandstone and lava rock. Young girls, their limbs brown and firm, stoked the open cook fires and baked blue corn piki on flat rocks. Marwood watched other women boil vegetables by dropping hot stones into gourds, as their forebears did thousands of years ago.

Naked children, boys and girls alike, ran between the big American horses, their dirty hands outstretched. Some had ringworm, bowed legs from rickets, or suffered syphilitic scars from birth.

Botis kicked at them. "Get away from the horse." But on sudden impulse he pulled light rein and threw down a handful of *tlacos*. The children dove and fought for the copper coins like cats. Botis chucked Acheron forward and left them scrabbling in the dust.

Presidio was a sad-looking *colonia* of mud-washed adobe houses, slumping *jacals*, and open-air *tiendas* with sagging *porticos*. Men from the *barrial* sat on the street under thin, leaning shade, and smoked coarse tobacco rolled in cornhusks.

Lovich smelled frying chili peppers. He dismounted, leaving his horse ground-tied. The Cajun followed in his wake. Following his nose, Lovich shuffled into a low-ceilinged *bodega*. Boxes, crates, and an old seat from a Concord wagon served for furniture.

"You speak American?" he asked the proprietor.

"*Sí*. A little bit."

"We need salt and beans and side bacon," he told the proprietor. The Cajun picked absently through a hooped barrel of old bones the local farmers ground and used for fertilizer.

The man who owned the *bodega* wrinkled his brow. "*No más tocino*," he said. He bore an old machete scar across his naked chest under a coarse-woven shirt. His pants were held up with rope and his feet were bare and horned with yellow calluses.

"What have you got if you ain't got bacon?" Lovich asked.

"*Perro*," the storekeeper said. He shrugged. "Just as good to eat. I promise the Virgin."

Lovich frowned at this. "No cabrito?" For, in truth, he was partial to smoked kid, more than any other man in the outfit, and loved to get it whenever he could.

"*No más cabrito*," the proprietor replied. He snapped his fingers under his nose, as if trying to awaken Lovich from a walking sleep. "*Perro. Perro.*"

"I'll be goddamned if I'm going to eat a dog," Lovich said.

"The men won't sit still for it, neither." The Cajun pulled a coyote jaw from the barrel to examine it. "Bad enough we had to eat one of our goddamn horses in the bush."

The proprietor shrugged. "Is all we have. *Lo siento.*"

"I'll bet you're sorry," Lovich said. "Are you telling me this goddamn town ain't got nothing to eat in the way of meat?"

The man standing before him shook his head. "*No más tocino. No más de cabra. Los Indios. Muy malo.*"

The Cajun's head jerked up. "*Indios*?"

"*Sí*," the man said. "Mescalero."

"Where are they?" He dropped the coyote jaw and came forward. "We been hunting them savages since we left Bexar."

"Ruidosa," Botis said.

Lovich nodded. His eyes slid toward the horizon. "That's what the man said, Cap. Up through the Chinati Mountains. He said there's a regiment of convicts who guard Ruidosa from Indian attacks. Mean bunch of bastards. They fight each other all the time. Seems to me we can get a piece of that ourselves."

Botis turned to Marwood. "Have you ever been that far west, Mar?"

Marwood shook his head. "I've been south to Saltillo." He didn't have to elaborate among these men what job he might have been doing there. "That's all rough country, though."

The abrupt gunshot made them turn as one. Calvin Zapata walked out of a *taberna*. He turned and lifted his hand as if to wave goodbye. Another shot from within the dark interior hit him square in the chest. He collapsed to his knees and toppled sideways. Immediately, two more shots from a bigger gun sounded inside the cantina. Jubal

Stone strode out next with a Walker Colt smoking in his right hand.

"Goddamn, Cap," he called, "somebody up and shot Calvin in the back." In Stone's other hand was a pocket five-shot .28 calibre Paterson. He showed it to them. "With this here gun."

The men gathered around Calvin lying dead in the street. "What happened?" Botis asked Stone.

"We was talking. This cobber from Kansas went to get him a drink, and when he came back he pulled his gun and shot poor Calvin in the back. Calvin lurched to his feet and this Jayhawker burned powder on him again. So I pulled my gun and put two .44s into him. He's in there. But he's dead now."

The men walked into the dimly lit place. There was an overturned chair in the middle of the room, which Marwood had to step around. An older, sandy-haired man lay on the dirt floor in a dark pool of blood. A frightened bartender stood in a far corner trembling like he had the ague. Botis kicked the dead man over with the toe of his boot.

"He ain't nobody we know," Botis said. "Mar?"

"I've never seen this man before."

Lovich spat and shook his head. "It don't make sense to shoot Calvin," he said. "He was just a boy. He never did nobody no harm."

Doc Quillen entered the cantina. His hands were bloody. "Calvin's dead all right, Captain. Ain't nothing I can do for him."

"Did Calvin have cross words with this here dead man?" Botis asked.

"What words, Cap?" Jubal Stone holstered his Walker and shoved the Paterson inside his coat jacket. "We was talking, and when he came back to the table he pulled out a gun and shot Calvin in the back."

"Goddamn," Lovich said, "he must have been looney. Why would anyone shoot Calvin for nothing?"

No one said anything for a long, dark moment. Jubal Stone removed his hat. He wiped the sweat from his wrinkled forehead with the ball of his thumb. "It don't figure out."

"It doesn't have to," Botis said. "It never has to."

The *alcalde* of the town questioned them briefly, but they had no more information than before. The *alcalde* said this red headed stranger had ridden into town two days ago on a malandered *burro* and was looking for piecework in the fields.

Botis and his band rode out of the *colonia*. As they were negotiating a narrow pass through the Chinati Mountains, stepping their horses around igneous boulders and scoria, Jubal Stone raised his voice in question.

"I don't see how you mean it don't figure, Captain," he said. "The world has parts, and they're knowable."

Botis led them on for another half mile. When they came to an open ledge he drew rein. Below were raddled lands and orange hills that wobbled and sheered in the awful heat. A long reef of blood-red herringbone clouds chased orange sky into black. Blue mesas with crimson tops rose like mansions on the measureless horizon.

Sitting his horse Botis took out his clay pipe and filled it. He lit it and flipped the match at the ground. "There is no order to the world," he said. He might have been talking to himself. "The order men perceive in Nature and the world around them is but a reflection of their disordered minds." He puffed his pipe. "Order has no natural existence in the universe, and the universe does not recognize man as an integral part of its own existence. Nor should it be so, for man himself is a being separate from all other things, even unto himself."

The pipe was out. Botis knocked the dottle from the bowl and pushed his hat back on his forehead. "The west is the best killing-fest there ever was," he told Stone, "or ever will be. That's what you have to remember."

His philosophical doctrine of red butchery rendered, he spurred Acheron down a steep saddleback ridge. Juniper and cactus grew in isolated hummocks between chines. Everything here was slowly being eroded over time. Marwood believed these rain-starved plants would one day tumble to the bottom.

The killers held their reins a little tighter and rode into the waiting cauldron below.

CHAPTER 12

They rode through the starwheel of night and into another day.

The wind picked up. Before long it became a maelstrom. Sand and rock chips struck Marwood's face and hands. The men tied canvas and cowhide to shield themselves, but the pellets left pin-prick bruises and mottled blood spots on every unprotected area. Later, when Marwood shucked off his boots, a half-cup of sand poured from each one.

The horses endured the worst. Their heads were hooded to protect their eyes. The riders dismounted to lead them best they could, but the horses kept trying to tail into the wind. Marwood dug in his heels and pulled at his mare. The remuda was whipped to drive them forward. As the day lengthened the howling wind would not let up. As the sky darkened into night, Marwood and the others were moving through the world more by feel than by sight.

By the meridian of the second day the sun was nothing more than a brown disk in a burnet sky. When Marwood looked up he saw turbulent roils of dust obscure its face. The coils would twist and writhe, and break into separate shards much like frightened dace in a millpond. Then, as quickly as it had begun, the wind died out and the dust storm ended.

Now he rode through a preternatural world of eerie silence. Naught was heard but the huffing of horses and clomp of hooves, kicking through overturned stone and scree.

"Goddamn this," Spaw said.

The sifting dust scattered aeneous light, making everything around the company glow as with fairy fire. The world became reversed—the sky rose dark and the ground was bright—and Marwood thought if a man was not careful he might begin to doubt his senses. Glare beat upward into the faces of the men. Dust continued to swirl, collecting in the creases of their clothes and brims of their hats.

Then, Marwood saw a thing he would have never thought possible. A column of rain clouds built up in the north and threatened to blow their way. The temperature dropped twenty degrees. Away to the west, a second, larger dust storm threatened.

The two forces collided directly overhead, transmuting with a thunderclap that shook the world and startled the horses. Dust and rain, wind and a wailing vortex. Marwood watched the collision, and the mud that formed. Immense rippling sheets, limitless lobes of aerial mud warped, bent, and torqued as unbalanced forces worked upon them. They spun, coacted into delicate helixes, were sheared apart, and fell.

It rained. It rained mud, and it did not stop. Marble-sized globules, some half-frozen, splattered the ground. Eyes and mouths of men became gummed, faces mired and unrecognizable. The men riding next to Marwood looked like they were wearing dirt masks and mud sluiced from their lowered hats. The horses walked with their heads down; their muzzles and long tails dripped. It continued to fall in a steady patter until Marwood believed they were being beaten by the sky itself—punished by irate gods for sins past, and future given.

The weather eased twenty minutes later. The mud shower ceased. Within an hour all was bone dry. Mud flaked like lizard scales from their flanks; choking dust rose from the horses' hooves. Men tied bandanas around their faces so they could breathe.

They rode on, watching the blue Cordilleras shimmer in the distance—from one extreme to the other. Marwood's tongue was swollen with thirst. Darkness rode up on their backs and Botis called a halt. There was no moon; clouds obscured the stars. All was black as pitch.

They endured a night's encampment with neither food nor fire. They were too tired to eat, too close to the Mescaleros to risk a light.

Marwood collapsed on the ground. He sat with his arms hanging at his side, palms up, eyes unfocused. It had been one of the most exhausting days of his life. Worse than the pit in Laredo. Worse than anything.

No one spoke. No man had the breath or the strength to speak. Usually, when they gathered around at night, they had time for talk. Tonight, Marwood watched men fall asleep while sitting upright, and they did not move again until morning.

Early light. The eastern sky burned. Botis went around kicking everyone into life. Horses saddled, they ate parched corn and a mouthful of water, and rode the sun full up.

By midday they came to a field of impaled Mescalero Apaches, and halted.

Lovich counted twenty-three naked bodies: men, women, and children, all frozen in horror—mouths torn open, eyes burned blind from the desert sun. All had been scalped and mutilated beyond recognition, their skin stretched like taut muslin over corded muscles and petrified bones.

The oaken stakes were set deep into the hard earth, with supporting rocks surrounding their base. Their points were fire-hardened. Sam Decker dismounted and, leading his grullo, stood in the middle of this grim planting. He lifted one of the base stones, examined it curiously, and put it back exactly as before.

Nothing moved. The air was filled with buzzing flies. Most of the male victims were impaled through the anus.

Two were upside down by their throats; one was transfixed directly through his trunk, with a leg hooked over his body, secondarily impaled. The women, five by count, were speared through the groin, the sharp tip bursting through their sternums. The top of the stakes were purposefully set underneath their lower jaws so gravity could not work them toward the bottom. Their breasts had been removed and their abdomens flayed open. Blackened viscera hung like mangled rawhide from the wounds. Two babies and a four-year-old toddler shared a stake. A metal ring was hammered two-thirds down so that their small bodies remained suspended above the hard-packed earth.

Lying against a large boulder were more honed stakes, and holes newly dug into the ground. Seven holes were already deep enough to receive both stake and the fresh weight of a struggling body.

The Cajun lifted one of these stout posts, twelve inches at base and ten feet in length. He levered it into a prepared hole. The bottom third of the stake chunked vertically into the rock-hard ground, and fit true.

"Leave that, Amos," Rota said.

"How come?"

"It ain't right to disturb a graveyard."

The Cajun looked at the pole he had planted and thought better of removing it again. He got on his horse.

Five miles on they discovered a deserted mission. The roof had caved in, the 'dobe walls crumbled and sloughing now that the main support was gone. The men kicked through the dusty ruin. Inside the sacristy Marwood found the remains of two Spanish priests called by God to anoint the heathens with the Blood of Christ. One was beheaded, his head placed in a brass *piscina*. They had been stripped, tortured, and scalped. Both men were castrated, and one had a crucifix tucked in his buttocks.

Lovich stood beside Marwood. He forked his hat back with a thumb. “They do love their jokes,” he said.

Spaw rode his horse between the open doors of the mission church and down the nave. His big dun stepped between the naked bodies and a boiling swarm of black flies. Buttresses of sunlight fell from shattered lathes in the ceiling, illuminating the bloated corpses. Their collective blood had solidified into a black ceramic glaze half an inch thick. It cracked like sheet ice under his horse’s iron shoes. There were more bodies in the chancel, where men had made a final stand. Fifteen more bodies from the *colonia* lined a dry *acequia* outside the church.

The Hydra regrouped outside and compared what it had seen and found.

“I guess they’re around here somewhere,” Rota said. He was using the extra time to whetstone the point of his harpoon. “All that’s left is we go find them before they find us.”

They rode on. They were half a mile from Ruidosa and could see the *azoteas* and stone walls of the city, when, five hundred yards off, three squads of Buffalo Soldiers crested a hog’s back, and with shortened reins, thundered down after them.

Even the Tonkawa scouts were taken by surprise. Botis and his men spun their horses and flew away north, into the open desert and sparse fields of sacahuista. Spaw and Jubal Stone turned in their saddles and fired with bouncing hands at the approaching horde.

“You’re wasting your shots,” Marwood warned them. He leaned close to the neck of his mare so his body would not impede like a sail. He held the little quarter-horse mare on short rein. She was running flat out and keeping good pace. So far.

“Come on,” he whispered in her ear. “Go for your life.”

Botis plunged them into a dry streambed filled with dense undergrowth. They followed a declivity, which opened on an alluvial plain of sand and gravel. They galloped across that, and back up the steep bank on the other side. Bill Rota, Jubal Stone, and Sam Decker rode a hundred yards perpendicular to the major line of fire. They took up station behind a rock outcropping and a stand of scraggly cholla.

The rest of the company jumped from their horses, hobbled them, and formed a straggled line along the crest of Pinto Canyon. Their collective volley of rifle fire smashed into the cavalry horses a hundred yards away. The soldiers milled briefly in the crossfire and fell back behind a ridge to regroup.

It wasn't much for prayer, but it was breathing space, and they were welcome for it. Marwood jumped into his saddle along with the other men and they were off racing again. His mare was lathered, and she was starting to flag.

They fought a delaying action along the dry streambed. Jubal Stone took a ball deep in his left shoulder. The remuda was scattered to hell and gone, and Bill Rota was missing entire.

When the cavalry tried a Cannae, Botis gambled with all their lives and, rolling the dice, turned his company back into the southernmost squad, guns drawn, blazing. He and his remaining men shot their way past the thinned-out ranks. The unexpected action was not, however, without casualty. Sam Decker took a ball in his leg. His femoral artery was nicked. Blood sloshed from the top of his left boot. His hand fell away from the reins and his head spun.

He was standing beside his horse on open ground, gripping the pommel and trying to regain his wits, when a Buffalo Soldier ran him down.

The soldier, a black sergeant of thirty-three winters, sat his big bay horse half a furlong away. He uncovered a buffalo jaw with a steel wedge fixed where the teeth had been. The dull steel curve was honed to a razor's edge.

The sergeant hefted his makeshift weapon. He leaned forward and spurred his horse in a wild gallop. He was running flat out, leaning off to one side. The sergeant looped his arm in a vicious, underhanded whip and hacked Decker's head half off his shoulders with one swipe. Sam thrashed in the dust, back arched in agony, and died.

The fighting along the perimeter of the battlefield stopped a moment. All were watching the scene play out.

The black cavalryman wheeled his horse around, his back straight, his head up, and dismounted. He used the tip of his biblical weapon to cut Decker's ears away and pocketed them.

Then he got back on his horse and rode off to rejoin his compatriots.

They could see the pinprick lights of the cavalry fires in the gloaming dark.

"How far do you make them to be, William?" Botis asked.

Rota had scrounged his way back when night fell. He had ridden after the scattered remuda during a lull in the fighting and drove them back. Now, at least, Botis had a force well mounted, but running low on ammunition. They counted fifty rounds between them. They had powder enough, but they couldn't risk a fire and run lead.

Rota squinched his eyes and judged the distance. They were up in a malpaís while the cavalry were camped on the lower flat. "I'd say right at twenty miles, Captain."

"I think we gained half a day on them when we doubled back," Marwood said, "and they got themselves turned around."

"We could head south across the border," Lovich suggested.

"They are looking for us in Mexico, too," Botis reminded him.

Doc Quillen wiped the blade of his surgical instruments with raw mescal. "I'm going to have to dig in your shoulder some," he told Stone.

Jubal Stone sat with his sweating back against a rock. His feet were splayed, his face a pale blur in the half-dark. "Do your worst, you evil bastard," he said.

Quillen gave Stone a piece of leather to bite on. He inspected the depth of the gunshot wound with a hook probe. The shoulder was one large bruise from neck to short ribs. Quillen pushed the probe deeper into the wound. Stone's lips pulled away from his teeth. His gums were white.

Tunk Quillen withdrew the bloody probe. He rocked back on his thin haunches. "I can cut her out before you get the blood p'isen," he said. "But it's liable to sting a mite. That ball is settin' up agin' your scapular bone."

Stone muttered something unintelligible. Quillen threw the probe into his black bag and rummaged with a blind hand for a scalpel. He made an incision and went to work. Stone sat in silence. His eyes bulged. The cords in his neck and arms strained like cables.

Five minutes later Quillen withdrew his brass calipers from the man's shoulder. A lead slug was captured between the points.

"You can tie it on your watch chain if'n you like," Quillen said.

"I'll tell your mother what you can do with it," Stone replied. But he was near wiped out, and not up to a prolonged verbal exchange with the resurrectionist.

Quillen cleaned the wound with mescal and flipped open a pocketknife. He cut bandage strips from a sugar sack, wound them around Stone's shoulder and tied the ends off neat. He gave the man a canteen of water.

"We ain't got much of that left," he said. "Sups it slow, so's you don' founder."

There wasn't anything much to eat, either. Their *mochilas* and food sacks were empty. They chewed handfuls of coffee beans. The night dragged. Acheron rolled in the dirt. His long tongue lolled out of his mouth.

"Wonder what that black bastard is dreaming about," the Cajun said.

The night advanced into grey dawn light. Colours washed out in their clothes and faces and the land around them. The men looked like shades vomited up from Dante's vision of hell.

Botis met them in the dawn holding a clay ewer with both hands.

The men looked at one another. Then, as if by unspoken agreement, they averted their gazes. They shuffled into a straggled line like reluctant participants in an unholy communion.

The Cajun thrust his hand in the ewer and drew out a white stone. He put it in the pocket of his breeches and stood waiting beside the horses, sharpening his Green River knife.

Rota also drew white. He picked up his filthy two-point blanket and his gun and saddled his horse.

Tunk Quillen dunked his hand through the opening and returned with a white stone in his wrinkled palm. He looked at it briefly, pitched it into a patch of scrub. He turned away, curious to see if his patient had survived the night.

Lovich was next in line. He grinned a knowing grin at them all. "You sons of bitches act like you're tupping your first whore," he said. He drew white and laughed at them for being fools and went to untie his horse.

Jubal Stone drew next. He allowed the white stone to tumble from his fingers. Quillen helped him to his feet and onto a waiting horse.

Ed Gratton stared at the white stone in his meaty hand. His salt and pepper beard was covered with dust. He suddenly started, like a clockwork automaton whose springs were engaged, and left to retrieve his possibles. Charley Broadwell dipped his hand in the ewer and walked away, his knuckles gripping white.

It was down to Marwood and Spaw. They looked at each other. Marwood stepped forward. The summer eyes of Botis were unreadable. Marwood's fingers closed on something with rough edges and he took out the black stone.

None of the other men looked his way. They were busy untangling reins, or bridling their horses.

Botis reached into the ewer, removed the final stone. This he pressed into Spaw's unwilling hand. Botis pitched the jug aside and it broke on an outcropping of rock. He went after his horse.

Marwood sat on a boulder cleaning the heels of his boots with a stick. One by one, the men filed their horses past him and disappeared down an incline of loose shale. No one looked back. Even Spaw refused to meet his eyes, though the latter man was shaken.

Leather creaked when Botis stepped into his McClellan saddle. He reined the big roan around. Marwood felt the eyes of man and horse on his back, but he did not turn to acknowledge them.

Botis rowelled his horse forward and followed his retreating men into the deep ravine.

Marwood saddled his horse and packed his equipage. Before leaving the campsite he checked his gun. He had four loads left in his pistol. He holstered it and picked up his Sharps rifle. He worked the breechblock mechanism and cleaned every surface with his shirttail. He opened the box of rifle shells. There were six .52-calibre 50-grain cartridges left.

Six.

They had left him half a canteen of water. Marwood slung it over his saddle horn.

He pulled his mare in the opposite direction the others had taken. He kept behind a high ridge, using the brush and scrag to screen his movements. It took him an hour to work his way a furlong down the mountain. When he emerged from the foliage he spied the glint of fires on the dark lowland. He circled around them, working downwind in case they had Indian spies like the Tonkawas who could smell a white man. He found a good position behind a rocky knoll topped with low bushes to break up his silhouette.

He would have preferred setting up a point or two east of the cavalry with the sun full behind him. But Botis was trying to manoeuvre his command that way and escape. It was up to Marwood to give the company cover, even at the cost of his own life.

There was one sign in his favour: dark clouds were blowing in from the northwest. Long tendrils of rain spilled from their black bottoms like gall ink. The clouds and their shadows along the intervening ground would make firing tricky, especially at this distance.

He loaded the rifle and edged the barrel through the juniper leaves. The cavalry was 500 yards away. Marwood saw tiny figures moving about the morning fires. His heart hammered and his hands began to sweat.

He pulled the rifle back, gave himself five minutes with the rifle butt resting on the hard ground and one arm over his knee. He thought of nothing at first. Then he thought of his past, which he could not remember, and that too was nothing. He wondered what kind of future he had, and where he might ever find a home. Then he remembered what the old Mexican *bruja* told him about his soul, and that, finally, was something, and he went into position.

The boom of the big gun rolled.

The first shot kicked up a fountain of dirt past the pickets. A second and a half later every soldier in camp started to their feet as the sound caught up to them. Marwood loaded another cartridge, picked a new target, and touched off the Sharps.

The leg of one of the Buffalo Soldiers collapsed while lounging on a settle. He went down, sprawled in agony. By now soldiers were either leaping for their rifles or throwing themselves flat. One man—sergeant or officer, Marwood could not tell—was on one knee barking orders. Then some unnatural sense warned him he was open-sighted and vulnerable, and he pitched himself behind an ammunition box. Marwood swung the barrel and instead killed a private crawling between the legs of the nervous cavalry horses.

Three shots left. Marwood pulled out and walked with long purposeful strides toward his horse. He swung up and rowelled her forward. The mare burst from the juniper and ran flat out across the open ground. Guns opened up behind him. Soldiers shouted. Something buzzed past his ear—the peculiar whine of a hot ball spinning through the air. Marwood worked his horse behind a ridge chine and let her chuff and blow.

He climbed away through more rock, and when he emerged in the clear he spied a mounted squad riding hard in his direction. They were using the lay of the land to close quarter on him. If he didn't do something he would be trapped. Marwood sawed back on the reins of his horse and yanked the Sharps from his scabbard, dismounted, and ran up a steep slab of rock. He lay flat on his stomach and wormed his way to the oblong tip of the rock finger. He brought the Sharps around his body, ready to pour lead into the approaching horses, but what he saw surprised him. The cavalry had turned around and was pulling out. A blue sheet of cold rain was approaching from their northern quarter, and they were riding into it to cloak their movement.

A good 400 yards, firing downhill and into a brisk wind. Marwood added up all the factors and forces that would act upon the 475-grain projectile. He touched the trigger. One of the lead horses plunged headlong into the ground, throwing its rider. The rain swept in and enveloped the squad and they disappeared.

Marwood quit the stone point and rode his mare parallel to the last compass heading taken by the retreating soldiers. He knew they were trying to circle around him, using the rainstorm as cover. He would keep moving with them, and in that way hope to lead them farther west, away from Botis and the men.

The squall hit with fierce power. The thirsty ground could not drink the water quick enough. Marwood entered down into a once-dry streambed and followed it up current to cover his tracks. Within the space of two minutes, however, the water roiled to his horse's knees, and he had to spur her out of there.

He was in a bad spot, much to his own making. He was too low in the canyon bottom. The cavalry was moving away and remained safely camouflaged. Marwood dismounted and led his mare up a washed-out slope. Water streamed from his hat brim and small rocks tumbled past his feet. Walking in a crouch to keep his balance Marwood reached the top of the bank and paused to catch his breath.

Clouds were breaking up overhead, but the racing shadows threw him a moment. He did not recognize the immediate country. He turned to look behind him. Nothing.

He climbed his tired body into the saddle. At least from here he was elevated and could check his backbearing for enemy movement. If he kept—

Without warning the soft ground gave way and his mare lost her footing. His saddle slipped and his horse rolled out from under him. Marwood threw his right leg over the pommel, using the extra momentum to quit the saddle as both horse and ammunition tumbled into space.

Marwood slammed to the ground. His breath was knocked from his lungs, but other than a wrenched shoulder, and skinned pride, he was alive.

His mare rolled helpless end over end down the slick mudslide. She plummeted a hundred feet and crashed backward into the violent torrent of floodwater.

He watched her dark head come up once in the boiling cataract. Then she, along with his smashed equipage, was gone.

CHAPTER 13

Marwood was drinking with cupped hands from a gurgling runnel of rainwater when he heard a single cough upstream. When he turned his head he saw a young Texas Ranger standing ten rods off, watering a bay horse. The Ranger filled a leather canteen. The bay lifted its head, water dripping from its long muzzle. It lowered its head to drink again.

Marwood backed into the brush and stole away. He would have shot the Ranger but he didn't know how many others were standing within earshot. When he heard raised shouts down water he stopped and crouched, his heart beating. Someone had found his dead horse.

It was time to get out of here.

The cloud-wracked sky allowed him no sun bearing, but he thought the main river lay to his left. That's the way this bed ran, anyway. Marwood turtled off, using whatever he could find for cover. His shoulder gave him discomfort and he kept working his arm so it wouldn't stiffen up on him.

He took stock of his bleak situation. He had nothing but his clothes, a gun, and a knife tucked in his boot. Everything else had been carried away by floodwaters.

To worsen matters, Marwood didn't know if he was headed north, or south, or skewed for hell. He should have reached the Rio Grande by now. He searched the heavy sky; it was impossible to compass the sun behind the lidded clouds. He kept walking.

He didn't see anyone else for the remainder of the day. He thought he heard gunshots but it might have been falling rock. With the crumpled hills and ravines in this part of Texas an echo could trick you clean. A man could run circles around himself trying to pin it all down.

He never reached the main river, which worried him not a little. Wind-flagged chaparral and wide, empty country stretched on all sides. He was lost in unknown territory.

He came to a deep canyon and stared into the abyss. He crouched behind a candelilla bush and quartered the land with his flint-grey eyes for half an hour. A lone turkey buzzard glided by. Its naked head was stark in the clear desert air.

Nothing moved on the canyon floor. A dry wash with fingering tributaries snaked between sotol stalks and scoria like the imprint of distant chains. Scrub brush and slag choked shallow ravines like brain coral.

The long day ended. Darkness rolled through the canyon in a quiet rush. Preternatural dark. Tiny free-tailed bats funnelled like sorcerers from a hidden crevice in the canyon wall. They scissored and chandelled, scrawling arcane signatures upon the darkness.

Marwood was about to climb down into the canyon when something flew through the air behind him and he froze. He put his hand on his gun and turned his head. Nothing there. His heart slowed. It had been too heavy for bat-wings, too distinct for an owl or hawk hunting mice along the brush lanes.

Marwood licked his parched lips. He knew well that horned and leather beat. He had heard it as a Union soldier in Glorieta Pass, and again at Sand Creek. It had accompanied him as a Kansas range detective riding railheads along the 98th meridian. It was a part of his life. It was him.

A martial drum roll. The secret beat of his red-muscled heart, which had shadowed all the years of his life, and found residence in the tattered remnants of his soul.

What had the *bruja* said? Ten thousand tears wept on his soul. This was one more in that awful multitude.

He did not descend right away into the canyon. Fragments of memory were returning in a rush of sound and colour. Half-forgotten years of an impossible past. If man was but the measure of his years, then Marwood thought he was little more than a half-finished golem of clay and blood and reason.

Images all—kaleidoscopic and puzzling. They drifted and sawed through his mind like warped glass, bounced like unsettled beads of water on a taut string, and fell into swelling darkness, nevermore seen.

More distant than anything he could imagine. Stone cities and dark men with tattooed faces, who spoke tongues long dissolved into time eternal. Men, and not a few women, called to stand against that which must be faced. Men who carried cold and ancient things inside them, awakened in times of need.

Marwood squeezed his fists to his eyes. He felt himself back there with those people. They were his reality. He was one. He knew he was one of those men. But he had left, or been taken from them, and now he was lost and could never get back. If he did return, he was not at all certain he would be accepted.

The overwhelming sense of anxiety ebbed. When he opened his eyes he was returned to the lip of the canyon. Lost and alone, yes, but he had a gun and the determination to survive. The memories faded beneath the amnesia that dominated his waking moments. Bits and pieces remained like the ember glow of a setting sun. He could sense their faint pulse, feel them move like distant thunder in the foggy crests and troughs of history. Tugging him. Always tugging him northward.

Marwood entered the canyon. He found shelter in a shallow cut where a section of cliff had given way in some distant cataclysm—a shallow cave once used by ancients. The floor was littered with bones of animals and lithic flakes. The domed ceiling was blackened from the soot of a thousand primitive fires.

Marwood folded his long body into the hollow and bundled himself in his torn and filthy deerskin jacket. He was thirsty, tired, and hungry.

He studied the sky outside.

The clouds rolled over the horizon with the last blades of light. A clear welkin and fractured moon stood high. But something was wrong with this sky.

Marwood did not recognize these stars. He watched the heavens for sign.

He did not know this world.

He crawled out of the cave, rubbing his eyes as bright day filled them. He saw a mourning dove fly the length of the canyon and whip behind a stand of cottonwood trees.

He walked toward the trees. Twenty minutes later he faced the terminus of a bleak cliff. The trees around its base sloped down along the edge of a precipitous drop-off. Marwood got on all fours and wormed his way over thick dry chaff. He crawled through a deadfall of honey mesquite and salt cedar, and chased the steepening flank downward, slipping and sliding on loose talus.

He found the water seep hidden between flat stones. Long haulms of grass grew between the cracks. The water was topped with white scum. He bundled a handful of grass to use as a filter and drank. He sat back, wondering if Botis and the men had made it out alive, and drank again.

With a bellyful of water he climbed out of the canyon and stood upon the immense plain. As he walked, his shadow stretched to his left. When the sun was at its zenith he sat down and rested. His head hurt and his shoulder ached. After an hour he rose and walked until his shadow flung across the hard ground to his right.

He made a dry camp in the open country. He had collected half a dozen sotol stalks, and scraped the root base with his front teeth and chewed the vegetable quid. The stars came out and chased away the blood-red clouds hanging in the west.

He knew these stars.

Another new star brightened and flickered on the far horizon. It was a campfire many miles away.

Marwood checked the loads in his gun and made for the camp. He lost the light when he dipped through low elevations between esker-like rills and fiddle-backed hummocks.

When he got close enough Marwood held the gun to his jacket to muffle the trigger cock.

"Hail the camp," he called.

An indistinct shadow in shaggy coat and wide-brimmed hat quit the firelight and moved behind a horse. A gun hammer clicked.

He was too slow. Marwood already had his gun out, and if it came to killing the man's horse to get his water, he would make that hell bargain.

"Who are ye?" the stranger answered.

"I want to share your fire."

"I got ye skylighted." The stranger paused. "What have ye got that's any good?"

"Trade tobacco for water."

"Ye got no tug?"

"I haven't had meat for days."

"I'll Carson some of the 'bacca if ye care to share it like a Christian," the man said.

Marwood drew up to the fire. It was a smoky dung blaze of white ash and crimson glow. A man in a stinking buffalo robe and shaggy leggings hid behind a slat-ribbed bay tacked with a bosal hackamore and horsehair mecate. He pointed an 1861 Navy Colt across the Mexican saddle. The saddle rig was fitted with tapaderos sewn from uncured hog skins.

"I don't like it when people point guns at me," Marwood said.

"I was making sure ye was white." The stranger lowered the gun and came out from behind the horse. "Although, under all that dirt it's hard telling what ye are. First off, I thought ye was one of them salt ghosts what track the desert night. Pleased to meet you, mister. My name is Lee Canton." He did not offer his hand.

"Evenin'."

Canton had a broad, seamed face and stooped shoulders. His black hair fell from the corners of his hat onto his collar. He was covered in trail dust and uncounted years of sun sweat and salt rime.

The man poked a pink tongue between his sun-blistered lips and put his gun away. "This country is full of Mexican bandits," he said. "I didn't know ye was a white American."

"I don't know that I am," Marwood said. "Are you going to unsaddle your horse?"

Canton looked at his horse and spat. He glared at Marwood. "My horse." He took in Marwood's own dirty clothes and gun. "Ye don't look none too prosperous yerself. I guess ye ain't fooling when ye say ye got no grub." He held out a hand with long nails. "I'll take that chaw if ye don't mind."

"Water first, Canton."

The man pitched him a canteen. "Easy sippers. It's all we got."

Marwood drank. He gasped and took another long swallow. He opened a rawhide parfleche and shook out enough Virginia kinnikinnick to make up a quid. Canton stuffed the coarse mixture in his cheek. His eyes gleamed with sprightly pleasure.

"I thank ye kindly." His long salt and pepper whiskers bristled like oiled quills as he chewed.

"Where are you from?" Marwood asked.

Canton tucked his hands in his back pockets, elbows knocked out. "I rode down from El Paso." He jerked his chin in the general direction. "I used to live up Fort Smith way, though. Ye ever been to Fort Smith?"

"Never." Marwood took one last swallow and stoppered the canteen with the heel of his hand. He handed it back to Canton. His head ached. He had gotten too much sun and too little water. He wanted to sleep for a year.

"How about Greenville? I got family in Greenville."

"I've never been to Arkansas."

Canton spat and rubbed his lips with the palm of his hand. "I worked all them flatboats on that river," he said, "until they up and gave my job to a free nigger. That's why I come to this here country."

He studied Marwood. He leaned over and spat at the fire. "Ye never said ye name, or where ye was headed. I been listening, but ye never said."

"My name is John Marwood."

Canton moved the tobacco from one cheek to the other. "That's half."

"I'm headed north."

"Mayhap that sun boiled your brain pan, Marwood. Most people are looking to shin it out of Texas."

"I lost my outfit in a creek flood."

Canton eyed him with suspicion. "Rangers ain't after ye, are they? I want to ride through the country unnoticed."

"I saw Rangers but they didn't give me any truck. I was supposed to do a job of work in Ruidosa when I lost my outfit. That's all."

Canton spread his hands over the fire. His nails were black glass grime. Knuckles crusted with old scabs. "Ye sure got a damnable habit of answering questions without answering them," he said with a sniff. "I guess I smelled law when ye walked up on me."

Marwood shook his head. "I used to be a range detective. It's not steady work. Ranchers won't pay anything once they get their stock back and the rustlers are hanged."

Canton juiced the quid. "Coming from ye that's damn near a political speech. Look it here. That's a sack of prairie chips at ye feet. Fetch one on the fire and I'll see to my horse before ye split your pants over it."

Marwood did so and collapsed in the dirt. Canton unsaddled the bay. He threw down bedroll, gun, and panniers beside the fire, but left an Indian blanket hanging over the saddle. The horse browsed on what meagre provender it could find.

Canton joined Marwood by the fire. "Wish I could pasture him a week or two," he said of his horse. "I ain't even got cottonwood bark for forage. He's damn near bottomed out, and so am I."

In truth, both horse and man looked abused beyond all redemption.

Marwood's shoulder ached something fierce. The dull throb accentuated the pulsing headache behind his tired eyes. He needed sleep. The warmth of the stinking fire bathed his face and hands.

Canton laid another chip on the fire. He seemed to burn all kinds of dung he could lay his hands on: coyote, human, dog, buffalo, cattle. It was as if his life's mission was to funnel the bodily waste from man and creature into his smoking campfires.

Canton's gun lay on top of his bedroll. Marwood eyed it.

Canton juiced the quid and spat another string of brown spittle. "Range detective. Is all ye did was air out rustlers and such?"

Marwood did not think Canton would have his six-gun positioned like that if he was planning dirt. Belike the man was who he said he was, a saddle tramp looking to pass through the country undetected.

"Something like that," Marwood answered. "I once did a job in Saltillo."

Canton's grin flashed between his greasy whiskers. "That's what I figured. I knowed men who hired out for such. I ain't judging ye. I'm passing along what I heard over whiskey."

"Sure."

"Ye killed some feller down in Saltillo, I take it?"

"I finished a job I was hired to do."

"Shoot him in the back?"

"Didn't have to." Marwood had shot the land agent through a window while he was at his desk forging permits.

Canton jerked a nod at Marwood's gun, holstered across his stomach. "My Pap worked the taxidermy and tanning yards when he wasn't jailed for drunk. That handle ain't no horn or pearl made. Ain't even ivory."

Marwood watched him close. "No."

Canton wiped his mouth. He laughed to himself. "Do tell. I've seen scrimshaw and jigged gun handles in my day. Damn if ye ain't a caution."

Marwood watched the fire. "I can't help what I am."

A block of silence froze between them. Canton settled back. "My stomach feels like my throat's been cut," he said. "There ain't no decent game in this country. If there was I'd a found it."

"I found sotol stalks yesterday."

"Keep 'em for your grandmother," Canton snorted. "I ain't one for eating roots like a dirty Apache. Look here, Marwood. I'm headed for Sabinas, myself. Got me a job lined up. Ye ever been to Sabinas?"

Marwood told him he had not.

"There's an ex-Colonel living down there in Mexico. Vickers. Used to be an officer in the Rebellion. After the surrender he bought an *estancia* across the border and churched a fat widow. Now he sells horses and Mexican cattle to the Texas Rangers. For a right good price, people say." Canton poked the fire with a short hook iron. He leaned over it, elbows crooked like branches. The hair on the back of his wrists was long and matted. "I met a ramrod in El Paso out to hire summer hands. Mebbe it ain't my look out, but this Colonel Vickers might want an experienced man like yerself on his payroll."

"I'm headed up country." Once more Marwood wondered if Botis and the men had made it out safely.

"Do as ye must think best."

The horse nickered and looked at them from the dark. Canton yawned.

"Ain't ye going to sleep none?" he asked.

"I guess I will." The fire lowered between them.

"I don't want to watch ye all night expecting a knife in my guts," Canton said.

"I'll bunk out here," Marwood said. "It's not the first time I slept on hard ground."

Canton dug thumb and forefinger on the back of his neck and pinched some small struggling life between them. He threw it into the fire.

"My horse ain't much, but we could spell him between us," he offered.

"Thank you, but I will keep pointed up north a ways."

Canton rubbed his hands over his britches. "Do as ye like. I'm only making conversation to pass the time."

"Sure."

Canton hooked the spent tobacco out of his mouth and flung it away. "Ye got a piece of tender chicken waiting for ye in Texas?"

Marwood lay on his side, elbow on the desert floor, head supported by one hand. "I feel I'm being pulled as from some great lodestone." Marwood didn't know if he was talking to himself or the other man.

Canton knuckled his mouth, nodded sagely. "I know what ye mean. There are times I feel I have to saddle and pull for the high country or I will bust."

"No," Marwood corrected him, "this is more . . . this is . . ." He turned quiet. How could he explain a thing to another person when he couldn't explain it to himself?

"Ye got any money?"

Marwood stared at the man.

"So's we can buy ye a horse. I guess we could steal ye one." Canton hitched a knee. The torn leggings draped his shin. "So long as ye feel no need for range detecting and hang us for our crime."

"I'm not a lawman, Canton. I have no money. I lost everything when I lost my outfit."

"Goddamn, Marwood, ye are a pitiful wreck on this empty desert. Damn near an orphan, and I ain't in the orphan saving business."

"Didn't ask it of you."

Canton pulled his hat down and turned away, arms crossed. "I'm quit with ye. Save ye turd in the morning—there ain't naught else to burn out here."

Marwood could feel the knife in his boot pressing against his leg. He closed his eyes. Somewhere in the dark the horse cropped thin shoots of grass. Sleep lapped the ragged corners of his mind. He did not let himself go under but rested on an uneasy shore of twilight. He needed to rest his eyes or he would fall asleep forever, and Canton's gun was lying well out of reach on the bedroll . . .

Canton had turned to sleep—without his bedroll.

Marwood's eyes sprang open. A filthy hand clapped his

mouth and the keen bite of a blade cut the skin under his ear. He corkscrewed off the ground and drove his own knife into Canton's thigh, sawed stringy muscle deep into his groin.

Hot arterial blood pumped over Marwood's fist. Canton screamed. It was a shuddering high-pitched wail that cut the desert air. Marwood kicked him away and rolled clear to his feet, chest heaving.

The horse smelled blood and snorted in fear. Canton stumbled backward and sat dumb on the desert floor. Blood pumped from his groin in black spurts. He tried to compress it with his hands, but the harder he squeezed the faster it pumped through his fumbling fingers.

"Ye cut me bad." His face was white-bone scared.

"I aim to finish it out," Marwood said.

He kicked away the hunting knife Canton had dropped. Something inside Marwood thundered and he saw naught before him but pain and death—a thing indescribable and of no comprehension to any sane man. But of all the things Marwood was, both past and present, he was not at that moment sane. All his rage and hatred centred on Canton's screaming face. Marwood felt blood boiling through his limbs like acid. His mind roiled with half-forgotten images and words from his distant past, coalescing as the coiled, wintry thing in his heart came fully awake and opened its black maw to demand Canton's life. And if it could not be sated, it would be fed the lives of others, of cities, of entire worlds.

He propped one knee between Canton's shoulders and forced his face down into the fire. He cut the man's throat with his knife. Blood hissed and smoked on the embers. Marwood took his time to work the slender blade between Canton's neck bones and, with a murderous cry of rage, flung his head into the desert.

He wiped his knife on Canton's clothes and folded it with care as the thing inside him coiled again in an uneasy sleep.

Then Marwood stripped the corpse of its stinking rags and threw them on the fire. They blazed and billowed greasy smoke.

Canton had little in his pockets other than a handwritten letter from a wife in Kentucky. There was a second letter from an uncle in Lexington, demanding a receipt for buffalo bones sold to a fertilizer concern in Dodge City.

Marwood looked at the remains of the man at his feet. “You aren’t from up Arkansas way,” he said. He tossed the correspondence into the fire.

Under the Indian blanket covering the saddle were three scalps. Marwood examined the scalphunter’s gun. It was in fair condition with three rounds left in the wheel. Low on ammunition, Marwood thought. Which was why Canton risked using a knife instead of an expedient bullet through his head. Well, a man too cheap to kill right deserves to die.

Marwood put the gun down and dragged Canton’s body into the desert. He returned to camp and searched the saddlebags and panniers. He found a pound of salt pork wrapped in stiff calico. Another leather bag of possibles contained seventeen dollars in Mexican silver. Marwood roasted the meat over the fire and ate.

Canton had also hidden a wolf’s hide waterskin under his saddle. Marwood shook it and drank, listening as the snarling coyotes tore Canton apart, wrestling with his head between their popping jaws.

CHAPTER 14

Marwood woke once again with the sun full in his eyes. He hiked into the desert and found no trace of Canton, just the circling tracks of the coyotes, who'd crept out of the low, bare hills, took the offering, cracked bone and meat, and left. There was nothing else but sand and wind-scoured rock for miles.

Marwood watered Canton's horse from his hat. What little remained he kept for his own use. But if he didn't find more water in the next forty-eight hours he would have to shoot the horse, and probably himself.

Marwood saddled up. Canton's horse wasn't much of an animal to stake his life on. The wretched, swaybacked creature had no spirit: the homemade hackamore rubbed raw, bleeding spots on the muzzle; the left foreleg had high ringbone. Marwood worked the pastern joint back and forth. The horse took the pain, but it would not be long before he walked himself lame.

Marwood mounted the horse and rode north. He travelled slow, pacing the horse and himself. As he rode he checked his backbearing. No sign of Rangers or the Buffalo Soldiers. They had departed for bigger game. No sign of any Pinkertons, either. Maybe they, too, had taken off after new game. He could live with that.

The following day Marwood shot a javelina nosing through a sunbaked streambed with Canton's gun. He made a dry and fireless camp. What he didn't eat raw he staked in thin sheets under the sun to dry. The trapezoidal head of the beast stared at him from a mesquite stob, black with crawling insects.

Late that night he reached a shambled collection of adobe structures and ugly mud hovels. He bedded down for the night under a thatched *portico*. The next morning he sold the horse, saddle, and Canton's gun in Gallina for three hundred pesos. In a cantina off the square, an elderly *vaquero* expressed an interest in, and subsequently examined, the scalps.

"Are they Apache scalps, señor?" he asked.

The *vaquero*'s name was Matias Antonio Sosa-Ruiz. He smoked black Maduro cigars. He wore brown on black and a silver *concho* belt. They talked business over bowls of black piñon coffee. The air swarmed with clouds of snarling flies and the tang of chili peppers assaulted Marwood's nostrils. Skinned goats hung in an open window, their blue bald eyes staring at the ceiling.

"I don't know," Marwood admitted. "Hair's greased. They're Indian, anyway."

He had the notion Canton cut the scalps off anyone he came across and greased them with tallow to pass for Indian. He might have done as much with Marwood's hair.

Sosa-Ruiz held one of the scalps toward the light. "The State of Chihuahua will buy Apache scalps," he said.

Male Apache scalps went for a hundred American in Chihuahua, fifty for women and children.

"I'm staying in Texas," Marwood said.

Sosa-Ruiz put the hair back on the table. He smoked for a minute and let his mind work. "I will pay one hundred Yankee dollars."

"That's not much."

"The *peligro* is mine, señor. If I am caught I will be hanged. Or worse. You are going to Texas, but this is Mexico. There is always worse for a man who remains in Mexico."

"All right, but make it gold." He could use gold on both sides of the border.

"Your terms are more than fair," Sosa-Ruiz agreed. "I will have your money tonight."

"I'll meet you at sundown," Marwood said.

They shook hands and parted. Marwood ate scrambled eggs and chorizo in a *taqueria*. He bought coffee, pinto beans, and salt. He also bought lead balls and powder for his gun.

He hung around the plaza until early evening. There was another man standing between two adobe buildings halfway down the street. He wore a black hat with a feather in it. When Marwood looked at him, the man backed off into shadow.

Sosa-Ruiz stood under an oil lamp hanging from a stone crosstree. Guitar music came from the cantina. *Malagueña*. Sosa-Ruiz took possession of the scalps, and Marwood pocketed five gold double eagles.

"I will ride to Chihuahua in the morning," the *vaquero* said. He folded the scalps in a white calfskin *mochila* and put them away. "There I will light a novena for my *hijo muerto*. *Veinte años* he is gone. How do you say it, señor?"

"Twenty years."

"*Sí*. Twenty years, my son, he is dead."

White moths dropped from the wooden rafters overhead and circled the lamplight. Their shadows flitted across the windows.

The *vaquero* smoked a cigar. "My son was the only person I lived for. Now I sell scalps. What can I say to God about that? If he would even listen to my petition, which he will not. *Los años no pasan en balde y cada gallo canta en su muladar*." He looked at Marwood. "I also light the candle for you, señor. *Perdóname*, but you look like a man who travels a dark path."

Marwood didn't know what to say to that. They shook hands a final time.

"*Vaya con Dios*, señor."

"Goodbye."

Marwood hefted his war bag and walked to the edge of town. Spaw was waiting for him with two fresh horses.

"They're all back at camp," he said when Marwood drew close. "We had a caution finding you. Those Rangers came out of nowhere and chased us over creation."

Marwood picked up the trailing reins of a chestnut gelding. It looked a decent enough horse. "Everyone make it out of that scrape alive?" he asked.

"Amos went under," Spaw said. "Caught a ball in his liver and died the following night. Wasn't nothing Doc could do. Goddamn Texans sold us out, Mar. Hope you're ready for a bloody, hard ride. We're headed for deep country. The pincers are closing in, and our necks are gettin' squeezed."

"I'm ready," Marwood said.

He chucked the horse and they rode off.

He found the men concealed in a hackberry grove at the base of a 175-foot waterfall in the Rio Grande Rift. Their bestial faces were quiet and withdrawn as they sat around the sparkling water pool.

Jubal Stone had deep pain lines carved on his face. The wound in his shoulder kept festering and had to be drained daily. They looked whipped and chewed up to a man, and their countenances startled Marwood.

Botis brought Acheron around and roused them to their feet. They rode through the night into the Cuesta del Burro hills. The range was covered with rhyolite and igneous shards of volcanic rock that split the horse's hooves, making them stumble and groan.

They rode out the next day over the Chihuahua Trail, through scrubby desert cactus. Flocks of startled doves flew up before them, their wings whistling with alarm. Toward evening Lovich shot a pronghorn antelope and they cooked meat over a fire on bayonets. The night after they gained the eastern reaches of the Glass Mountain Range.

While they rode Marwood noticed the men stared at Botis in spells and turns. Their own faces were unreadable and enigmatic. It was as if they were trying to fuddle something out, and either could not comprehend what they knew to be true, or trust their own sanity.

They had to shoot two lame horses in the course of the week, and were down to their last one in the remuda when they happened upon a cluster of wooden buildings that shared a communal water well.

Seventeen men and five women, all Mennonites, emerged from their respective abodes and stared in astonishment at the feral men dressed in cannibalistic vesture: animal skins, furs, and disparate parts of human beings worn as ornamentation. Teeth, blackened ears, a necklace of fingers and shells, tooled belts and bridles cut from human skin, clattering scalps hanging from the horses like black moss. They were blood stained and reeking—men who rode the brim of Hell's expanse, and supped on the devil's scat.

"Do you have any horses?" Botis asked.

"Not for sale, mister," replied an aged foreman dressed in black with a fringe of whiskers under his chin.

Botis dropped all pretence. "I wasn't asking to buy."

They had to shoot one recalcitrant Mennonite to make their position clear. Dan Lovich flipped a rope around the wounded man's neck and dragged him back and forth over the ground. When he finished he threw the rope down in disgust. The torn and bloody body lay where he left it. No one moved to touch it.

They ransacked the shacks, turned over beds, and emptied cabinetry. There was little to eat other than collared peccary, feed corn, and a wheel of goat cheese.

The settlers did have guns and powder at their disposal. The Hydra took it, along with all the lead shot and percussion caps they could find.

Botis was prying open a small button chest with an iron pritchel, looking for hidden valuables, when a settler filled the doorway of the single-room structure.

"Get out of my fucking light," Botis growled.

"We are peaceful men of God," the man told him. "I will pray for your soul."

"That's the least you can do before I whip your goddamn ass for standing in my light," Botis replied without turning around. He returned to work once the man's shadow departed.

They gathered the stock and were about to depart when a dark-haired woman ran past Marwood toward Botis, who was already sitting in his saddle. She carried a loose bundle of clothes pressed against her breast, possibly everything she owned in the world. She took hold of Acheron's bridle.

"Take me with you," she begged. "There is nothing left to build on. I will be your woman."

Botis kicked her in the stomach. "Let go the goddamn horse."

Her knees buckled. She dropped her bundle of linen but stubbornly held onto the bridle, jerking the horse's head down.

"No," she said. "You have taken everything. These men are too weak and cannot protect us."

"Acheron."

The blue roan snapped his teeth onto the woman's face and hair. He shook the upper half of her body like a dog with a rag, tearing skin and ripping hair from her scalp.

She screamed wildly, her arms flailing. She fell back on a pile of gravel, wheezed with pain and stunned surprise. Blood dripped in her eyes and soaked the front of her cotton dress.

Acheron shook his head, bridle rattling. Gore and foam flecked off his muzzle. He wickered. Maimed and bereft, the woman covered her head with folded arms. She shrieked and rocked back and forth.

Botis and party left the settlement in their backwash; only slowing later in the day so the horses could blow and regain their strength. Otherwise, they would have ridden the animals into the ground. They were but that desperate to put long safe miles under them.

They rode on. Men slept and ate and lived in their saddles. They relieved themselves without stopping. The Tonkawas would leap from their horses, put their ears to the ground to listen, then vault back onto their animals without breaking stride. They kept going all through the night and the next day, and the night that followed. The horses were played out. Marwood's body ached from the never-ending ride; his eyes burned with sand, sun, and overwhelming exhaustion. Water scarce, food little. Hope none. This was the mixture they rode on.

By mid-afternoon of the following day, when they believed they had placed enough distance between them and the Texas Rangers, Botis called a halt.

They had crossed canyons, doubled back, and laid many false trails. Marwood more fell from his horse than dismounted. If anything, he left the saddle with less grace than when he lost his mare in the flash flood. So too did the others, dismounting in similar fashion. They staggered into a small clearing and dropped and sprawled.

Spaw and Marwood joined the beaten company. The Tonkawas also drew near. This was to be a major council of war. Every man had a living stake in the decisions that would be made over the next hour.

No one said anything for a space. Botis used the time to quietly load his gun. His clothes were smeared with blood and streaks of caked mud, but otherwise he looked no worse for wear. The same could not be said for the remainder of his crew. Every man had a wound of some kind, and was damaged near the point of inaction. Gratton had a deep gash on his face sutured with cactus thorns. He had shaved part of his beard to repair the wound. Lovich had one knee wrapped with rawhide and used a broken rifle as a crutch. Blood and foul yellow pus seeped through his crude bandages. Quillen drained the pus and cupped him for good measure, but his fever wasn't breaking.

Rota whet stoned his harpoon. The harsh rasp of stone on steel caused the men to look up.

"Goddamn, old man," Charley Broadwell growled, "can't you be quiet?"

Bill Rota lifted his eyes toward Charley then bent back to his task.

The other men were too tired, or too hurt, to do anything but sit in a mute circle. Much like a ring of Paleolithic savages off the short end of a bad mammoth hunt.

Botis took a powder flask and charged an empty chamber of his gun. He patched a ball and levered it into place. He did the same for the other chambers and centred percussion caps over each. He spun the cylinder, checked the gate and hammer action. Satisfied, he thrust the gun through his belt and glanced at Lovich.

The Dutchman took this as his signal to open the floor for discussion.

"The Captain wants to ride into Comancheria," Lovich said, tapping a hobble rope against his leg. He waited for a reaction.

There was none. The men were looking down at the ground. Even Rota had stopped sharpening the point of his harpoon. If Lovich was disappointed by their response he did not show it. Men studied their boots, their dirty nails, or contemplated a horned toad sunning itself on a rock. No one looked up, and no one dared look at Botis.

"That's a mistake," Marwood said.

Botis swung his head and eyed him hard. Marwood was not put off. He returned the man's stare.

"They won't follow us into Comancheria," Botis explained.

"You're goddamn right they won't," answered Marwood. "They won't have to."

"Cibola is there, Mar. I saw it, again. So did these men."

Marwood remembered the unknown star-filled sky. He looked at the men, who were reluctant to add their voices to the discussion. Perhaps they had differing opinions on Botis, even as to his sanity, but they trusted him. That went a long way between men desperately fighting for their lives in the desert bush.

"I want to find Cibola," Marwood said. "Or whatever this place is that haunts me and has stolen my memory. I want to know who, and what, I am. I think you know the answers to these things, Captain. I think you're keeping them to yourself because it gives you power. It gives you power over the world, over yourself, and over me."

"We can't head back west," Botis said, not gainsaying Marwood's words. "Not on this same track. That's certain death."

"No, I agree." Marwood frowned. He kicked at the dirt. He was not a man who often gave vent to frustration. "Going west would be like running us through a slaughter chute. Texas border narrows down at El Paso. All they have to do is put the stopper in to bottle us up. No way we will ever get through El Paso into New Mexico Territory. North of that lies Comancheria. South of El Paso is all of Mexico. It's a huge death trap for every one of us here."

"We might have an easier time in Mexico," Jubal Stone said. "If we keep jumping the border we could get both sides chasing their tails."

"I am not so sure about that," Marwood cautioned. "The Federales have warrants out on us by now. We can hold up somewhere down there until the heat comes off. But I wouldn't want to bet my life on the good graces of Mexican hospitality."

"I agree with Mar on that point," Botis interjected. "So what do you suggest?" The last question had been put back to Marwood.

Marwood looked at the big man whose secrets he wished to know. "You know my answer. We need to run hard back up through Texas. We will have a much easier time in Hill Country than the flat waste of the Sonoran Desert or that Chihuahuan hellhole. Or anywhere in West Texas for that matter. There are more settlements and towns up central way, which is to our benefit. It will allow us the opportunity to stay ball and powdered, and find fresh horses."

"I suppose if I got to be shot I'd rather it be by a Texas lawman than a Mexican one," Spaw said hopefully.

"I don't want to be shot at all," Marwood countered. "I am looking at this situation from a narrowing field of choices. They are all of them bad. But some are less bad than others. We can fight our way out of this, but we have to be smart about it."

"I spent time in a Mexican *cárcel*," Lovich said aloud. "You don't want to know what those bastards fed us, or what they did to us. I don't want to go back there again. I'm for Texas."

"What about Cibola?" Botis asked. His eyes remained on Marwood. In truth they had never left his.

"Hang Cibola," Marwood answered. "I want to get my ass out of this trouble first."

The rest of the men had nothing more to say.

Marwood walked up to Botis and said low so the others could not hear, "I want to find Cibola, too, Captain. That I am willing to hold off on something I have wanted answered my entire life . . . that should tell you where I'm standing right now."

Botis faced around to the Tonkawas. "What do you say about this, Red Thunder? I want your opinion as well."

The younger Tonkawa drew a deep breath. "Comancheria is a death sentence for every man who enters," he said. "Despite what white people think, Indians are not all alike. Tonkawas have no special immunity from the savage leanings of the Comanche nation. I hold the best course of action is the one proposed by Mar. These are my words, and I want my counsel to be considered."

Jubal Stone leaned into Bill Rota and elbowed his ribs. "That sly old Tonk speaks better American than you do, old man."

"Aye," Rota said, "he's a smart old dog." He lowered his voice to Stone. "We are a long way from the sea, Jubal."

"You speak it plain enough," Stone muttered back.

"So where do we go?" Spaw asked aloud. "I'll ride anywhere you boys say. I don't care none."

"I say we ride through the state and kill every goddamn Texan we see," Ed Gratton said. His black eyes burned with hatred.

"Ed's right," Jubal Stone said. "We can't let these people push us around."

"I'm for that," Broadwell echoed. "I'm tired of being hoorawed by these motherless sons of bitches."

"Well, we can keep west a little ways out and ride up through Santa Angela," Marwood said. "I would study on that."

Doc Quillen lifted his head for the first time. "Fort Concho is at Santa Angela," he warned. "And to get there we got to ride right past Fort Stockton." Someone groaned. None of them wanted to see Buffalo Soldiers ever again.

"We can whip them," Ed Gratton said. "They ain't nothing."

"I've been to Fort Stockton, Ed," Doc Quillen said quietly. "You think that bunch we ran into out west was a bugger bear? They got the 9th Cavalry in Stockton, boys. Them mean niggers is known all over this here back country. They ain't near a patch to fool with. There ain't a man alive who can tie a can to their tail, believe you me."

"Yes, Doc, but they are looking for us everywhere," Marwood said. "This is all empty land. The Mexican border is more settled than West Texas, until you hit the really deep desert. And what good are we there without food and guns? At least in Santa Angela we are near enough to Comancheria to jump if we have to. That's all Comanche borderland up that way, and it leaves us the option if the captain wants to take it." Marwood shrugged. He was out of words. "That's all I have to say. I guess I've spoken my piece. I'm like Spaw, I'll do whatever you boys want."

An unsettled quiet fell over the company. They waited for Botis to decide their final fate.

"It's your decision, Cap," Lovich said gruffly. He leaned on his rifle to take the weight off his bad leg. "I'll kick their peckers in line if that's your call."

"I agree with Mar to this extent," Botis began. "We have to get out of this open country. Santa Angela is our best bet for now. We can re-provision and . . ." He stepped back and motioned for Marwood. "Mar, I want to talk to you."

The two walked off together until they created some distance between themselves and the weary band.

"Look, I am not hiding anything from you," Botis said. "I want you to know that much."

"I think you are, Captain," Marwood said. "I think you have been all along. I think all this taking on jobs and working for the Governor to kill Apaches has been a ruse that works to your benefit. I think you have a definite plan of what you want to do. Like I said before, I am not kicking about it. I want to get out of this trap and make some breathing room before we push on."

Botis mulled this over. "I mentioned at the bodega you

might jump one way or the other," he reminded Marwood. "Or for yourself. I continue to remain of two minds on that point, son. You're a good man, but you're a hazard."

Marwood refused to speak to that.

Botis kept silent for a bit. "I know you had reservations about that village in Mexico," he allowed.

"I got to thinking what a man told me in Laredo about a line crossed. I saw it crossed in Sand Creek."

Botis scowled. "You know what a line in the sand is, Mar?" he asked. "It's something a man can erase and redraw for his own benefit."

Marwood removed his hat. He looked at it in his hands, put it back on and squared the brim. "Botis," he said in a clear voice, "I don't want to set myself up against you. But if I wanted to light out I'd do it, and neither you or any of your men, or your damn Indian spies, would be able to stop me."

"That's not the point I am trying to make," Botis said. "I'm not Chivington. I will let no man step in my way. Not even a man I respect. Not even a man I would die for. Not even you."

Botis turned on his boot heel. His hands were in the deep pockets of his leather jacket. The sun burned full on his face.

Standing before them was a massive juniper tree. It rose seven feet high, with thick intertwined limbs. Long, snake-like trailing branches sprawled over an expanse half the size of any decent town plaza. It was petrified and brown, of ancient lineage and with a hard, sapless core. The berries were brittle, desiccated by red-hot winds. It had been dead so long there was no chaff under the limbs or piled around the base of the trunk. The needle-like leaves had been blown away. The only living thing it housed was a spider, which staged its silk net across a V-shaped branch lying close to the ground.

Botis ranged his eyes over the ancient plant.

"Hard to believe something that big could ever die," he said with wonder.

CHAPTER 15

Pecos County, fifty miles south of Fort Stockton, west of the deep blue green and cavernous, Pecos River. Mid-June day, sun hot enough to sear skin, and a drum-rattling wind.

They rode past old tipi rings and wickiup sites overgrown with thick scrub. Charred stones that had once ringed age-old fires. The obdurate ground was covered with flint shards and other prehistoric artifacts of no modern use to anyone.

It was in this field Bill Rota dismounted. He passed the reins behind his back and kicked through the thin stony soil, searching for arrowheads.

By this time his thoughts were often of the sea and the whaling ships upon which he had worked. Stone's reminiscence about his sailing days brought all the old memories of harvesting spermaceti rushing back with untrammelled ferocity. The white curve of sail; the bite and splash of salt wind. A whale breached to leeward and you went out after it with your heart pounding and blood in your eyes. When you made the kill it was a feeling you had conquered something so immense it would one day roar back to life and overwhelm you with its crushing power. So you had to hold it back as best you could, and live with the knowledge of what you had done. But, that, too, was a kind of immortality, and every whaler knew it when he set out from Nantucket, with the shadow of the ship long across the morning sea while he stood at the rail smoking a clay pipe.

Rota squatted on his boot heels and furrowed his stubby fingers through the dry dirt, turning up flint flakes. He had garnered a large collection of arrow points in his fifty-odd years. He long wondered at the slow progress of making war upon men and animals alike with spear, harpoon, and iron. Long blood rivers of time and civilization. He looked up and behind him. The rest of the party had kept on riding, and did not notice his absence.

He watched his horse cropping mouthfuls of grass and studied the dry, futureless land around him, and the dry, futureless future still before him. *The sea, the sea.* One last time, he thought, before he died. Dip his hand into salty spume and taste the yesteryears of his life. How far to the sea? Weigh anchor and ride a southern course to Del Rio. Find a way across the Seminole Canyon without breaking his damn neck. Follow the del Norte back down to Laredo. Then set a new course and ride the evenstar until you reach the Port of Corpus Christi. Perhaps he could work passage on an outward-bound ship. A ship to anywhere. The Mother sea. Salt water tied to the coursing blood of every man's veins. The sea, his life. Was Mary alive? He turned the iron wedding ring on his finger. They'd all be grown now, his sons. *Storms in my heart. Before I die*. The idea took hold. He nodded to himself. *Yes. One last time, before I die.*

He looked up trail. Botis and the men were gone. Rota felt the silence and the ever-present sense of solitude men experience in the desert when faced with a decision that will change their lives.

He walked to his horse, picked up the trailing reins. He wasn't quite sure yet. He swung the free ends across a cactus flower, making up his mind. He placed his foot in the stirrup and lifted his body into the saddle.

Before I die, yes, he thought, and before the storms of old age send me under the chop one last time.

He reined the horse around and rode south into the welcoming desert, and was never seen again.

Charley Broadwell was the first to notice Rota's absence. He rowelled his horse and caught up to Botis riding point.

"Cap, Old Bill done lit a shuck on us."

Botis looked over his shoulder at the tired string of riders cutting through the awful dust and heat. He spoke into Acheron's ear, and kept riding.

Broadwell decided this was an invitation to offer up more information. "He was bringing up drag last I saw."

"Very well, Charley."

Broadwell figured he had done all he could. He rolled his bay back around and took up his usual position in line.

Red Thunder and Little Shreve were three furlongs out and riding swing. Botis made a slight motion and the two Tonkawa scouts came flying back on their bareback ponies.

Marwood watched Botis address the scouts. They peeled off and rode back down the train until their separate figures melted and warped into the forsaken desert heat.

The following day yellow dust clouds filled the sky ahead of them. Two-dozen cowboys were driving a long herd of bone-thin cattle along the Pecos River. Many of the cowboys were blacks, Mexicans, even a few Indians. They were headed for Sante Fe and parts north. Four thousand head stretched from sun to compass point, endless and unending all.

The mounted killers watched the tall, rangy beasts pass like a living river, and walk collectively into a wavering horizon of shimmering, blistering heat. Dirty, speckled beasts, bedecked of colour: brown and yellow-pale, bright black or blood red, and every combination thereof. There were great mossy horns on the steers, like fantastic medieval weapons. They ate anything in their path: mesquite bark, cactus paddle, the spines of cholla, and dead leaves. They could walk all day on a sup of water. They were more bone and sinew than muscle meat. They were even known to kill horses, and could stand their ground before packs of javelinas or rattling snakes. They were rumoured to chase coyotes come morn, and could walk all night under the stars.

The afternoon shuddered and waned and finally gave up the day. The lowing river of cattle ended, and the cowboys riding drag passed by without a word or a nod.

Botis and his exhausted men turned east and rode into their own shadows. An evening star rose above the low bare hills.

Jubal Stone spied smoke threading the pecan trees ahead. They were a mile out from the Pecos River when they neared the Horsehead Crossing ford. They heard a rhythmic clunk of an axe cutting through wood. They made for the spire of chimney smoke, halting in the yard of a log cabin, with chickens, pigs, and a few head of miserable stocker cattle.

It was a hardscrabble homestead. The ground was littered with cow and horse dung. A boy of fourteen chopped pecan wood beside the corner of the house. Another boy, a tow-headed lad of eight winters, collected wood splints for kindling in a blanket folded over his back.

Botis sat his horse while a man holding a short and deadly Mare's Leg rifle emerged from the cabin.

"We have come for water," Botis said.

The farmer stood in his tracks and looked them over. He turned his head and spat. "We have water."

"I thank you, kindly."

"Proud to offer," the farmer said.

Botis came down off his big horse. He picked up a wooden pail and worked the handle of a pump. Sweet spring water gushed. He sat on the stone coping and let Acheron drink before he lifted the pail and drank himself.

The rest of the men took this as sign and slid from their saddles. They stood in line, patient confederates all, and waited to water up.

"How long have you settled in these parts?" Botis asked the farmer. Before he could answer, a woman appeared in the open doorway of the little farmhouse. She wore a pale yellow dress and black button shoes. Her face was lean and pinched, her pinned hair brittle and greying. She looked dry and used up, as if the land was killing her by small degrees.

"Get back in there, woman," the farmer said. She disappeared back inside the house. The farmer turned back to Botis. "We've been here nigh on twenty year' all told," he said. "Paid for in blood. My eldest, Quentin, got hisself killed on by a Comanch' war party two years ago."

"I am sorry about your boy," Botis said.

"It's a hard life," the farmer replied.

"Yes." Botis stared philosophically at the darkling sky, and the dark doorway into which the woman had disappeared.

"Texas is hard on dogs and women," he said.

"Ain't that a truth," the farmer agreed, earnestly. The fourteen-year-old boy ceased his chopping. He listened to the men talk.

Botis picked up the drooping reins of his horse. "We would like to stay the night on your place. We'll be out of your way come early sun."

The farmer pointed. "There's a crick down in the bottom of that draw. Good shade trees. You're welcome to build your fire there."

The creek lay fifty yards away. Botis walked toward it, leading Acheron. Marwood and the other men in the party followed, walking their horses.

They unsaddled the animals, kicked leaves into passable beds, pitched down their torn blankets, and collapsed like broken marionettes. Spaw got a fire going. The men drew near and let the miles of the long, deadly ride slough from their minds like old snakeskin. They cooked a tierce of white-tailed jacks Little Shreve had killed before going after Rota. He always carried a pouch full of rocks and could whizz one from the back of his pony. They ate the meat from the points of their knives.

They talked among themselves but little. Each man sat by the fire and kept his own counsel. Some smoked, or repaired leather reins and clothes. Ed Gratton unfolded a sewing pouch. He drew out a bone needle and white thread, and went to darning his torn stockings.

The night rushed in. Pale moon fire filled the sky. A coyote yipped on the flat and dropped quiet.

"You better come out of those trees," Botis said to the gathering dark.

A shadow broke away from one of the trees and crunched through leaves and twigs. It was the fourteen-year-old boy come alone. He stood at the edge of the firelight where Marwood sat. His eyes were filled with curiosity.

"Step up to the fire," Botis said.

The boy hesitated like a deer caught in the open. He drew near.

"What are you doing here?" asked Botis.

"I want to ride out with your men."

They looked at one another, directed their collective gaze back to the boy.

"You don't know anything about us," Botis said.

The boy looked like he might cry. "I know you're living," he said.

Some of the men looked down at their blankets or cleaned their guns. Botis held the boy's gaze.

"What's your name, son?"

"Franklin Perry. I'm called Frank, though. Mostly by my Pap."

"Frank, belike your father needs you to stay around the house and chore," said Botis. "You'd best head back before he gets to missing you."

"Aw, he don't care none what I do."

"He might strap you some, he finds you here."

"I guess I've been whomped a time or two already," Frank said.

"He comes out here looking, I don't want to have to shoot your daddy."

The boy must have heard something in Botis's voice—a welcoming tolerance. He did not quit the firelight.

"I have a gun," he told them.

Botis raised his eyebrows.

"My Pap keeps it locked up. But I can shoot it good. We go hunting of a Sunday, him and me."

Marwood scrunched aside. Frank squatted beside him on his thin shanks, eyeing the ring of fire rocks.

"I ran away from home once already," he told them. His slender hands were clapped before him. A log popped in the fire, sparks flew. He shifted his weight to another leg. "I had enough of working daybreak to backbreak, so I lit out. I lived off the land for two weeks. I killed rabbits with a stick and got my leg tusked open by a wild boar. I was some kind of cold and hungry so I came home whipped dead. It was near midnight. I crept back in bed and lay there waiting for my Pap to hide me good. I heard his footsteps, and he stood in the doorway, and you know what he said? He said, 'You got it out of your gut?' And I said, 'Yes, sir, I guess I did.' Then he went back to bed. That was last year. We never talked about it again, him and me." The boy licked his mouth. "But I didn't get it out," he said with fierce pride. "I don't think I can burn it out if I tried."

"Your Pap doesn't want you to leave, son."

"Aw, you can't know that, mister."

"Your Pap doesn't want you to leave."

The boy expressed his doubt, but you could tell he wanted to believe Botis. "Maybe. Ma doesn't do much for nothing after Quentin got killed by Comanches. Anyway, Pap has Nelson to help him. He's my little brother."

"Your Pap needs a man to help pull stock. Nelson is between hay and grass."

"I ain't no man yet," Frank admitted. "Will be someday, though."

"Mayhap you are closer than you think," Marwood said.

Frank thought that over. He looked as if the idea might appeal to him. "I'm good with horses," he reflected. Then, "You men hunt out Indians? I seen them scalps."

"We hunt everything," Botis acknowledged.

"Ain't there nothing you don't kill?" Frank asked. It was clear the thought intrigued him, as all things apocalyptic attracted young boys.

Botis pointed a dirty finger at the night sky. "Do you see Old Father Moon up there?"

The full moon was like yellow cream in a barrel. "I guess I ain't blind," the boy said.

A few of the men laughed. Botis grinned in turn.

"If I could," Botis said, "I'd kill that moon. I'd kill its light and erase every thought and deed and word ever said or written about it. I'd do it for no other reason than it was within my power to do so. That's the kind of men we are."

"Aw, hell, you're greening me." The boy stood up and brushed his pants. "I can bring you something to eat in the morning. If'n you want me to, that is. Ma said it was all right."

"We are leaving before first light," Botis told him. "But I thank you for the offer."

"You ride back through here, you won't be able to stop me. You hide and watch."

"I will take your caution under advisement," Botis promised. Frank slipped back through the trees and headed for home. They could hear his feet rustling the leaves, then nothing.

When they were sure he was well out of earshot, they laughed among themselves, yet quietly. It was not mocking laughter, but the laugh of men sharing the pain and hurt all boys who grow into men must carry in their hearts.

CHAPTER 16

They left the arid lowlands of the Pecos Valley, never to return. Ten miles farther on they brought the horses through Castle Gap, a mile-long pass of rimrock and natural blocks of limestone. Colossal mesas stood on either side of the pass like terminal gateposts opening onto some distant Brobdingnagian acreage.

Seven days sequent they rode through mansions of dust and wind. Rattlesnakes lay in the shade bush and under flat rocks. The men never saw them, but heard their buzzing when the reptiles felt the ground tremble from the passing horses.

They came upon a rebuilt *colonia* on the Rio Frio they had all but destroyed during their winter scourge. Botis and his men drove into them with murderous intent, firing their guns into the fleeing backs of farmers and ranchers, tradesmen and cattlemen and coopers. A dozen settlers formed a ragged skirmish line. The vanguard of Botis's company rode into them, guns blazing. They used ropes to pull down the skeletal frames of half-finished houses, and tossed flaming brands into the shattered woodwork. They burned tents and wagons. They scalped and docked ears, and they shot Double-barred V-branded cattle and poisoned stock tanks with bags of lime.

Three days later they rode into another Double-barred V *colonia* on the same river. White settlers had erected, on the understructure of the routed Mexican squatters, a wood-frame church with a white steeple. They had done this in the hope a fully constructed church would attract a man of the cloth this far out to oversee their congregation. The pulpit was torn down and the church set afire by Lovich. The survivors were rounded up and brought to stand before Botis.

Botis sat in a leather chair before the flames, dressed in rancid skins and wearing his black galero. His face was like a sword, and he was prepared to pass judgment on those men who had declaimed him. Buzzards sat perched in the high branches of tall juniper trees along the riverbank. The ground below was carpeted with a bed of their long, stinking feathers.

Botis picked up the tortoise-shell pince-nez with his customary dainty ease. He set them on the end of his nose and addressed the frightened congregation by the light of the burning church.

"I am Abram Botis," he said. "I ride with demons. I have come among you to judge all things past and future given."

Men and women wailed. Some fell to the ground in abject terror, for the name of Botis, old and ancient as it was, had come to be known by them through rumour and revered whispers.

"Hear me," Botis said, lifting a hand for silence, "for the grave stands naked before you. Your destruction has no covering in this land. My lieutenants will carry out my orders. Their only lust is revenge, and to a man they cleave unto the blooded wife of murder." He half-turned in his chair and beckoned each one forward.

"Know them by their names," he said.

And thus he named each man in his company, and they stood at his elbow with weapons drawn and the glint of red murder in their fierce eyes. When he got to the last three he called them forward one by one.

"Know him, Abaddon, the destroyer," Botis said, "and

Moloch who seeks revenge. Here, Merihem stands beside them with the fires of Hell between his hands."

Captives were brought under gunpoint from a temporary holding place—a rope corral strung between tree trunks and fence posts. Botis required each man to confess his worldly sins.

Many did so willingly, recognizing the face of sheer madness before them. Others did not, insisting they were innocent of any wrongdoing under any known reckoning of God. By what method Botis evaluated the evidence heard, or arrived at sentences of absolution, none could fathom.

Death sentences were meted out. Acheron was brought forth in harness. Those destined for execution were given over to him, and thereupon his back did ride to their deaths. Marwood tied their hands with baling wire. They were laid across a charred tree stump in a welter of gore, each prisoner beheaded with a two-man crosscut saw. Wine red blood pooled on the sand and grass, and the nine headless bodies were strung swinging from the creaking limbs of trees.

When it was finished, the men and women left alive were covered in ashes from their own homes, tied to singletrees, and scourged naked into the desert to wander like aimless penitents among rock, cactus, and scorpion.

The company collected their horses. Rising columns of smoke marked the blown site of the last Double-barred V *colonia*.

Botis climbed back on his horse and led his men out. He did not look back, or ever think again upon the awful destruction he had wrought.

They rode around, aimless for the most part. At the headwaters of the Middle Concho River the Tonkawas caught up to them. The company sat on the clay banks of the river eating freshwater mussels. The cliffs overlooking the sporadic pools of green water were chiselled with Native American pictographs. The primitive carvings depicted deer, rabbit, buffalo, and snake. All manner of creature were mixed in with other odd geometric designs that represented grass, water, and sky. Alongside these were pictures of men, and painted handprints of the authors revealing themselves in signature.

Red Thunder rode lento across the grassy plain. His humpbacked cousin, Little Shreve, was behind him on a piebald pony with painted chevrons. They closed the distance. Red Thunder looked to Botis and made a negative motion with his hand.

Botis received the news, speaking not a word in return. The Tonkawas filled their waterskins and pulled out to scout the terrain ahead. Botis mounted his horse and kept his eye fixed on the horizon.

From that hour on the name of Bill Rota was never mentioned again by any living man in the troop.

PART IV

The Thunder of the Plains

CHAPTER 17

For what is man's mind but a caution of madness?

The words haunted John Marwood. They spoke to the aching doubt growing from an acorn stone in the centre of his heart, and to the increasing madness so evident in Botis and his wild, inexplicable actions.

Marwood was not yet of two minds, as Botis had put it, as to which way he would jump. However, following an obsessive man purposefully drowning in madness was not a path Marwood wanted to travel under any circumstances.

Nevertheless, there remained salient elements to Botis's searing madness, which Marwood dared not deny and wanted to understand for himself, if for no other reason. In particular, they either answered, or raised questions, relating to Marwood's own existence. Or, put more simply, events that highlighted his own singular brand of madness.

True, then, any man's mind was his own. Marwood knew his private madness well, though he did not understand its relevance, and admitted as much to himself on any given day. Therefore, he continued to look to Botis for answers, because Botis was the only other man he knew who lived with a demon coiled like a watch spring in his marrow.

But the haunting feeling he carried with him from this moment on did not cease. It echoed in his mind like restless ghosts, and he wanted answers.

They pushed the horses through a thicket of mesquite and out the other side. Riding behind Marwood, a stray limb level with Jubal Stone's stirrup passed between his boot and the metal dowel. The branch ran clean through the stirrup loop, stripping leaves, as Stone, unknowing, continued to ride ahead. When he did notice something was wrong he tried to saw back on his horse. The animal spooked and reared and bolted wild until the unyielding tree branch bent and stripped away rider, saddle, blanket.

Stone's foot became entangled in the stirrup and a fork of the tree limb. The big horse dug its hooves into the ground and kicked forward with every ounce of power until the man's leg tore from his knee and lay twisted up with the wrecked and entangled saddle.

"Oh, God," Stone cried. He sat on the ground. One pants leg was empty up to the blood-soaked knee. A naked hairy leg with a cocked boot hung from a mesquite branch, along with the saddle.

Stone lay back, his shirt wet with sweat and fear and pain. "Dear, sweet God," he said.

Tunk Quillen dismounted and strode quickly to the downed man. He examined with a glance the awful, mortal wound and the enlarging puddle of blood beneath him.

"There ain't nothing I can do for him," Quillen told Botis.

"Then do for him," Botis said from the back of his horse.

Quillen drew a hunting knife from his belt. He crouched beside the dying man.

"Captain says I got to," he told Stone in a sorrowful voice. "When your leg tore off the ends of your blood vessels twisted themselves up. It might take you an hour to bleed out, but you are going to bleed out."

Stone's face was colourless. "I guess there ain't nothing left for it," he said.

"You want a drink of water?" Quillen asked.

"What the hell for?"

Quillen put his hand over the dying man's face and

turned it aside. He carved the hunting knife across the carotid artery and underlying vessels. Blood spurted two feet across dry chaff. Quillen held Stone down until his struggles lessened and all was still.

Botis watched the mercy killing from his saddle. He saw the tired and drawn faces of his men. "We will camp here," he said.

Quillen packed a tent with his additional belongings. After Spaw built a fire, Quillen erected the structure under a spreading soapberry tree. He carried Stone's limp body inside. Then Quillen returned to his horse and retrieved the black medical bag, a separate leather satchel filled with old books on anatomy, and a lantern.

He ducked back inside the tent, drew the flaps down, and did not emerge.

The day darkened into night and gibbous moon. The men watched Quillen's shadow move behind the yellow-lighted canvas. It would bend, straighten, elongate, stand still.

"What is he doing in there?" Charley Broadwell asked.

"You don't want to know," Ed Gratton said, and went back to wiping down his gun.

Broadwell watched the shadowy apparitions behind the canvas, trying to discern some meaning from them. "How come you all call him Tunk?" he asked the men around him. "I thought his first name was Joshua."

"He picked it up during the war," Gratton said. "It was the sound surgical instruments made when he dropped them in an alcohol bath."

"You rode with him in the war, Ed?" Broadwell asked.

Gratton looked up, annoyed. "Are you soft-headed? And him a Confederate slaver?"

The men finished their tug. They sat relaxed about the fire. Sometimes they glanced at the shadows moving inside the tent. They hauled out their pipes and makings and smoked.

"It's an evil thing that happened today," Spaw said, nibbling his square of leather. The other men nodded.

Botis sat perched on a fallen tree trunk well inside the light of the campfire.

"Not so, Lewis," he said. "The eradication of life, the destruction of all that God has wrought, is man's one great work. If he cannot accomplish that, the earth itself must one day reach out and strike him down."

"I've heard you say that before, Captain," Broadwell said. He picked his teeth with a mesquite thorn. "But the Bible says a man is made in God's image, and God can never die. Therefore, man can never die."

Botis smiled at this sophistry. "Man is sinful by nature, Charley. Thus is his corruption manifested by all else that is evil in the world."

"God created the earth, Captain," Lovich said, coming to the defence of Broadwell with what little religious instruction he could recall from his youth. "You can't never deny that."

"True, Daniel." Botis folded his broad hands on his knees. "God did indeed create the green earth and the mysterious fires of Heaven." He leaned forward, his face gone hard. "But I tell you this, Man himself is the sole artifice of the devil. He is the vomit of the devil's creative energy, and thus, of greater portent than anything else of God's work. For who but the devil could bring forth into the firmament a creature with the willpower to deny God? God could not, and would not, create a being to doubt his existence. We are, all of us, the devil's own sons."

"God makes a man to choose the path of his own life," Lovich said, knowing full well he was out of his depth.

"Did Jubal choose his path today?" Botis asked. "Of what

use is the interpretation of books, man, when the interpreter is by artifice himself a corrupt and ignoble nature?"

"You are a spry cobber with words, Captain," Lovich allowed, "I will give you that. But what happened to Jubal today was an accident. It was not evil by intent."

"The warp and woof of life is itself an accident, Daniel. It was never meant to be sanctified, though man continually tries to find ways to do so. The earth is a lone green spot in the void. A flicker destined to be extinguished. Only then can God ball up and die, and only then will Man reign supreme."

The men turned in and were soon snoring. Marwood sat beside the low fire thinking about what he had heard. The night wore on. He got up and approached Quillen's tent. He opened the flap, ducked inside.

A single lamp hung from a centre brace. Doc Quillen wore a blood-smeared leather apron. The dissected remains of Jubal Stone were laid out on a three-and-a-half-point blanket—heart, liver, and other undefined organs rested in clay bowls awaiting closer examination. Quillen's dissecting tools lay in a shallow pan of mescal, his only nod to the science of disinfection.

Quillen held one hemisphere of Jubal's brain in his left hand. He poked the ridges and inspected the whorls of grey matter with a steel probe.

The air inside the tent was heavy, reeking of blood, formaldehyde, and a sweet ripeness that threatened to bring up Marwood's gorge. Open books lay all around, pages earmarked and heavily annotated, including a leather journal in which Quillen had sketched, in India ink, the circulatory network of Jubal's left arm.

Quillen looked up, clearly annoyed at the interruption. "What do you want?" he asked. He viewed Marwood with a critical eye. "You ailing?"

"Not until I came in here."

"Never mind that. Get out."

Quillen had erected the tent over stones large enough to serve for seats or tables. Marwood sat on one. "I want to talk about Botis," he said.

The resurrectionist did not appear surprised, or unwilling, to pursue the subject once it had been broached. If anything, he behaved as if he expected it from Marwood. He put Jubal's brain in an empty dish, laid the steel probe in the pan with the other instruments. He wiped his hands on the leather apron and sat on another table rock on the far side of the tent.

Quillen put his hands on his thighs and stared at Marwood with unblinking eyes. "What do you want to know?" the resurrectionist asked. "I warn you, my knowledge of Abram Botis is extensive. I have studied the man every day for every year I have known him. Which is a considerable length of time."

"Tell me who he is."

Quillen patted for a cigar in his vest. He nipped off the foot with his front teeth, spat it across the tent. He bent to the chimney of the lamp and lit it.

"Tell you who he is," the doctor mused aloud, sitting back. "I expect you already know who he is. Or, more importantly, why he is. But I take your question as well meant and I will attempt to elucidate an answer you will find satisfactory."

Quillen smoked a minute to gather his thoughts. "I met Botis for the first time in the spring of 1865. Baltimore, it was. I'd lost my practice and was performing abortions for a high-end whorehouse in Locust Point. I was coming out of this particular establishment one morning, via the servant's entrance, when I encountered yon Botis standing on a street corner big as all life."

Quillen had been so engrossed with his story his cigar had gone out. He relit it. "Botis was dressed much as you see him today—galero, furs, mule-ear boots. He didn't have his beard then. Appears he had experienced some undefined, yet ineluctable difficulty in recent Continental past. We talked for an hour on that street. I knew then he was mad, and yet he fascinated me in a way no other man has since. He was a study, Botis, and is today. Later, we happened upon Lovich and drew him inside our circle. Then came young Spaw, who was turned out of an insane asylum for incorrigible children when he came of age. It seems he killed a governess in St. Louis and had eaten part of her womb. We made quite a fellowship."

"St. Louis?"

"What?" Quillen had lost the thread of his story. "Oh, yes. By that time we decided to leave Baltimore and come west. As I said, Botis was already on the run. Had been for years. I think in truth he was born on the run. He has a foot in two worlds: the world of men and the world of hell. He is a cambion of exceeding lineage. I traced his existence as far back as La Tour des Sorcières in Thann on the mouth of the Thur River. Where he came before that no man knows. But he is a single-minded individual who would crack the world if it were within his power to do so. Witness his furor and obsession with finding Cibola."

Quillen rose from his rock and puttered with the plated organs. He stacked them, put them aside for future analysis. He returned to his rock, puffed his cigar a moment, and continued his reminisces.

"I remember the first night he told us about Cibola," Quillen said. "It is seared in my memory. Oh, we listened. We listened with the patience of men in the presence of a mad dog. Botis has a preternatural light about him. I have seen this blue aura crackling from his body on nights when no other man experienced the searing touch of St. Elmo's fire."

Quillen tapped cigar ash between his boots. "We came west. There was no place other for men like us. Botis said there are men destined to stand against that which must be faced.

There were beings, he claimed, who initiated this work. He called them Eternals. Not of men or God, but things eternal in and of themselves."

"The Cambions you mentioned," Marwood said.

"Yes. Half-human offspring resulting from the union of demons and human beings. Creatures who take men from places they call home and send them across worlds. Well, this is what Botis believes. But, as I told you, he is quite mad."

"He wants to go into Comancheria, Doc."

Quillen shook his head. "He will not die there. Botis has foreseen his death. He knows the day. He knows the very hour."

"Was he always mad?" Marwood asked.

Quillen threw down his cigar stub and ground it under his boot heel. "No. I suspect it is a condition that has worsened over the years. He's eternal himself, you see. I believe it is the weight of this eternal memory that is slowly ossifying his brain. The human memory is being dripped from his mind, falling like black rain into his bottomless soul. It leaves a swollen, empty darkness. It is a hot hell dark which will ultimately consume him, and us, if we allow it."

"I don't understand this," Marwood said. "I don't know what he is."

"I will put it to you simply," Quillen said. "Botis is the devil, and we are his apostolic demons. All of us have our parts to play. You're here for a specific reason, John. The play is joined. Botis stands centre stage. Another will join him there. I believe you know who that man must be. Botis is a man apart. The One Man—a lone man. I have studied him long enough to recognize another of the species, my boy. How you get there, if you get there, and by what tortures and punishments you must endure—I cannot say."

Quillen got up and stretched. He came across the tent and placed a hand on Marwood's shoulder. "You have not asked for it, but I offer you this advice. Or take it as a warning from a learned man. On this earth, there is but one guarantee. God makes the wagons roll on time. Man shoes the horses."

Quillen looked at Marwood with all seriousness. "But it is the devil who holds the wagon's reins, and that devil is Botis."

CHAPTER 18

They followed the Middle Concho River into Santa Angela and bought supplies. They saw Fort Concho in the distance. Not every army fort was necessarily after them, and the danger from cavalry lay mostly in the deep bush. Nevertheless, Lovich cautioned, there was no reason to poke a sleeping bear.

Additionally, cavalry were always more concerned with depredations from Native American attacks on the frontier, along with Mexican incursions to steal Texas cattle across the border. Bandits and comancheros were left to the Texas Rangers and other civilian law enforcement entities.

Santa Angela was also small enough not to matter in any political sense for Texas. The company often saw paper on Botis posted outside a town marshal's office, but that was not unusual, either. Botis had warrants dogging him from Europe, and, as he often claimed, "One more sheet to wipe my ass does not distress me."

They rode north from Santa Angela, thinking they might try their luck at Buffalo Gap. There were ranches there, and plenty of opportunity to steal stock in one county and drive it to another for profit.

They were three days out when Marwood's horse stepped in a prairie dog hole. It broke its cannon bone and dislocated the fetlock joint. Marwood heard the bone snap and the horse collapsed with a piercing scream. He was thrown off the saddle into a stand of prickly pear cactus.

Marwood rushed to his feet, ripped his hat from his head, slapped it against his leg, and walked away in disgust. The horse struggled to rise, and could not. Marwood came back and shot the lamed horse in the brain, then stomped across the prairie for fifteen minutes thinking of every swear word he knew, cussing everything—God, Botis, horses all, and prairie dogs in particular.

The men sat their mounts, laughing and throwing out a jibe now and then to get his blood boiling. He let loose a string of new invective, excoriated them and Texas, and the men hooted and howled and hazed him on to new heights.

He cut a tall claybank out of the remuda and saddled and bridled the horse.He mounted up, refusing to speak to the others. But during the long day's ride men warned him of invisible prairie dog holes, or said, "watch that pebble there," and other broad sallies.

Marwood rode on in stony silence.

"Goddamn if you ain't hotter than a whorehouse on nickel night," Lovich said. The men laughed anew, but try as they might, they could not draw Marwood out.

The Tonkawas returned after scouting the country up ahead. They reported a big group of Texas Rangers camped on the South Concho River with guns and horses.

"How many?" Lovich asked.

"Six Rangers, twenty hired men, and four Indian scouts."

"Dammit. You think they're after us?"

Red Thunder shrugged. "They might be looking for stolen stock."

"Not a party that size. At least they won't be able to move very fast if they're that big. You see anything else?"

"Large troop movements," Red Thunder said. "Regiments and heavy patrols probing the southern border of Comancheria."

"I can't believe they are spending that kind of manpower on us. But now we can't go in that direction, either. It's plain we are being pushed farther north, much against our will."

"Whether it is intentional on their part," Red Thunder said, "I cannot say. But it would appear the result remains the same. We are left with little else in way of choice."

Lovich went to Botis and delivered the news. "Looks like we got to keep pushing north, Captain, or they'll get the bulge on us. If we are not careful they will trap us in a Cannae. We could turn the table on them, ride back into them and fight our way clear in the opposite direction."

Botis faced Marwood. "What do you suggest?"

"I'd rather put off a trip to the Llano as long as we can avoid it," Marwood said. "But it looks like we're being forced into doing exactly that. Or turn into these people behind us and fight. Like Lovich I prefer the latter course. But the safe decision is to keep driving north. As far as that goes, we could ride clear across the Red River and hide out in the Nations."

"What would you prefer to do?" Botis asked him directly.

"I hate Texas," Marwood said. "I want to find the other ranchers who sold us out and kill them."

"Lewis?"

"We could ride out this day and night," Spaw said. "Put sixty miles under us and burn a couple of farms to the east. That might pull some of the law here off, and we can double back and sneak through their thinned out lines."

"Ride through their lines unchecked? But we can do that now," Botis said. "The problem is water, gentlemen. They will be watching for that and guarding all the holes and springs. As for the rest of your plan, Lewis, we would have to bottom out the horses, and we can't be certain we will find fresh ones to see us through to safety." He thought a minute. “We will head into Buffalo Gap and locate what news we can find there. If it looks like a trap, we will head onto the Llano Estacado.”

“If we do go up there, Captain,” Marwood said, “have you considered what it will take to ride safely across Comanche territory and into New Mexico?”

“We will have to travel most of it by night,” Botis said. “Unless there’s a moon the Comanche won’t trouble us at night.”

“Yes, but my concern is lack of water. Water, as you said, is the key. All the creeks up there run east-west. To find water we’ll have to scout north-south. But the quickest way through the high plains is a direct run west.”

“We cannot make it through Comancheria without finding water,” Botis said, “and we cannot take the time to search for it. Is that what you are saying?”

“I don’t see how,” Marwood said. “We will have to travel hard and fast, and trust to luck. Otherwise, we will never get out of there alive.”

“Luck.” Lovich spat on the ground and shook his head. “We haven’t had much of that in our favour so far.”

Someone had built a line of box cabins on Elm Creek and set them up as a trading post. Botis headed toward them. One of the cabins was a post office established more than a decade prior. Down water stood a mercantile store and the main trading post.

The men rode past the post. There were hide hunters and Indians in abundance, which the Hydra considered most unusual. Big hide and meat camps ranged up and down the creek, and were sprawled out on the grass. There were hundreds of people here, and they appeared to be waiting for something.

“What are these apple knockers doing?” Ed Gratton asked.

"They got meat and hides and horn stacked up everywhere. Why haven't they taken it to Fort Griffin and sold it?"

"I do not know," Spaw said uneasily. He rode beside Gratton and Marwood. "But I fear something is dreadful wrong."

"It's not right, that's for sure," Marwood said. "I never knew a buffalo hunter yet to leave his skins rotting in the sun like that."

Buffalo Gap was long a winter staging area for hunters. Buffalo hunters and tradesmen of every sort gathered during the winter months prior to transporting their hides up to Fort Griffin.

"Why they should be encamped here during high summer, and not out killing the last buffalo of the southern herd, is a study," Spaw continued.

Botis dismounted Acheron and walked into the empty store. The shelves were bare. A wizened clerk stood in one corner of the store counting axe helves in a barrel. He was balding, dressed in black trousers, suspenders, and a clean white shirt. He had a pencil stub tucked behind his right ear.

"Good morning, sir," he said, straightening. "What can I do you for?"

Botis stood in the centre of the store, studying the barren shelves and hollow barrels. "What the hell happened here?"

"It's the plague, sir," the storekeeper said.

"Here in town?"

"Oh, no, sir, not here. Up in Fort Griffin. Cholera. Killed goddamn near everybody. No sane body wants to go up there now, and you can't blame them."

"That's what the buffalo hunters are doing outside," Botis said.

"You perceive the problem correctly, sir," the clerk said. "The hunters are skeered to ride into Fort Griffin or into The Flat while the plague is raging. They can't leave their hides unprotected and go hunting, either. So they stand guard here and watch it rot. Fort Griffin is much worse off than we are. There are entire acres—hell, city blocks, of hides and horn and rotting meat no one can get to. Mountains of it. Well, that's always the case in Griffin. But now no one wants to go in and bring it out. It's the goddamndest mess I ever saw, and I am fifty-one years old."

Botis nodded at the wooden barrel the clerk had been handling. "What are you doing there?"

"Well, sir, every morning fair I open my shop and come in to count these here axe helves. As you can see they are all I've got left to sell. That ain't much hickory standing between me and starvation."

"We were wanting to buy powder and shot," Botis said.

"Good luck to you, sir. The hunters won't sell the lead pigs they've got. They are hoarding gunpowder in the hope the plague will end and they can get back to killing buffalo out on the plains."

"How far to Fort Griffin?"

"Two days hard ride." The clerk blinked in astonishment. "You ain't thinking of going up there, are you? Oh, no, sir, you can't do that. Hell, all the spoiled doves are gone. When a whore leaves a town, you know it's dead."

"What about the Buffalo Soldiers in the fort?"

"You mean the fort on the bluff? All dead, sir. Well, that ain't half right. They are keeping to themselves, but the cholera got them, too. Hit them hard. Croaked a lot of the white officers' wives and children. They couldn't bury the kids fast enough. Most of the Indians who stay to trade, they're dead, too. Like I said, it's a Biblical prophecy. One of the seven seals has been broken, and pestilence is upon the land. You mark my word, sir."

The clerk walked Botis to the door. "Are you thinking of going up to Fort Griffin?" he asked. "Excuse me, mister, but if you do, they might let you in, but they will never let you out."

"That is what I am counting on." Botis tipped his galero. "Good day, and thank you for the information."

They smelled the dead before they ever saw the fort. Five miles out they caught the scent of rotting flesh and corruption on the prairie winds. The horses shied, afraid to ride nearer. The men rowelled them forward, held a tight rein.

Marwood came upon torn fields of broken wagons where the dead awaited burial. Men, women, and children. Wagons with thrown rims, shattered wheels, and split crosstrees. The corpses piled like cordwood in buckboards. Cemeteries were full. A self-appointed delegation of whites and Native Americans went from wagon to wagon. They poured kerosene and lit them with flaming brands and stood back. Botis and his men rode between these smoking markers of death into a miasma of putrefaction and pestilence no prairie wind could ever scrub clean.

The wagon-burners watched them ride for Fort Griffin. They didn't speak to, or warn the riders what was ahead. If a man wanted to commit suicide by riding into Fort Griffin during a cholera outbreak, he was welcome to do so. But there were other wagon-burners who carried rifles and guns. They would make sure no man left the fort, spreading the contagion to other towns and settlements in Texas.

The company crossed beneath the base of a cliff upon which stood the main army fort—ninety-odd buildings housing Buffalo and Federal Troops, their servants, and their wives. Marwood could see the flat *azoteas* of the buildings, and the smoke from cook fires, but little else. The American flag flew at half-mast. Two Mexican boys guided a solitary wagon drawn by windbroke mules down the road. Marwood looked into it when it passed by. The wagon was full of dead soldiers, covered with lime.

They rode into The Flat and saw acres and acres of stacked

buffalo hide, bone, horn, and meat. The meat was set out to dry under the prairie sun. But it had rained, which added to the overall misery of everyone in attendance. The meat had rotted, with foul seeps running from the rancid slag.

The roads were impassable quagmires. Big Studebaker wagons were stuck axle-deep in the ooze. Weary men tried to dig them out, threw down their tools in frustration and quit. Sud's row, where laundresses did the daily wash, was a ghost town. Empty tubs, bottles, and rags were strewn over the muddy pockmarked ground. Abandoned wash hung in trees to stiffen and sun rot, like the markers of temporary graves.

There was some life left to the town of Fort Griffin. Three thousand people and 1,500 buffalo hunting crews could not be killed off overnight. There were saloons, bars, hotels, and mercantile shops built of soft cottonwood. But Marwood could plainly see people weren't living here as much as they were surviving.

"And damned little of that," Spaw said, riding beside him.

Everywhere they went they saw people dressed in mourning black, weeping, praying, hoping for the best. One man went around town with the pages of the Bible pinned to his clothes to ward off evil spirits. Whole families had been devastated by cholera. Entire swathes of townsfolk laid waste, and the disease had yet to burn itself out. A hundred people were dying in The Flat every day. As one old cobber told Marwood around a fire that night, "There ain't enough open ground left to bury them all in."

They rode through the middle of the devastation. "What if the law decides to come for us after all?" Charley Broadwell asked.

Botis listened to a man in the street preach about the End of Days. He had a respectable crowd of faithful around him, listening to his apocalyptic sermon.

Botis turned from the scene, a smile touching the corners of his lips. He was a man much in his element.

"Then we will kill them in this place of worship," he said.

They dismounted and led their horses to a livery stable.

CHAPTER 19

"I know how it began," an old man told Marwood. "I was here when The Flat was founded. I will be here when it turns to dust."

They sat around a communal bonfire behind one of the saloons. Spaw had built the fire for the company, but the light drew citizens from all parts of the surrounding town. To be certain, there were other fires scattered throughout the streets. But these wild men dressed like buffalo hunters, with the faces and manner of warm-blooded killers, were strangers who'd come to Fort Griffin of their own merit. They were, therefore, a curiosity to the inhabitants. After all, where else could townsfolk get news of the outside world, and perhaps find a glimmer of promise in the midst of their own desperation?

Ed Gratton boiled coffee. The back street they inhabited was a mud pit filled with refuse and sodden filth. The old man holding court held out his tin cup. He was dressed like a monk, in a mud-splattered white robe and creased leather boots with wooden soles.

There were a few women in the crowd, intermingled with the men. One of the women went off with Charley Broadwell. Another held a baby to her breast: her face was ashen and drawn; her slack clothes were mud-stained on a scarecrow frame. The baby in her arms did not move and it did not cry. It was only later Marwood surmised it must have died that very morning, and she was loathe to give it up.

"We are looking at the face of God's punishment," the old man said. He slurped his coffee and smacked his lips. "It is a dreadful countenance." He stared up at the night sky and drew his attention back to the fire. "Fort Griffin has always been an evil place. I used pull stock for John Melkin. He had a ranch on the Clear Fork. Mr. Melkin went into New Mexico Territory one day to buy short-horned Mexican cattle. He trusted his foreman, a man by the name of James Fisher, to watch the ranch in his absence. Fisher rebranded all of Melkin's steers and milled them into his own herd. When Melkin returned he hired nine men and they went after Fisher thinking to steal the cattle back. But Fisher outsmarted them. He ambushed Melkin and killed every man out by Bush Knob. They never did prove nothing against Fisher, even though Melkin and his nine gunfighters were shot in the back. Later, Fisher built a nice ranch house for his wife on the Butterfield Stage Route. Out by Camp Cooper, I think it was. One day, when he was out with his spring herd, she packed her bags and flagged down the stagecoach. They say she went to San Francisco, but others believe she died in Arizona Territory, and was scalped and raped by Mescalero Apaches."

The old man swirled his coffee, took a drink. "Killer, cattle thief, Fisher became the first sheriff of Fort Griffin. This was before the buffalo hunters came in with their loud stink and took it over. This place wasn't nothing but a grease spot on the map in them days. Fisher, he remarried, and hired two Irish stonemasons to build a limestone wall around his ranch house. When the time came for payment he and his deputy shot the Irishmen in the heads, weighted them down with stones, and threw their bodies in the Clear Fork. The house was struck by lightning and burned down during a big thunderstorm, but you can see the walls and foundation if you ride past it."

The old storyteller coughed and shook his head with deep sorrow. "Yes sir, Fort Griffin has always been a bad place to die, and a worse place to live. Five thousand buffalo hunters, crooked ranchers, prostitutes, drunks, and criminals in one place can't never be no other thing but ripe pickings for hell."

The old man talked through much of the night. As men came and went from the central fire, they heard different parts of another story. Later, when they got together to compare what they had heard, they discovered each man had listened to something quite different from the other.

Some men said the old man talked about his life back east, where he had a wife and child in Charleston who died of pneumonia. Others claimed he had been a hilljack in California, and had made—and lost—a gold fortune there. Others swore he talked about his life as a trapper in the High Rockies, and how he travelled shank's mare to the western coast and gazed upon the blue Pacific waters, and even saw whales.

Every man heard something different, because no man stayed at the fire for the entire night. Even Marwood had gone off to relieve himself at one point, and then went into an all but vacated restaurant to eat a plate of pinto beans and mule deer backstrap. When he returned, the old man was still speaking, and Marwood sat down and listened to what to him was the same story.

But every man present heard their own bits and pieces, and they cobbled together the thread of a tale they would take with them the rest of their lives—a tale they'd tell others, or their children, or their grandchildren. And the stories, bits of stories, lies, and half-truths would be written down as Texas history and taught to generations unborn as the truth of the west.

A red band of light shone like a sash in the eastern sky. Tunk Quillen stepped up to the firelight.

"Captain," he said, "you better come see this here."

Botis, Marwood, and Lovich followed the resurrectionist. They squelched down an alley and across another mud-filled street, and stood behind the corner of a hotel turned into a temporary deadhouse.

Half a mile away, riding between blazing wagons of newly dead, was a big party of Texas Rangers, hired guns, and Kiowa scouts. The Rangers had caught up to the Kiowas. The scouts were pointing to the plague town.

"Goddamn," Lovich said, "do you think that's Jack Hays out there after us, Captain?"

"Hays is retired in California, fucking his fat wife," Botis said.

Lovich leaned and spat. He hooked his thumbs in his pockets. "Well, whoever this Texas Ranger sumbitch is, he has a tenacity like old Hays."

Botis and Doc Quillen returned to the bonfire and gathered the rest of their company. Everyone walked their horses through the dead city toward the deep running waters of the Clear Fork. Marwood paused at the edge of the river. It looked deep and fast.

"How do you aim to get across?" Lovich asked.

Botis's face was grim with determination. "If they are any smart they have men waiting to ambush us at Daws Crossing. We can't wait to find another ford. We will have to swim it out here and trust to chance."

"That's a bad current to fight," Charley Broadwell said, "with a lot of snags and tree roots. A man could go under and you'd never see him again."

They were preparing to leave when they heard an uplifted cry of surprise behind them. The people of Fort Griffin were shouting as with one voice in praise and mortal fear.

Across the sky, a great bolide crossed from eastern fire to western night. Huge fiery chunks splintered off the blunt head of the thing, and again into smaller firework fragments. Spaw and Lovich thought they heard a deep whistle from the meteor as it streaked across the sky, but Marwood and Broadwell were not so certain.

The shooting star disappeared to the west, its fire sputtering out somewhere over Comancheria. But even then an auroral shimmer remained, for close to a minute showing where it had whipped across the sky.

The killers gathered up their their guns. They did not speak for they had become adept at pulling out of a place in silence. They brought the horses quietly down the bank, past the deserted laundry site, and entered the cold river water. Marwood held his gun above water in case he had to shoot his way clear on the other side. The men around him spurred and larruped the horses up the far bank and through a spindly stand of juniper and pin oak. They followed this tree line until they came upon open prairie.

"Expected to see someone guarding this side of the river," Spaw said.

"This way lies Comancheria," Marwood told him. "They don't have to guard it."

They rode without stopping. All through the day men looked up at the sky with wondrous eyes, searching in vain for some new portent of their future.

CHAPTER 20

Charley Broadwell got sick three days out of Fort Griffin. He vomited clear water early one morning after he woke up. Later that hour he lost control of his bowels and passed rice water. Doc Quillen pulled the shaking man aside while they rested the horses. He examined Charley's sunken eyes and felt his wrinkled hands.

"He's got the cholera," he told Botis.

"Oh, Lord," Spaw said.

"Will he live?" Botis asked.

"That ain't but for God to decide."

"Bind him to his horse so he can ride."

They did. When they accomplished this task Quillen turned to the men.

"You boys listen good. Don't eat or drink nothing after Charley. I mean it. Don't wear his clothes nor take his boots even if'n after he dies. Not even his gun."

Spaw looked at Charley sitting the back of his horse, doubled over and shivering. The man's pants and saddle were soaking wet with diarrhoeal water flooding out of his body. It stank of raw fish.

"You think we might catch it, too?" Spaw asked Quillen.

Quillen studied the man's boils and face warts. "You will know for certain in another two days," he said. "We are in the middle of the incubation period. If we make it past that . . ." he lifted his hands and let them drop in a helpless gesture.

The miserable day surrendered the sun. Broadwell's health worsened.

They rode out the night and half the next day before arriving at an encampment of sod and mud-brick structures stuck in the middle of the wide-open, sun-baked prairie. They sat their horses on a grassy rise, watching for signs of life or a flicker of movement between the two houses.

"I don't see nobody around," Lovich said. His knee had gotten better over the past few days and he was much his old self. But the eeriness of the silent prairie, along with its appalling vastness, unnerved him. They were sitting downwind, but neither horses or Tonkawas smelled anything amiss.

"Maybe they got some medicine for Charley," Gratton said.

"These sons of bitches ain't got nothing." Spaw spat from his saddle. "That's why they're out here."

"And what about us?" Gratton asked.

"Let's not go into that right now," Spaw said.

Botis laughed, for he was always one to find humour in even the direst of affairs. "You boys best take hold of your shrunken pizzles," he said. "You get the wim-wams out here you won't never make it out alive."

Spaw and Gratton approached the house and the smaller shed out back. Marwood had his Sharps rifle out and was covering them from afar. When they were within a furlong of the first house Rangers pushed their guns out the doors and windows and opened fire. Botis and company lifted their guns and fired back.

"How did these whore sons get ahead of us?" Lovich asked.

"They didn't." Marwood jumped from his saddle and pulled his horse behind a hummock of grass and bristle. "These are new men."

Gunfire became sporadic. Botis turned and addressed his command. "Make sure Charley is tied down so he doesn't fall."

Marwood was closest to the dying man. He checked the knots and walked Charley's horse past Botis, with

Charley slouched over in his saddle, hardly knowing what was happening.

Botis brought out a hobble rope and lashed Charley's horse across the haunches. The horse started across the prairie at a rocking-chair gallop, angling away from the house. Several Rangers on the other side, hiding at the bottom of a trash ditch, popped up and banged away at the fleeing horse and rider. Botis and his men poured lead into them, sent two men reeling back with mortal wounds. Charley's horse stumbled and fell, a half dozen bullets buried in its heart.

A man quit the smallest house, little more than a round barn built of prairie sod, and walked toward Charley's body.

"Can you get him?" Botis asked Marwood.

"No," Marwood shook his head. "He's too far even for the Sharps."

The lawman walked across the flat prairie directly toward Charley. Charley reached out to the man in a plea for help. The ambusher brought out his gun and shot Charley in the forehead. Then he walked back to the shed.

They fought for three days, along the dry hollows and grassy hummocks, in a 500-yard circle around the two sod huts. The other posse from Fort Griffin joined the battle on the third day, catching Botis and his men in a murderous crossfire.

Botis held the higher ground, and with it a tactical edge. One morning the lawmen made a foolish charge on his strong position. Botis beat them back and they retired to the sod huts to lick their wounds and count their dead.

At night, both sides lighted false fires and sat on the ground a quarter mile away, hoping to decoy the others. The day following they set fires with the wind. Walls of flame and smoke raced over the countryside. Around them, men rode for their lives. They hooded their horses and rode straight through the fire before falling to the ground and batting their smouldering clothes.

They kept fighting. There was no end to it. The huts had all the water, while Botis had the high ground. Neither side would quit.

One night, when they were at the end of their tether, Little Shreve looked at his younger cousin. Red Thunder did not say a word but gave a quick nod. Little Shreve rose from the decoy fire and walked away into the closing night.

Botis watched him leave. They all did.

The men listened and waited, barely breathing. They heard nothing other than the night sounds of the prairie. Whispering grass and the click of insects. They were exhausted, but they could not sleep. If they were men of prayer, they would have worn out the knees of their breeches.

An hour before first light Little Shreve returned. He dropped three bloody scalps in the dirt beside Spaw. He had also stolen four horses from the lawmen and hid them in a secluded draw a mile and a half away.

He sat beside the coal fire without speaking and scratched himself. Lovich offered the Tonkawa the last of their water.

"Take it," he urged.

Little Shreve crossed his arms and turned his face, refusing to drink.

By the fifth day both sides were out of ammunition. They fought hand-to-hand—men used their guns and rifles as clubs. Water was short to nonexistent—they drank their own urine when they had anything to drink at all—and there was nothing to eat except raw horseflesh. Marwood killed two men with a brush hook, hacking their bodies apart to retrieve their waterskin. When he reached it, it was empty.

Red Thunder, Lovich, and Spaw crawled onto the larger of the two sod huts and cut through the roof. They dropped one by one inside the barricaded house, which was being used as a temporary hospital. They killed men with their knives, and cut the throats of five wounded lying in stinking pools of blood and foul, gangrenous rot. They scalped the dead, taking ears, noses, teeth, and scrotums, and left the sod hut trailing blood and gore on their clothes, hands, and beards.

By the end of that same day Botis calculated they had whittled the other side down enough to attempt a break out. They brought the horses up, the animals all but dead themselves, and stepped wearily into saddle.

Marwood was tired, torn, and bloody. He had lost the brush hook somewhere. He sat saddle with reins in one hand and a knife in the other. The blind ancient thing inside his heart had long awakened; its red roaring hate filled his whole head, and thrummed his chest.

"Ride through them and ride them down," Botis said. "Kill them all."

The Hydra reined their horses around and kicked into a phalanx. They held short rein, leaned as close to the necks of their horses as they could. Men rose from the high grass to meet them, holding sticks and knives and metal rods. Marwood hacked at a defender, missed. There was a brief flurry as the horses slowed and men fought. Acheron reared and brought his sharp hooves down, ripping one man from throat to stomach. Botis forced his way through the salient, his men strung out behind and racing for their lives across the flat red plain.

They were a quarter mile out, and safe, when, with the capriciousness so often seen on those plains, a prairie storm blew in from the north. Cold, drenching rain. Botis and his men reined their horses and looked at one another, water dripping from their faces and hats. Nothing was said between them. As one, they turned back. They rode with faces grim and knives out. They plunged into the unsuspecting Rangers, lawmen, and Kiowa spies gathered around the sod huts filling canteens and leather sacks with rainwater streaming off the eaves.

They rode into them from blowing clouds of sand, grit, and rain, and they threw themselves from their saddles screaming incoherent war cries. They killed, and they kept on killing.

Little Shreve ran in a bowlegged frenzy from dead man to dying, scalping and disembowelling. His arms gleamed with blood, and it dripped from his knees. Marwood pushed one of the men hired by the Double-barred V cattle barons into the ground as the rain beat upon his head, and he stabbed that man in the face, leapt up, and looked around for another victim.

The Hydra feasted. They killed, and when the killing was done, they tore the sod huts apart, using what little lumber and lathes they could scrounge—buffalo chips, cut saddles, clothes, everything that could conceivably burn. They built a tremendous bonfire, and into these flames they cast the bodies of the men they had all but destroyed.

As the flames consumed the bodies, blood, fat, and grease ran in sheets from the charred bodies, which swelled as their internal juices expanded. Their hides burst from the massive heat amidst cracking bone and brains whistle-steaming from ears and noses.

Little Shreve sat cross-legged beside the fire, holding the scalps he had taken on the end of a forked stick. The hair was turned inward so it would not burn. Clear grease dripped from the scalps into a small trench he had dug with his knife.

When the scalp grease cooled, Little Shreve dipped his fingers into it, and rubbed the tallow through his long hair.

The horses were not up to riding through the night. For the truth of it, neither were the men. They were ripped and blood-chewed. Marwood felt he was coming to the end of his rope.

They dismounted so the horses could rest, and walked for a lone hour through the grass spanning the horizon. While they walked they sometimes stopped to look behind before stumbling on.

The early night was warm, the stars bright. Grass and wind smelled fresh and clean. Red Thunder and Little Shreve peeled off to find a watering hole. The company made camp in a buffalo wallow as large as a community amphitheater. Marwood was so exhausted he slept on the bare ground without blankets. In the morning everyone pulled out with hollow eyes and empty faces.

The land was studded here and there with scrubby hackberry, clumps of mesquite, and wind-flagged trees. They saw buffalo grazing in the distance, a small herd of twenty. But they had no powder or lead, and could do little but watch the beasts graze unmolested.

"What is that in the tall grass?" Lovich asked. He pointed to a lanky object walking their way. "By God, it looks like a woman."

Indeed it was. A naked woman stumbled aimlessly over the prairie a half-mile away. She had come around the low neck of a hill. Her shoulders and face were burned, blistered red by the fierce sun.

The men rode close and brought their horses in a ring around her. She had been scalped. The naked red bone of her tonsured skull gleamed through a ring of wispy blonde hair. Her eyes were gouged out. She carried the broken shaft of an arrow in one shoulder. Dried blood stained her thighs and calves.

She reacted slowly to the presence of horses around her and the sound of men talking. She sat down upon the prairie.

Tunk Quillen swung off his horse and went straight to her. "She's hurt for fair," he said. He squatted on his haunches so he could look directly into her face. "They cut out her tongue, Captain."

"Wouldn't think they'd let her live like that," Spaw said.

"They probably thought she was dead." Quillen lowered his voice and addressed the men behind him. "She is, she just don't know it yet."

"Get her a blanket," Botis said.

"Captain, that ain't going to do her no good."

"Go ahead. So she can cover up her shame."

Quillen fetched a blanket from his saddlebag and draped it around the woman's bloody shoulders. "It's all right," he told her. "You gonna be all right, now."

"I wish them Tonks would get back with the water," Gratton said.

"They will get here when they get here," Botis said. "Which direction do you think she walked from?"

The men looked around from the backs of their saddles. "I'd say she followed the run of the land," Marwood said, studying the land around them. "Dying animals don't go uphill. So I don't expect she did any climbing."

"She couldn't have walked far," Botis said.

"No."

They could make out her trail, where she had cut through and trampled nearby grass.

"We will backtrack and see what we find," Botis said. "Mount up, Doc."

Tunk Quillen finished tying a bandage around her lost eyes and got into his saddle. Marwood lifted the woman and put her in front so Doc could hold her while he rode.

They followed her winding trail for five miles. The Tonkawas returned with filled waterskins, and they drank and watered the horses. No matter how much Quillen tried, the woman would not take water. He wetted a handkerchief and pressed it to her lips, but she turned away.

Red Thunder lifted a corner of the woman's blanket. He examined the broken shaft of the arrow embedded deep in her shoulder. He turned his eyes to Botis.

"Penetaka," he said, and let the blanket drop.

"Oh, damn," Spaw said. "I feared as much."

"Where did you find water?" Botis asked.

"Seven miles," the scout said, pointing in the opposite direction.

"This woman didn't walk no fifteen miles. We will continue on her trail. Let's go."

"Captain," Doc Quillen said.

"Yes."

"She's dead."

"All right, Mr. Quillen. Wrap her up and lay her down here."

Quillen reposed her on the ground and left her body covered with the blanket. He climbed back on his horse. He looked at the body and shook his head.

They followed her winding trail back farther and discovered a private stockade built on a rise of gold and yellow grass. There were cottonwood trees down in a coulee, and smoking cornfields, which had been trampled and burned. Fat hogs fed upon the ruined bodies. Some had gorged themselves until they lay bloated and supine under the hot sun, their big chests moving like a bellows.

Marwood rode in silence between the massacred bodies. Botis called a halt. They got off their horses and searched for anything of value they might take from this wasted place.

Everyone in the settlement was dead. Caught unawares with the gate to their stockade inexplicably left open, whole families had been trapped inside their homes and roasted alive. One or two fires were burning freely. Marwood saw incandescent skulls and hacked bones of children half buried in the quaking coal beds.

Men and boys trapped in the open had been tortured and castrated, grinning mouths stuffed with their own black genitals. Everyone, far as Marwood could see, had been scalped, stripped, and left to die before the Penetaka Comanches had pushed on.

Botis found the settlement leader hanging from a creaking cottonwood limb. His body was pincushioned with arrows. The war party had hanged him upside down over a slow mesquite fire.

Lovich found a woman tied to a wagon wheel. She'd been scalped to the bone, and the wheel set afire. A girl lay outside the stockade gate, stripped and disembowelled. Her bruised white and purple flesh stank and festered with swarming maggots.

Ed Gratton discovered what at first he thought to be a pile of skinned rabbits at the base of a tree. The children's heads had been smashed with stones.

Marwood walked through the middle of the devastation. He remembered Sand Creek and wondered why the world was so dark, and he knew it was because he was here.

"They all dead, ain't they." A lone hunter limped up the dusty road into camp. He bore a slouch hat and scraggy brown beard. He was leading a pack mule. The mule was burdened with coyote and wolf pelts.

"I saw it happen," he said. He stopped and greeted Botis and the men of the company. "My name is Gerald Causey. I was camped up in them high rocks out of sight." He turned and pointed behind them. "They came out of yon woodline with the sun on their nakedness and their lances glinting like steel. Their horses bit and snapped at the shreds of morning fog like wild dogs. You never heard such a caterwauling. Hell, in half an hour it was all over."

"You saw who did this?" Botis asked.

"Comanche warriors. Penetaka. Biggest party of red niggers I ever saw. Must have been fifty, sixty of the bastards. They are hitting military *presidios* and Catholic missions up and down this country. Got the army all stirred up. Some say they might head south and kill all the way to Galveston. They've done it before, mister. They have a great reverence for the sea." The pelt hunter spat. He looked at the men. "They took a little girl with them."

Marwood said, "Belike they mean to ransom her back to the army for guns and ammunition."

"That's how I figure it," Causey agreed.

"They take anyone else?" asked Botis.

"Children, dead. Skewered by their heels from pad saddles. Likely skin them out on the prairie. Their pelts are much coveted by the women of their tribe. Stole the horses, but you would figure on that."

"Any chance getting that girl back alive?" Ed Gratton asked.

"Hell for," Causey said. "They like to never got that Parker girl back, and when they did she was no longer white. Mister, I watched a buck rut her right where you're standing. She's ruined for life and God. Ain't nobody can do right for her now short of putting a bullet in her head."

Marwood turned and walked away.

"What's eating on him?" Causey asked Botis.

"He's seen this before. Out to Sand Creek."

There was something in his voice bordering on awe when next the hunter spoke. "That man yonder fought at Sand Creek?"

"Yes."

He studied Marwood's retreating back and swallowed. "Goddamn."

"Yes," Botis said, "that's what he says about it, too. Do you have anything to trade? We need lead and gunpowder."

"I ain't got nothing to trade on, mister."

"Either you trade with us," Botis said, "or we take what you have."

Causey poked a thumb at Acheron. "Okay, I will take some of those scalps off'n your hands, if you want to cut a deal. I can sell them in Austin."

The bargain was cut and they shook hands on a price. This, along with what little ammunition they gleaned from the destroyed colony, saw them in better stead.

Spaw and Lovich found cartridges, pigs of lead, and a horn of powder under loose floorboards in a clapboard shack. Marwood pulled a .50-calibre Hawken rifle from under the bodies of two young men lying dead in a corncrib. The rifle had not been fired.

Botis and his men ended up with three rounds between each of them. Marwood had two for the Hawken gun. "We are headed into Comancheria," Botis informed Causey. "You are welcome to join our expedition."

"No, thank you," Causey replied. He packed his scalps into a jute sack and tied it to his mule. "I am for home. I got a cabin on the San Gabriel. You ever in the area, you come see me. We can trade for scalps again."

Botis sent the Tonkawa scouts ahead to cut for sign. The day waned. They made camp twenty miles farther on at the bend of a creek. Spaw built a fire from buffalo dung and spitted and roasted an antelope Lovich shot.

They sat around the fire, tearing into the charred and bloody meat with their teeth. Juice and grease ran into their beards. Their eyes glittered with hunger, and they gorged themselves like ticks.

CHAPTER 21

A week later they camped beside a vacated dugout at the root of a limestone bluff. The entrance to the bunker was overgrown with scrub and tall thistle. There was good water nearby, and the horses were rubbed down and allowed to drink and graze their bellies full.

Marwood stood inside the dugout, the floor of which was littered with small bones. He smelled earth, rock, and an ancient, muddy past. He exited. Red Thunder stood outside waiting for him.

"I must speak with you," Red Thunder said. He stood with the sun behind him. Black tattooed lines covered the entirety of his body and he wore a soft breechclout of human skin. He held a Spencer rifle crooked in his right arm. The oiled barrel gleamed in the daylight.

Marwood smelled rancid grease, which Red Thunder had covered himself with. Down by the creek Botis and the riders filled skins and canteens amidst hawberry shrubs.

"What do you want with me?" Marwood asked.

"I do not approach you as an enemy," Red Thunder said. "I consider you ta'en."

Marwood considered this. "All right."

"We are riding into lands which belonged to my people," Red Thunder said. "We will fight, and my brother and I will die there."

"Little Shreve? I thought he was your cousin, not your brother."

"When my first wife died I married Little Shreve's sister.

It was then he became my brother. But you cannot go with us into the lands of my past. You must go north. You are Long Blood. You are like Captain Botis, but you are also not like him. You must go north."

Marwood shook his head. He stared up at the trees and then at Red Thunder. "Why do Indians keep telling me to go north?"

"I do not understand."

"Red Thunder, I am staying with the band."

"No. You must not ride onto the Llano Estacado. Your destiny lies elsewhere. I tell you this as ta'en. I learned many things when I was taught in the Christian way. When this happened, I forgot some of the things I had learned as a boy growing up in the shadow of my father. But one thing I never forgot: there are men like the captain, and yourself. You do not belong with us. You must find your real home. You must find the place where you will die, because that is your true home."

"You're not making sense." Marwood remembered the incident in Piedras Negras with the ancient Mandan. "What does *numank maxana* mean?"

A flicker of recognition passed across Red Thunder's face. "That is a Mandan word of great medicine and power. No man may speak it lightly."

Marwood was a tall man, but still he had to look up into Red Thunder's face. "I know it is a Mandan word because a Mandan spoke it," he said. "What does it mean?"

Red Thunder watched the men washing their hands and faces at the river ford. Botis was combing his beard with a cactus thorn. He focused his black eyes back on Marwood.

"I will tell you something of my people," Red Thunder said. "We hold the wolf sacred. We never kill the wolf because we believe we are descended from it. When the wolf runs among men we cannot kill him. But the wolf remains a wolf."

Marwood started away. Red Thunder stepped in front of him. "No. I speak to you as ta'en. I cannot use the words you want because their power would blacken my tongue. Let me tell you a legend of my people. Coyote found a woman crying in her tipi. She told him an evil monster had killed the villagers. Coyote promised he would kill the monster. Coyote went to the river and made a fire-hardened spear. The monster appeared the next day. It was red above the waist, and black below. Coyote and the monster fought. Coyote called upon the wolves, and together they killed the monster."

Red Thunder stepped closer and lowered his voice. "I tell you this because you have a destiny. There is a Great Spirit inside your heart. Botis has this ancient spirit, too. If you do not defeat it, the monster will consume you, and the spirit will walk away, red above the waist and black below."

The men were coming back from the sandy creek bed; they were eating red haws and talking cheerfully among themselves.

"I have a Christian name," Red Thunder said. "My Catholic name is William Stuart Miles. But I remain Tonkawa. I was born upon the prairie, where there is no roof to break the light of the sun. When I die, you will remember my Christian name, and my Catholic spirit will live on in this world. But my name Red Thunder will be forever in the spirit world of the Tonkawas, with that of my brother. Do not cross the Llano Estacado, John Marwood. If you do, Abram Botis will become your enemy. He will be red above the waist and black below."

Red Thunder turned and went back to his horse. He checked the bridle and swung onto its bare back. He looked at Marwood one last time. Little Shreve joined him on a sleek pony, and they rode side by side without speaking another word.

The company crossed an undulating sea of trackless grass. Ahead lay the prominent Caprock Escarpment, which Francisco Vásquez de Coronado and his conquistadors came upon 300 years past. They, too, had been searching for Cibola. But now the gears of time had turned, allowing Botis in all his madness to come, under this sun and this sky, to find what had eluded him his entire life.

Botis glassed the natural rampart; he thought it safe enough to climb. They found a defile and rode up a craggy ramp of caliche and lime. Marwood watched Red Thunder, but the Tonkawa paid him no further attention—and in truth, never spoke to him again.

When they reached the top they rode a full mile onto the High Plains. The grass came to the bellies of the horses. Farther on they spotted the Comanche war lance, and a man tied to it with his own intestines.

The poor, naked wretch sat cross-legged, head bowed, arms bound behind his back with raw buffalo hide. The hide had contracted, squeezing blood out until his hands were blackened stumps. He had been scalped, and his ears were gone. From a small red hole in his stomach, a wrinkled rope of purplish-pink gut lifted in a bow and was fixed to the middle of a fourteen-foot war lance, plunged into the earth twenty feet away.

At the top of the lance, a black hawk feather lifted and snapped in the wind. The supple bois d'arc shaft vibrated and straightened. There was no sound but the keening wind, and the rustling grass.

Botis and his riders regarded the grisly tableau, which had been staged as a warning meant solely for them.

"This just happened," Marwood said. He turned and

surveyed the empty country from his saddle. "They tortured him and staked him out here for us to find."

Lovich looked over his shoulder at Botis. "Captain?"

"We can't waste ammunition on this man," the apostate said. "Unless you want to cut his throat, then let's go."

The riders reined their horses around the prisoner and left him to his fate. They rode mile after waterless mile toward an empty horizon.

By late afternoon they were well within the ambit of Comancheria. Botis spied a lonesome hill through his field glasses. They rode around it, slowly climbing, and made camp on the side opposite from which they had approached. Red Thunder and Little Shreve gained the crown and stood as sentinels, watching their backbearing.

They ate handfuls of dried apples and hard biscuit. Each man took a sip of water from a buffalo paunch. They sat like brutish Neanderthals around a pile of smoking buffalo chips.

The night was filled with a reef of stars. Spaw looked at the great Northern Cross and wondered aloud, if the stars were but pinpricks, how could there be so many?

Botis was seated on a buffalo skull across from Marwood. The horns curled out from behind his knees. "Remember the atlatl," the apostate said. "The stars are the immortal expression of God. But, so is man himself immortal. It is not through government or architecture or family issue he finds this divinity. Man finds immortality expressly through the art of killing. Or, more specifically, through the specialized institution of war."

Botis looked at each of their faces. "I have always believed war is a manifestation of man's ultimate will," he said. "Does history show us otherwise? As the stars manifest the sublimity of God's own thoughts, so does war mirror the glory of man. War is considered evil, an abomination. It therefore reflects the corrective shape of man's soul. This *long blood* of violence should never be avoided, but instead embraced, and worshiped."

Marwood's heart hammered. *You are Long Blood.*

"But why do men make war?" Tunk Quillen asked, chewing his biscuit. "Ain't we ever for naught else but killing one another like apes?"

Botis faced the resurrectionist. "War is a manifestation of man's practicality, Joshua," he said. "Laws are made by the weak to limit the will of the strong. A strong man has no need of law. He shuns the very idea of restraint on his ineluctable right to elevate himself above others."

He poked the fire with a bone and leaned back. "Man walks the red plain of life and, being man, demands an audience. As he fights, so do the women watch. Through war, he creates an evil beauty, which surpasses anything imagined by God. War dwarfs the infinite stars, and frees man from the shackles God himself imposed. It is a freedom God never intended man to have—it is the reason God detests war, and man embraces it. Therein lies its subtle power."

Botis leaned close to the campfire, elbows rested on his knees and thick fingers interlaced. His naked upper torso and face were highlighted by red flame.

Behind him, in shadows, stood Acheron. The campfire was reflected in the horse's eyes.

"War is man's creation entire," Botis declared. "God created the world. The Devil created man. Man created war. It is a singular progression to a summit upon which man stands alone and unchallenged." He lifted his black eyes and stared directly at Marwood. "As the son destroys the father, so, too, will man destroy God, with his mathematical machines and cold science and dread will."

Botis looked like a dark elemental from another plane of existence.

"God is nothing more than a gasping wretch," he said,

addressing the fire. "Why not put the poor bastard out of his misery?"

After sleeping several hours the men awoke, stretched, and moved about camp. It was midnight. They could not spare water so again they were left to chew dry coffee grounds. They brought the horses in, unhobbled them, and pulled out.

They rode until midday when they saw five Comanches sitting on horses of ancient Iberian lineage. The animals were barely fourteen hands high and painted with chevrons, stars, and other strange signs and mystic symbols of power.

"They ain't doing nothing but watching us," Lovich said.

"Belike they can't believe how stupid we are," Marwood said.

The Comanches wheeled their nimble ponies about and disappeared over a rolling hill.

An hour later, eight more reappeared on an altogether different point of the compass. They rode parallel with the company, dipped into a fold of land, and disappeared again.

"They're trying to draw us into ambush," Lovich said with stout conviction. "Thank God they do not know how little armed we are."

"I hope they stay ignorant of that fact," Spaw said.

Botis led them onward. They saw nothing and no one else for the remainder of the day. The Tonkawa scouts could not find water, so they cut fresh horses out of the remuda and rode through the night. Blue heat lightning shimmered and quaked the barren sky to the south until the sun rose in the paling east.

The company put as many miles under them as they could without bottoming out the horses. When the sun was high on their backs Botis called a halt and they made camp. Marwood pulled first watch as the men slept. Evening came warm and soft. They broke camp and rode on.

The following day they crossed a desolate playa. The ground was hard and cracked under the horses' hooves. The sun reflected off the pan like a mirror; the men had to black their eyes, and the eyes of the horses, or they would have gone blind. They rode on seeing moon, then sun, then moon again.

They continued over the escarpment. Botis did not head directly west but rode a great analemma on the unending plain. They saw no sign of Cibola. They kept riding and they kept searching.

The days passed like beads on a string. Their water grew very short. The Comanches did not harry them.

"I don't understand it," Marwood said, watching as a large party of fifteen Comanches shadowed them on the horizon before disappearing in the searing heat.

"Maybe they recognize the captain's power in this place," Doc Quillen said, riding beside him. He had a neckerchief over the lower half of his face. "A man like him can make his own reality where he wants it."

"I don't know," Marwood said. Botis was riding ahead, a distant figure. "I think maybe we're so deep onto the Llano they don't care for this here part of the world."

"You mean like it's sacred?" Spaw asked. "Well, let's hope they don't change their minds about it."

The land would not change, either. There was always one more flattened hill, and beyond that, more seas of grass. Marwood felt diminished in a calculable way by the scorching, endless prairie. He felt swallowed and lost within the enormous space, which never changed, never altered its terrible and absolute face.

They came upon dead things—white bone, sun-bleached skulls, grass-choked ribs strewn across the ground. Beasts trying to reach some distant watering hole but died in the attempt.

The riders approached another playa. This one held an inch of water, but it was poisoned—alkali, through and through. They whipped and rowelled the horses past it so they would not drink.

Marwood's eyes were haunted caves as he looked upon the sky reflected cotton blue on the water's briny surface. The water hole was surrounded by dozens of blanched skeletons—some partially embedded in the hard pan, the grass growing through the bones they had been there so long.

The scouts found a little water one day and they kept going. Lovich cut a notch in his pommel for every day they were on the Staked Plains. He counted them one morning and he could not believe there were so many.

"We been out here goddamn near sixteen days," he whispered to Ed Gratton one morning. All the men had taken to talking in low voices as if they were afraid to break the great silence surrounding them.

"The captain, he ain't one to give up easy," Gratton said.

"I'm near clinkered out," Spaw replied. "Come on, he's ready to go."

They mounted up. The horses snorted and stumbled through the high, dusty grass. Thick foam and lather dripped from the mouths and nostrils of the animals. Their lungs blew and rattled like great winded engines. They were dying. The men were dying with them.

Marwood observed that even Acheron, that monster, was labouring.

He saw no more bones in the grass. Saw nothing but the empty world.

"I think this here string is about to play itself out," Ed Gratton said one afternoon. They had stopped to rest the horses. He was sitting on his saddle on the ground, smoking a pipe.

Marwood nodded, his blood pounding in his ears from the stifling heat. He had never felt so lost and alone in such awful emptiness. The silence itself was oppressive. It was as if this vast emptiness had taken over the world and everything he ever thought he knew.

"There's not much left in me," Spaw agreed, lying flat on the ground. His lips were cracked and bleeding. "Too much more of this and we're all going to go crazy."

Botis got up from his bedroll and started to saddle Acheron.

Gratton took his hat off and wiped his forehead with his sleeve. "I think we've been that for some time now," the black man said.

They rode on. They were so worn out—both man and horse—Marwood didn't think they made more than ten miles that day. The next day they faced an inescapable fact: they had no water left. Marwood and Spaw stopped to cut a horse out of the remuda. Red Thunder killed it with his knife, and the men drank its blood. They urinated what little they could in their canteens. When a horse in their string would stop and stale, the nearest man would jump off his saddle and fill his canteen.

"Don't drink yer piss for the salt," Quillen warned them. "Swish it in your mouth and spit it back into the canteen. It will last longer that way."

Botis would not stop. They kept riding, searching that great void. Another waterless day, another horse killed. In the morning and night that followed, Marwood searched the barren sky for doves flying from, or to, water. He saw nothing. The Comanches had also disappeared. At night he heard no sound but the wind scouring the grass. Not even coyotes were this far out.

There was nothing. There was nothing here at all, he thought. Not for him, and not for Botis.

The men were as scarecrows. They ate leather for the food was all gone. They killed another horse and Marwood chewed the bloody meat in his saddle. Scabbed blood dried in his beard and the cracks of his hands. His hot breath rasped in his tortured lungs.

Doc Quillen's horse collapsed and died under him the following day. Its heart had burst. The men opened its neck and crouched over the animal in a mad pantomime of camaraderie.

Quillen doubled up with Ed Gratton, but his horse could not carry them both, and the resurrectionist would not give up his tent and dissection tools. They took turns riding and leading.

When Marwood looked behind him the men were strung out in a long, staggered line, like dots on the prairie. Another horse died.

The next morning they saw Cibola.

They saw it to a man. They got off their trembling horses and stared in stunned disbelief. Spaw slowly sank to his knees in the high grass, his hands clasped over his heart. Giant ramparts and warping towers rose from the flat plain. They were mirrored with separate spires bisecting a thick line hovering through the sky. The city and its dark grey spires lined with gold and silver filigree, warped and twisted as if a dream brought to life, flexing its power over the broad earth.

The men mounted up and rode toward it, and as they came close the Fata Morgana melted and disappeared. They saw purple buttes in the distance and headed straight for them. Beyond those were blackened canyons and plateaued badlands filled with cactus, mesquite, and blackened juniper scrub.

Marwood fixed his eyes thoughtfully on Botis's back as they rode.

Shadows of distant clouds raced up the vertical faces of cliffs. A lone turkey buzzard fought the wind sheared off the canyon floor.

"There is water here," Red Thunder said.

They went down into the earth. The interlocking system of canyons had suffered a savage wildfire many years ago. Amid blackened mesquite trunks, charred lumps of cactus, and stumps of juniper, small green shoots poked from the lampblack ground.

"It is nigh impossible to eradicate life," Botis said, "but man has taken it upon himself as his one great mission. Washed in blood, and sanctified by God."

Away to the west, dark rain clouds lined the horizon. Long streamers fell from their swollen bottoms, like skirts brushing the canyons and limestone bluffs. They turned and rode toward the rain.

They reached the place where they thought the rain had fallen, got off their horses, and walked through the early morning sunlight. The trees and scrub around Marwood glistened and sparkled. The dry ground under foot and hoof had swallowed every last ounce of moisture.

Botis spotted more rain clouds building in a separate quarter. They headed for them, and missed the rain again.

"Goddamn this," Lovich said. They stopped in the middle of a bone-dry ravine. The horses could not, and would not, go any farther. "We ain't doing nothing but chasing our tails."

Botis sat staring at a lone juniper bush growing on the point of a limestone break. "Daniel," he said.

"Captain?" Lovich replied.

"Watch my horse."

"Sir."

Botis dismounted and stalked to the base of the sheer bluff. He tilted his head back and studied the juniper bush hanging precariously above him. He started to climb the sheer face of the break. The men watched him, mouths open. He crawled like a black and brown spider along crevice and ledge until he gained the crown, one hundred feet above them.

Botis took hold of the juniper. He tugged and wrestled it out of the unforgiving ground. Rock and sand spilled from the point. Marwood, standing near the base, had to back up to avoid getting pelted.

Botis ripped the bush from the soil. He lifted the green shrub over his head and hurled it into the gorge. Then he sat on the rocky promontory with the wind fingering his clothes, and watched the clouds, daring them to ignore his offering.

Fifteen minutes later, a single cloud cut the sun's track. Blessed shade fell across the canyon. More clouds appeared, pregnant with warm rain. Soon the sky was covered with them.

Water poured upon their bare heads. The killers filled their canteens from rivulets dripping off the bare rock, while Botis's laughter vied with the booming thunder overhead.

CHAPTER 22

They worked their way through the tangled web of canyons and out the other side. Marwood stood beside Botis on the rim of a high bluff. The two of them were studying the trail they had negotiated.

"This canyon," Botis told him, "the entire west, covered in blood. This is my home, Mar."

Botis took a deep breath. His eyes swept over the land. "When man first crossed into this country he looked around and went to killing. Not every man, and not every tribe, but kill he did. Then came the white man, and he killed, and both killed together. When the red man is finally eradicated, as he must be, then will the white man begin to kill himself. As he must. So the circle of history is joined. Is it any wonder a man like myself loves this country so much?"

"I'm still trying to understand what happened on the Llano Estacado," Marwood said.

Botis looked at him and smiled. "If Cibola were easy to find all men would find it," he said. "But one day I will have it in my grasp. I have foreseen it. Come on, let's get the horses together."

They rode into a small trading village called Muchaque. The post was little more than joined tunnels and shallow dugouts carved into arroyo walls. There were crude ladders extending from overhanging caves shaded with brush arbors, opening into other caves below. To the naked eye Muchaque looked more a chaotic anthill than a village.

"We need provender," Botis said to the villagers.

The Ciboleros who lived here claimed they had nothing to take, and nothing to give.

"Comancheros come here all the time and abuse us," one man said. He was dressed in mouldering buffalo skins and used an old Comanche war shield as a hat. He had set himself up as de facto *jefe* of Muchaque. "When we do kill buffalo they come and take what we have, and leave us dust to eat."

A young boy pressed himself upon Marwood, meaning to sell obsidian flakes, polished shells, and bone awls from a wooden tray slung around his neck. It was all he had to sell. Marwood bought a *quena*—a whistle carved from buffalo bone—because he had never seen the like before. He gave the boy four bits for it, twice what he asked. The boy stared at the coins in his brown palm and wept. He had never held such treasure in his life.

"Where might we find these Comancheros?" Botis asked. Such men would have guns, powder, and food.

"Take this trail leading out." The *jefe* pointed to something that aspired one day to be a goat path. "That is *La Pista de Vida Agua*. You will find them, or they you."

"Where does this trail end up?" Lovich asked.

"Across part of the Llano, señor. In the territory of New Mexico."

"What about water?" Spaw said. "We already had a time on the Llano."

"There are seepage springs a day's ride from the trail," the *jefe* explained. "But the comancheros will not let you use them. They will kill you, and your body will become dust."

"We'll see about that," Botis said.

Four days later they fell upon a Comanchero wagon train like tatterdemalion demons conjured from a nightmare. They killed everyone, including a family of settlers from Maryland who had bribed the Comanchero raiders for safe passage across the Llano.

The family had a daughter of marriageable age. Lovich dragged her screaming behind a clump of cholla and tall flowering yucca. When he emerged, he had a dripping scalp in one hand and her bloody crinoline dress in the other. He wiped his sweating face with the hem of her dress and tossed it into the bush.

They burned four of the wagons but kept one of the rigs for themselves. The new horses and two jacks were turned out into the remuda. Botis parcelled out guns and ammunition stolen off the dead Comanchero raiders. They had lost but a single man: Ed Gratton was laid out on *La Pista de Vida Agua* with a bullet lodged in his right eye, and two poisoned arrows in his lower spine. His blood had splattered Marwood's face and he was wiping it off with a neckerchief when Botis walked up.

"Get his gun and fold his horse into the remuda with the rest of the stock," Botis ordered. "We ain't got time to bury anyone."

They rode through grass baked into yellow dust. Cholla grew in small dark clumps like weird, wind-blown candelabra scattered over the plain.

Doc Quillen drove the wagon until it threw a rim and broke its whiffletree, bouncing too fast across a washout.

"Goddammit, Doc," Spaw groused, "you kill everything you touch."

Later the Tonkawas reappeared and hove their horses to.

"Looks like something's got them riled up," Spaw told Marwood.

"I can think of only one thing that would do that," Lovich said with worry.

The band rode back with the Tonks, accompanying them like an honour guard. They sat their horses staring at two bodies hanging like spoiled fruit from mesquite stobs—an unimaginable harvest of violence and savagery.

The dead men were skinned. Their red, mottled flesh was networked with white sinew and lumps of yellowish fat. The sharpened mesquite stob, with its black thorns, penetrated their lower jaws, and exited their mouths like caustic demon tongues.

"Are they white?" Botis asked.

Lovich leaned off his horse and spat on the ground. "Hard to tell, Captain. They might be white. Indians who done it all the same."

"I will ask you one more time: Are they white?"

"Yes, sir, I believe they are."

"Cut them down."

"Yes, sir."

Spaw and Marwood were tasked with the job. Spaw climbed the tree, holding a branch with gloved hands to protect himself from the poisoned thorns. He raised his boot and pushed against the chest of the dead man. The body inched along the mesquite stob but got hung up in the thorns. He hacked at them with a machete. The branch cracked. The body jerked and fell half a foot. It swayed, a sickening red mass of pulped flesh. Spaw kicked it again, his boot squelching, and it fell to the ground with a wet spongy thump. Marwood whipped a lariat around the legs of the second dead man and pulled while Spaw hacked the limb. It, too, fell in a slump.

"You want us to bury them, Captain?" Lovich asked Botis.

"What the hell for? This country has to eat, too. Let's ride."

They were almost off the Llano for good when they were beset by Comanche raiders.

They were Quahadi, and their faces, and the faces of their horses, were painted black. They rode in a counterclockwise wheel around Botis and his men. Little Shreve lay dead in a pile of cactus, scalped, his heart taken as prize.

The bandits again had the good fortune to hold the high ground—a bald limestone break surrounded by tall yucca. Botis's men husbanded their shots. When arrows landed nearby Marwood grabbed them and broke the shafts so they could not be used again.

The Comanches possessed a few guns, mostly eighteenth century flintlocks with slanting frizzen pans and other obsolete muzzleloaders. One Comanche warrior possessed a modern breech-loading rifle, but without forestock or sight. Another, dressed only in top hat and tails, carried an *escopeta*, the only decent working gun among them. Once the initial volley was over, during which Doc Quillen was crippled, they resorted to more traditional weaponry.

They rode bareback, slipping over the offside of their horse with one leg across its back, shooting their short bows under the horse's outstretched neck. They wove in and out of the standing yucca plants. Marwood could not draw a clear bead on them. Spaw took an arrow in his leg and sprawled helpless on the ground.

After a somewhat curtailed flurry of violence, it was over. A second war party crested a grassy rise to the north. They stole the remuda and added their own covering fire until the first raiding party had disengaged from battle. Then they formed up and rode away together, into the Staked Plains with the stolen horses.

Red Thunder looked first at his dead cousin and then at Botis. He walked to his horse and flung himself on its back. He lifted his Spencer rifle, reined his horse around with a violent jerk, and flew after the retreating band of Comanches.

The men watched his dust plume shred up and disappear on the high desert wind.

"You want us to go after him, Captain?" Lovich asked.

Botis shook his massive head. "No. He is a man riding to his destiny. I can respect that."

He started away, stopped, gazed back to where Red Thunder had disappeared, and continued on. "He will find Cibola," he said with something like envy.

The arrow had pierced Spaw's calf, transfixing the meat of the muscle. Marwood cut the iron head away, yanked out the shaft, and washed the wound with water. He peeled paddles of nopal and tied the green pulp to the entrance and exit wounds with jute. Spaw lay back on his elbows, his face ashen. His fancy ostrich plume had lost its fullness, and was naught but a naked quill.

Doc Quillen was in a great deal of pain. He had taken a full load of rusty nailheads from the *escopeta* at close range, shredding his left leg from hip to knee. The damage was too extensive to sew up. The men did what they could to make him comfortable, and waited for him to die.

Meanwhile, they held another war council and decided to pull out and make for higher ground. Spaw was down a horse and they had no spares, so he doubled up with Marwood. Lovich built a travois and they strapped Quillen to it with blanket strips. Quillen puffed a cigar while they dragged him along the bumpy ground. He held a tattered bumbershoot made with bone ribs and a sagging human skin canopy to protect his face from the fierce sun.

Spindles of dust wobbled in the distance. As the company rode, dust devils tracked alongside them for the remainder of the day, like loyal shepherding dogs.

They rode off the staked plains and struck out cross-country. They hit the Pecos river, camped and rested for a day, and followed it north into the territory of New Mexico.

They came upon *rancherias* and prosperous *estancias* on the western rim of the Llano Estacado. Many houses had already been burned out by Comanche war parties. From those that had not, Botis took on water, food, and horses, and forced his men to keep riding.

They rode into Fort Sumner, bought supplies and powder, and crossed the Goodnight-Loving Trail. Quillen was taking a long time to die. His leg had worsened, and though he was now able to ride horseback and could cup himself, he knew he was done in and ready for the casket.

Marwood sat beside him one evening as they camped in an arroyo. The sky to the west was crimson. Petroglyphs engraved on the rocks along the arroyo walls shone snow white in the distance. Marwood remarked how he could see them shine. Quillen said he could not, that they only showed themselves to a man ready to see them.

"I want you to have this," the resurrectionist said. He handed Marwood a gold locket and chain. "That there belonged to my mother."

Marwood stared at the shiny locket in his calloused hand. "I don't remember mine," he said.

"No," Quillen said, "you would not."

"I have been thinking about what you said that night, in the dissection tent."

"Have you now?" Quillen puffed a petite cigarillo.

"I don't know what I am," Marwood said in an embarrassed, confessional tone. "I don't think I have ever known."

"No man does with any assurance," Quillen stated. "Only Botis. Every other man must solve that mystery for himself."

"I believe I will go north, Doc."

Quillen studied him without speaking. "I believe that is the right thing to do," he said at last. He fell silent, then said, "You make sure I get buried, Mar. Don't leave me on the road like they did poor Ed Gratton."

"All right."

"You keep that locket, too. Give it to a girl one day."

"I will do that." Marwood stowed the locket away. "What do you want me to do with your books and journals?"

"Burn them," Quillen said. "They don't mean nothing anymore."

They limped into Agua Negra Chiquita on the first of September. The day was cold and bracing, and the wind felt as if it cut the flesh from their bones. Marwood sold his Hawken. He purchased a good Sharps rifle off a buffalo hunter who had married a twelve-year-old Cherokee girl and called it quits.

"It's a hell of a world," the buffalo hunter told Marwood. "I killed those big shaggies from sunup to sundown. We used to piss down the barrels of our guns they got so hot. We'd dig slugs from their hearts and use them again. Made and lost a fortune twice over. Now I'm going to pick up their bones and sell them for fertilizer. You think God's not laughing at that?"

Botis and company left the tiny settlement and headed west. They passed between red and yellow sandstone cliffs, through more adobe *pueblitos*, and into the dirty, narrow streets of Santa Fe.

Botis hitched his horse in the *alameda*. Marwood went off to buy a horn of gunpowder. Dirty, unkempt children ran through the street selling huge bundles of grass forage for a dime. Botis bought some, cut them open and threw them down in the street so the horses could feed.

Marwood found a telegraph office in a sandstone building fronted with mud adobe. He paid for, and sent, a wire to Laredo. When that was done, he purchased his horn of powder and a new shotpouch from a *bodega*.

He found Botis and crew eating heaps of boiled mutton and fried onions in a restaurant facing the Santa Fe River. The walls were planked with piñon. A hooded fireplace smoked and blazed, the wood popping. A Mestizo woman stirred a pot of red chili with a long wooden ladle.

Marwood sat down. It had been another long day and he was glad for the break. They ate, drank a gallon of black coffee between them, and hammered out their plans.

"We will have to hire new men," Lovich said. "Scouts, too, if we can find any Indians we can trust."

"Some of these Tiwa know the country," Marwood said.

"Leastways we won't have to pay them much," Spaw said, reaching for the coffee pot. His injured leg was propped on another chair.

"I think we four horsemen are enough," Botis countered. He forked a mess of onions and peppers into his mouth. "Remember," he said, chewing, "that morning in my office. In Piedras Negras? It was the four of us then."

Lovich sipped his coffee and contemplated the turn of events. "Looks like we've come full circle."

"Is that what you want, Captain?" Spaw asked.

Botis wiped his mouth with a napkin. He glanced at Marwood and smiled broadly. His white teeth glinted behind his black beard.

"It is what I have been praying for all my life," he said.

PART V

Numank Maxana

CHAPTER 23

They were not men who could remain inside buildings long. The only roof they needed was the sky. They gathered their horses and rode six miles out of Santa Fe.

Spaw built an outlaw's fire at the mouth of an empty slot canyon. They crouched around the fire, surrounded by snow-capped mountains; they were like a band of Paleolithic savages more comfortable with knapped stone tools than gun, powder horn, and saddle.

They rode into the Taos Pueblo the following Friday and attacked a government payroll wagon. Then they went up into the mountains with their gold and buried it. They lived like bears—sleeping during the day and coming down from the mountains at night to forage along the El Camino Real.

In the weeks that followed there grew whispers and rumours of four horsemen who were attacking pack trains throughout the Sangre de Cristo Mountains. It was said these horsemen rode from mountaintop to mountaintop with lightning between their hands, and they used unholy darkness to hide their movements. When men gathered in saloons at night, or in plazas during the day, they sat or stood in a close circle, drinking from a shared bottle. They assured one another these *bandido yanquis* fed on the souls of men, and dressed themselves with fire and burning ash. No mortal man was safe from their depredations, and their gold cache filled a great cave.

When Botis and company rode through the Arroyo Seco one morning they discovered a crude *bulto* carving of four horses nailed to the front door of the Spanish mission. Below the carving was a clay bowl filled with gold and silver. Botis divided it among his men, and they mounted up and rode past the deserted village.

They were making their slow way through Ratón Pass when Marwood spotted a white dove flying overhead. After a while they heard a creaking wagon beyond the trees behind them and stopped in the middle of the road. They took out their guns. A man driving a two-wheeled ambulance wagon, his *burros* hitched in tandem, came rattling around the bend. He wore a knee-length *serape* with faded bands of yellow and blue.

The rickety Civil War wagon had broken leather springs and jounced like a child's toy on the stony road. Their curiosity got the better of them and they drew nigh. While the driver sat patiently under their guns Botis pulled the wagon cover aside and peered into the back.

"Are you Mestizo?" he asked the wizened old man.

"Spanish, señor."

"What have you got in this here chock barrel?"

"A *quintal* of salt."

"Salt?"

"I am taking it to Pueblo."

"You mean Colorado?"

"*Sí.*"

Botis pulled the triangle of canvas back over the barrel. "Well, I will be goddamned," he said.

They rode alongside him. He told them his name was Domingo de Salazar. He was taking salt to his brother-in-law who lived in Pueblo. He said he thought many men were coming up behind them from Taos, men with evil on their minds, but he could not be sure.

Five miles farther on they came to a hanged man in the bend of the road. Grackles flew from his chest and shoulders when they approached. The man had been strung up without his boots, his chest laid bare to the wind. Carved into the muscle were two letters.

"Guess they don't cotton to horse thieves in this neck of country," Spaw said. "It will make for thin living on our part."

Marwood heard this but said nothing in reply. Spaw rode on, nibbling his already champered square of man leather with more than his usual preoccupation.

They made camp and shared fire and meat with their new companion.

"Are you looking for work, señor?" Salazar asked.

"We are always looking for something," Botis answered.

"You will not find it in Pueblo," Salazar assured him.

"Why is that," Lovich said.

"There is nothing in Pueblo. No work. No women. No salt. I am bringing them salt. I can do nothing for their other problems."

"How did you get picked for this here job?" Lovich asked.

The night was cold and the stranger pulled his *serape* close around him. He shrugged. "I volunteered. There was nothing to do in Chihuahua, either."

"Wait a minute," Lovich said. "You hauled this hundredweight of salt all the way from Chihuahua?"

"Yes."

"Are you crazy?"

"No more than any other man, señor."

Botis laughed. "They have salt in Pueblo, old man," he said.

"Yes," Salazar agreed, "but not this salt."

"What's special about this here salt?" Lovich was becoming nettled.

"It is salt from Cibola."

Botis's head jerked up. "Come again with that."

"This salt is from the city of Cibola. It is blood salt."

"Blood salt."

"Yes. It is the salt of the dead."

The men looked at one another. They went to the ambulance wagon and ripped away the sun-stiffened canvas. There was a loose angle iron lying on the bed. Marwood and Spaw used it to pry the lid off the cask.

The inside was filled with pale red crystals the size of pencil points.

Botis licked a finger and dipped it into the barrel. He tasted, then turned to gaze at the man slouched by the campfire. The other men tasted the salt, and they, too, looked at Salazar sitting unconcerned beside the fire.

They went back to the old man. Botis squatted in front of him, gun cocked out at his hip.

"Who are you?" he asked quietly.

"I think you know my name," Salazar answered.

"And you know mine."

"But of course."

"I am searching for Cibola," Botis said.

"Then how fortunate it was we met each other upon this road. Of all the roads in the world, señor, we met on this one. Do you not find that strange?"

Lovich hovered in the halflight of the background, hand on his sawed off shotgun. "You speak damn good American for a greasy Spaniard."

The old man lifted his head with a slight grin. "*Ik kan spreken elke taal die u wilt, meneer* Lovich."

"Old man," Botis warned, "I am not impressed by your parlour tricks. Tell me about Cibola. Tell me about the salt. Or I will kill you here and now."

"Cibola is a city of eternal men," Salazar said. "It existed upon the desert, long, long ago. But men dreamed, and so it disappeared. The salt—that is another matter. The salt is a pinch of blood from every man who died searching for Cibola. All men, throughout their lives, search for Cibola. Or something very like Cibola. It is an inexpressible burden all men share. It is the burden of Long Blood. I carry the salt of Cibola. I seek the Lone Man. I carry the salt of the dead. I collect it. It comes to me but gives no comfort, as does a winter rain upon a graveyard."

"We saw a city on the Llano Estacado," Botis said. "It was only a mirage. I know Cibola exists. I have known it all my life and in all the . . . all the pasts I have known. But what we saw that day was a mirage."

"You have not listened to a word I have said, señor." Salazar turned his head and stared at Marwood. "This one. He is listening. He knows. Now he knows."

Botis looked down the dark trail behind them. He faced back around. "Who is coming up behind us?" he asked.

"As I told you, evil men from Taos. They will kill you and your compatriots, and bring your bodies back to Taos. When I return there, I will collect the salt of your blood. Just as I have done for ten thousand years."

Botis watched him a long time. "You know what I think," he said at last. "I think you are a crazy old man who thought he could get a bounty on us. That's what I think."

They saddled their horses and stamped out the fire. Spaw cut a branch and swept the ground where they had been trampling it before he climbed on his own horse.

"We will leave you here," Botis said. "You can walk back to Taos." He pulled his gun and shot both *burros*. The somber old man watched them drop in their traces. The four horsemen wheeled their mounts around and rode away into the night.

"We will keep to the high rocks so they can't track us," Botis said. "Then we will kick for Pueblo."

They rode through a long night and into a grey morning. The sky was filled with dark clouds threatening rain. Spaw rode beside Marwood, his face glum.

"What's wrong?" Marwood asked once Botis and Lovich had gotten a little ways ahead of them.

Spaw chewed his bottom lip. "I got a standing warrant on me in Pueblo," he said. "I can't go back there."

"What happened?"

"I shot a boy." Spaw rode a little more before he started talking again. "It was an accident, but I killed him. I can't go to Pueblo, Mar."

"We don't have to go to Pueblo," Marwood said. "We have to get clear of this posse chasing us. That's all."

They rode hard, keeping to the Santa Fe Trail to make better time. It began to rain with great force. They pulled out their slickers, which were little more than capes and *serapes* hacked from raw leather. It was raining when they stopped in Trinidad, at the foot of the Ratón Pass, to buy food and extra gunpowder.

As Lovich was coming out of a cooperage with his hands full of packages, two lawmen stepped around a corner and blasted his back open with double-barrelled shotguns. The Dutchman fell face down in the mud and did not move. Marwood was across the street sitting his blood bay. He pulled his Colt's Dragoon and fanned five shots, giving Spaw the cover he needed to jump on his own horse and clear out.

Botis walked out of the barbershop where he'd been getting his beard trimmed carrying a cocked gun in hand. He shot the two lawmen dead where they stood. The rain was heavy and freezing cold, and it poured like hell from the leaden sky.

Someone opened up with another shotgun from a second-storey window in a clapboard hotel. Botis, in the middle of this ambush, took a pellet in his thigh, and two more in his left arm. The air was thick with buzzing lead flying in all directions and at oblique trajectories. The last Marwood saw Botis had reached Acheron and was racing up the Ratón

Pass, back into New Mexico Territory. Spaw, on the other hand, had pulled north, opting for the quickest way out of Trinidad.

Marwood went north, too.

He paused under a tree long enough to reload the chambers of his gun, then kicked hard, trying to cut Spaw's tracks. The rain was so heavy the ground was already washing out. He kept riding, looking for sign.

The rain quit sometime around midnight. Marwood found the muddied tracks of Spaw's horse. There were three others on his trail. Marwood pressed on.

Dawn brightened. Marwood stopped in the pale light to feed and water his horse, and let it blow. He would be no good to Spaw with a dead horse on his hands. He ate a handful of parched corn himself and mounted back up.

He tracked Spaw and his pursuers for two days. He was working his way over a pine-covered ridge when he spotted Spaw in a narrow rock valley a quarter mile below. Two riders were tearing across the wet ground after Spaw. The third rider had frog-jumped him during the night and was cutting off the only escape route with well-spaced pistol shots.

It is nigh impossible to hit a crouched man on the back of a fleeing horse fifty yards away. Hitting the horse, however, was another matter entirely. Three good shots slammed into Spaw's dun horse. Its head whipped up and to the left, and its legs buckled. It broke its neck when it hit the ground.

Spaw was thrown hard. He rolled like a crushed doll in the soggy field. He tried to get up, but his right leg was bent sideways at the knee. The other two lawmen reined their horses around and drew to a full stop, mud flying from their horses' hooves.

One of the men slowly got off his horse and approached Spaw. Spaw scrambled over the grass, searching for his lost gun. The lawman pulled his pistol and shot Spaw in the head. The lawman stood over him and shot him five more times, spacing each shot so their echoes blended with one another.

Marwood dismounted and draped the reins of his horse across a convenient tree branch. He pulled the Sharps from the scabbard and walked through the sparse treeline.

The lawmen were standing around Spaw, talking to one another. One of them had lighted a pipe and was writing something down in a small book. They picked up Spaw's body and tied it head down over a saddle. Marwood loaded the Sharps, not hurrying at all. Two lawmen had to double up on a single horse. The third led the horse carrying Spaw's limp body.

When they passed directly beneath him Marwood lifted the Sharps, sighted down the ladder, and killed the first man.

The .52-calibre 475-grain slug knocked him clean off his horse—damn near took his head off his shoulders. While Marwood reloaded, one of the other two remaining laws jumped from double riding onto the now-empty horse. The second man fired his six in Marwood's direction. Marwood heard bullets cut and chatter through the trees above him. The second man grabbed the reins of the horse carrying Spaw's body, and they both raced free and clear out of the valley.

Marwood walked back to his horse. He drank water out of his canteen and ate a piece of hardtack as he thought about the day. Then he gathered up the reins of his blood bay and mounted into saddle.

He rode down and regarded the man he had killed. He had always been of the opinion if you were willing to do it you might as well look at it. The man was a bounty hunter out of Santa Fe. Marwood left him for the wolves and followed the tracks out of the secluded valley.

The direction of their sign made it clear they were headed back for New Mexico Territory, and in one hell of a hurry. Marwood followed. Six hours later he shot the second man as they were watering their horses at a mountain stream.

It was a good shot, well over 600 yards, and down a thirty-degree mountain slope, which made the trajectory more difficult to judge. By the time Marwood got the Sharps reloaded, the third bounty hunter had disappeared with Spaw's body in a scraggly copse of young pine trees.

Marwood mounted up and went after him.

The day waned. Marwood eventually came to the horse with Spaw's body. The animal was tied to a creosote bush and was browsing grass. A white sugar sack was knotted to the pommel.

Marwood left Spaw's body and went after the fleeing bounty hunter. He killed him from a quarter mile away as the man transversed a bald ridge, attempting to double back in hopes of losing Marwood in the high country.

Marwood went back and retrieved the horse carrying Spaw's body. He then rode north for two days, until arriving at Pueblo. He walked into the sheriff's office.

Spaw had a 500-dollar bounty on his head, dead or alive. Marwood signed for the bounty and the sheriff told him he had to wire for the money. To pass the time, Marwood went to a café and ordered coffee, ham, and eggs. While he was eating four lawmen came through the back door with their guns out and arrested him.

He was held in a jail cell for several long days. They had taken his gun, boots, and belt. He sat on the edge of the bunk and thought about Spaw, and Botis, and the others. He closed his eyes and tried to remember the pieces of his past. He could not see how it all fit together. He felt alone, incomplete, and without direction. And for the first time in his life he felt as if he needed to change that in some real manner. An action or method that would give final meaning not only to his existence as a man, but his life—who and what he was, including his past. But how to find it?

"Cibola," he said low.

Or, if not Cibola, some other place. Some distant place meant only for him, waiting, maybe needing his presence.

Two deputies came for him on the third day. He was given his boots, taken from the cell, and walked across the mud-torn street to a hotel and up a flight of dingy stairs. There was a door at the end of a long hallway, with oil cressets set in the wall. The sheriff used a skeleton key and opened the door, and Marwood walked inside.

Judge Creighton sat at a low desk in front of a bright window, smoking a cigar.

CHAPTER 24

Marwood sat down in a straight-backed chair. Judge Creighton leaned sideways in his seat as if the angle afforded him a better view. He looked at Marwood with a deep critical gaze and no amount of wonderment.

"It has been a while since we last saw each other," Creighton said.

"Yes," Marwood said.

"I suppose you know what this is about."

"I figure it's about the bounty on that boy I brought in. I want it."

Creighton was not put off by Marwood's abrupt tone. "We can start there if you like. We dug those bullets out. They were .45 calibres. You carry a .44 Colt's Dragoon, and a .50 calibre Sharps. Can you explain the discrepancy?"

"I lost that gun."

"Which gun?"

"The .45 I killed him with," Marwood said.

"You lost that gun."

"That is what I said."

"Goddamn, you have sand."

"I want that bounty."

Judge Creighton got up from his desk. He took the cigar from his mouth and stared out the window. When he turned back around his face was grave.

"You are not going to get that bounty." He pushed aside a sheaf of papers on his desk, picked up a telegraph wire.

"'I am in Santa Fe.'" He looked up from the wire, pitched it fluttering back onto his desk.

"That is the only time I heard from you," he said. "Never expected it, to be frank. It was late reaching me because you sent it to Laredo. It took a while to catch up to me here. You don't know this, but I've been reposted to a new territory."

Marwood said nothing.

"I don't know why you sent that telegram," Judge Creighton said. "Or, maybe I do, but I don't want to believe it."

"I don't know why I did, either," Marwood said. "I felt it was something I needed to do. Maybe for myself. I don't know."

It was Judge Creighton's turn to not speak.

"I'm not trying to sull on you," Marwood said. "I can't explain why I sent that wire. Maybe because I don't know anyone else. Judge, I want the bounty on that boy."

"You are not going to get that bounty. To get that bounty you need my approval, and I am not going to render it."

Judge Creighton came around the desk. He stood and smoked and remained silent.

"If we are going to work together we have to trust one another," Marwood said. The room was very quiet. He could hear the panes of glass in the windows rattle at a gust of wind. "I won't work for a man I don't trust."

"Are we going to work together?" Judge Creighton asked.

"You wanted to. Your bastard sheriff down in Laredo made a fine point to tell me to ride north to a certain watering hole he knew."

"And that was as far as you took it."

Marwood motioned to the desktop. "Until I sent that wire. I didn't have to do that much. The fact I met Spaw was more luck than anything else, and you know it. Judge, I am only one kind of man. I will never change. I was not going to betray the men I rode with, any more than I would betray the man who went out of his way to help me in Laredo." Marwood got up from the chair and made to leave. "If that's the kind of man you're looking for, then you better look elsewhere. That has never been me. That will never *be* me."

"Despite the fact you killed squatters and land barons who made a pact with the devil and got what they deserved, I told you the chances you would end on my gallows," Judge Creighton said. "Son, the trap door is under your feet. My hand is on the lever."

"I am not a lawman."

"I don't want a lawman. I want a warm-blooded killer."

"I will be carrying a badge."

"John, what makes you think western law is anything other than an arm of civilization operating under the licence to kill? Maybe one day there will be schools and ice cream parlours in this part of the country. But we are not there yet. If history tells us anything, law and order are ever born out of chaos. Order is not a natural state of the world—it never will be where men are concerned. Law has to be built. It has to be killed for. Why are you grinning?"

"You sound like somebody else I know," Marwood said. "Look, I've never built nothing in my life except a reputation."

"That's all I want from you. Make no mistake. I am going to send you against men like yourself. One day you will fall. The question is how far you tote up the other side of the board, so self-righteous chickenshits like John Calvin and Mary Hoopskirt don't get their dainty hands dirty."

Creighton opened a side desk drawer. He pitched a U.S. Deputy Marshal's badge. Marwood caught it in mid-air.

"I will tell you something every judge and lawman knows," Judge Creighton said. "That badge doesn't mean a goddamn thing. History alone decides who is right, and who is wrong. We both will be long gone by the time those pages are written."

Marwood knew Judge Creighton was playing a role. He doubted the man felt as intensely about the uselessness of the law as he pretended. It was an act, and Marwood saw it was an act. But it was for his benefit, and he appreciated it.

Creighton wanted him to understand the stakes, and the enormity of the decision that lay before Marwood.

Marwood moved his things into the room beside Creighton, which the judge had booked for him. He stretched out on the bed, hands behind his head. As he stared at the ceiling he heard horses and wagons trundle past the open window. He listened for church bells, but there were none in Pueblo.

He thought about what had transpired in Judge Creighton's chambers. How he had taken the oath and signed his name to several official documents, and Judge Creighton sprinkling sand over the wet gall ink. He wondered if it all meant anything. He didn't feel any different.

He got up from the bed and went to the dresser. He stared at the badge resting on top of the polished wood, next to his gun and skinning knife, but didn't touch it. He got back into bed.

Maybe it did mean something, after all. Maybe this was something he was going to have to puzzle out on his own.

The next week was spent in the company of Judge Creighton. They ate every meal together, and at night Creighton brought out a bottle of Kentucky bourbon and they drank and smoked cigars.

Creighton expounded upon the law. He covered everything from Hammurabi to Moses to Manusmriti. He defined the difference between jurisprudence and jurisdiction. He touched on evidence, property, casuistry, and contracts.

Their conversation turned to Marwood's time along the Mexican border and up through Texas. He told Creighton all he knew about Abram Botis: the way the man thought, how he moved, his tactics.

"You were in a good position to observe it all," Creighton said, "even though you weren't officially undercover. Come the day you ever pick up his trail again, you will have to bring him in. That will go a long way to afford you amnesty for the questionable actions you took while riding with Botis." Creighton held up his hand to forestall Marwood's response. "I know you don't care about something like that, John. But considering your past with this man, is that going to be a problem for you?"

Marwood thought it over. "It will not be a problem, Judge."

"Good. If anything does happen to you, is there someone I should contact?"

Marwood shook his head. "I have no one like that," he said.

Creighton leaned forward and refilled his glass. "That's best," he said. "A lawman can't afford to have worries that slow him down. I'm not talking about your gun hand; I'm talking about your mind. Not being able to think yourself out of a tight situation, that, more than anything else, will get you killed."

"When am I going out?"

"Very soon. I'm getting things together now." Creighton ventured a tight smile. "You that eager to get shot at?"

Marwood looked at the whiskey glass in his fist. "I figure if I'm going to wear this badge I might as well do the job right."

The following day Marwood went to the livery stable to see about his horse. The man there said, "That blood bay of yours isn't going to hold up. He's got a fractured coffin bone. I've got a bay gelding here you might want to look at instead."

"How much you want for him?"

"Don't worry about money. Judge Creighton will pick up the tab."

"All right, let's take a look at him."

One night, when he and Creighton were finishing up, he asked Marwood, "What happened to you boys out on the Llano?"

Marwood would not answer, for that was a bridge too far. He felt it was betraying a confidence to the men he had ridden with. Judge Creighton did not press him, and the matter was dropped.

The next morning, following breakfast, Judge Creighton said, "I have had my jurisdiction amended. I am preparing to work Montana Territory now. Have you been up there?"

"No, sir."

"That's where you're headed."

"That's a long ride."

"You can catch a stage in Auraria."

Marwood packed his war bag and went downstairs to kit out coffee, salt, and gunpowder. The store clerk wore egg-shaped spectacles and had a tight collar that squeezed his fat throat. He licked a pencil nub and totted up the charges.

"Where you headed with this bundle?" he asked.

"The Territory of Montana."

The clerk stared in admiration. "You that new deputy marshal Judge Creighton done hired, ain't you?"

"I guess I am."

"Good luck," the clerk said. "Last man the judge hired was skun by rustlers. Goddamn if he don't chew through men faster than a javelina eats pecans."

Marwood was ready to pull out by the tail end of the next day. Judge Creighton met him on the street in the rain. They shook hands.

"I will see you in Fort Benton," Creighton said.

"Yes, sir," Marwood replied. "I guess you will."

Marwood left Pueblo on his new bay gelding. That night he camped on top of a caprock somewhere between Pueblo and Auraria. He ate a pan of cornbread and greasy side meat. Beneath the stars he watched snow-capped crowns glimmer in the northwest—the eastern reaches of the Rockies.

In Camp Collins he was told about a little-known pass that would cut 150 miles off his journey if he hit it before it froze up. He went through, riding well above the timberline. At night he huddled under his horse, blowing on his freezing hands and cursing Creighton and the world. He was cold, tired, and hungry, but also happy.

It took him seven days to climb through snow and rock ledges encrusted with thick shale ice. At one point he had to chop his way through five yards of ice wall with a hand axe. He came down the other side and the air warmed, and he rode through forests of dead pine for two days and two nights running.

He glanced up and saw the dead trees converge at a centre point in the sky. The only other living things were ravens gliding between the trees, and chipmunks chattering at him from mossy stones.

He rode past breaks and ledges of limestone and quartz, and passed a shelf unearthed by some ancient upheaval. Preserved in the rock were tracks of antediluvian monsters that had roamed the earth before man. Marwood ran his fingers along the depressions, trying to read the size and structure of these animals. Later, he entered an aspen forest and rode through white pillars and green canopies. He came into the wide-open territory of Wyoming on Thanksgiving Day. In Billings an official telegram was waiting for him. He replied, and when he went to bed that night he thought of the men he would kill in Tomah.

He rode 'tween the Gallatin and Bridger mountain ranges. Upon emerging from the Bozeman Pass, after being snowed in for four scary days, he saw Cibola.

He got off his horse and held the reins, waiting for the mirage to disappear.

But it did not vanish. It was Cibola. Gold ramparts and spires of sparkling onyx. It lifted from the ground like a translucent bubble. He looked up. The stars were different, and he did not recognize them until they changed back and Cibola was gone, and he was back in the world again.

On Christmas morning, 1869, he tied up outside a taproom in Tomah. A thin snow mixed with light rain was falling. He got off his horse and checked the loads in his gun. He pinned the badge to his vest. He pushed through the batwing doors and stood in the smoky red barroom light.

"I am looking for Henry Pickett and the Ketchum brothers."

Three men standing by the bar turned around. One of them carried a Spencer rifle with a fresh Indian scalp hanging from its brass butt plate.

Marwood came out of the saloon five minutes later and walked across Last Chance Gulch, a mud street that meandered between tapped-out gold claims. There was a large mud-spattered U.S. Army surplus tent with sod cloth in the back of Reeder's Alley. Marwood went inside, sat down, and ordered biscuits and black coffee.

Gold miners and Chinese labourers crowded the tent opening. Marwood looked up from his breakfast—the canvas storm flap dropped back down and they were gone.

A waiter came by to refill his coffee cup. "They are carrying those men out of the saloon now," he said.

"All right."

"You centre-cut every one of them. They'll wait until it stops raining before they bury them."

"That so."

"You looking for a place to stay?"

"I'm going to need a room. I don't know if Judge Creighton has made arrangements."

"There's a hotel off Reeder's Alley. My brother-in-law works there. He can set you up nice."

"I appreciate that."

"You need anything else, you only have to ask, Marshal."

"I'll keep it in mind." Marwood took out his wallet.

"No, sir," the waiter said. "This one is on the house." He turned and left.

Marwood drank his coffee. There wasn't a lot of light here; tin candleholders were fixed to the wooden frame. A striking young woman sat beside a dripping tallow candle on the far side of the tent. She wore a crisp white blouse with a dark green jacket and a long heavy skirt. Her auburn hair was caught up at the back of her head with a tortoiseshell comb. She saw him looking at her and rose from her table and walked across the packed mud floor. She sat down opposite Marwood and arched her dark eyebrows at him.

"You're the new marshal we've been expecting," she said.

"Yes, I guess I am he."

She spooned sugar into his coffee cup and stirred it slowly. "You and me will be good friends." She smiled.

CHAPTER 25

It had started to snow heavily. Marwood watched it pile up outside the hotel window. It was a year to the day he'd been suffering in Rex Brookstone's mud pit.

The woman he'd met in the tent stood in front of the window in his room wearing a white cotton linen chemise with pin tucks and French lace. Her name was Carlene Minker. She had green eyes and long, dark lashes. She said she thought she had a husband somewhere, but he was out killing buffalo or being killed by Lakota Indians—she didn't care which.

"I haven't seen him in eighteen months," she said. "Last I heard he was trapping for skins up around the Bitterroot Range and had himself a squaw wife. I never did use his name when we got married anyway."

Carlene stood at the foot of the four-poster bed. She bunched the linen of her chemise and wiped between her legs. When she let the material fall back into place there was a wet spot where her slim fingers had probed herself. She reached up to pin her loose hair. Her breasts lifted under the dirty chemise.

"I don't mind being your woman," she said. "But if Clete comes back you'll have to kill him. He ain't going to like what we did."

"I thought you said you haven't seen your husband in eighteen months."

"He might come back." She finished fussing with her hair and faced him. "He will come back."

Marwood grabbed her wrist and pulled her to bed. She sat on the edge of the mattress, pale-limbed, loose red hair smelling of stale perfume and sweat. It was cold in the room and she had goose bumps on her arms.

"We can live here in this room if that is what you want," she said.

"That is what I want."

She looked at her hand in his, and his strong fingers. "I guess that's the way I want things, too," she said quietly.

Lawing in Montana Territory kept Marwood busy, with little time for self-reflection. The years passed quickly enough, and his knowledge and talent for the job grew alongside his reputation. Judge Creighton handed him warrants, and Marwood went out after the men and brought them back. Most days Carlene was waiting for him when he got back, even when he sometimes didn't want her around. But for the most part he accepted his fluid relationship with her; she asked very little of him and he was not the kind of man who gave a lot. The only thing hanging over them was the ever-present danger of her husband returning.

It was 1873 and he was down around the Three Forks when two Mandan Indians rode into his camp. One was the old man from Piedras Negras but dressed this time in heavy buffalo skins. The other, at his side, was his interpreter, a rail-thin boy of nine wearing white cotton duck pants and a shirt that hung below his waist.

"My grandfather says it is time to come to the village," the boy said. They squatted beside Marwood's campfire without invitation. "You must come when the trees leaf out."

Marwood studied the old man. He asked the boy, "Who is your grandfather? I have seen him before."

The boy spoke to his grandfather briefly. The man replied at length.

"His name is White Sky Heart, the last son of Mato-tope," said the boy. "He is a man of great medicine power. He knows the sun, the wind, the sky, and how to use their medicine. He says we will take you to the great Medicine Lodge. You will fast for four days and you will be lifted into the arms of the sun. There you will find the path you have lost. We do this because it is our path, too. That's what he says, mister."

The boy listened to his grandfather speak again. He turned back to Marwood. "My grandfather wants you to know this is a journey which will change you for all time. It changes all men. Some die, but those who live through it are forever changed."

The old man spoke again. The boy listened carefully, nodded, and translated the words.

"There are two worlds," he said. "There is this world of rock, water, and sun. When a man dies he crosses into the Spirit World. When this happens, sometimes a spirit will cross back the other way, into this world, where he does not belong. This has happened. There can only be one *Numank Maxana*. One must die so the other can find peace."

The old man had finished speaking. The boy looked at Marwood and shook his head.

"I do not understand everything my grandfather says, mister. But this is something he has waited for his entire life. He believes it is the reason he was born, and when his work is done, it will be the reason he dies. I do not want my grandfather to die. I love him. But this is a stone in his heart he must dislodge. He has asked me to help him. So I will help him."

"What is your name, boy?"

"I am William Red Corn." He pulled his canvas shirt aside to reveal a wooden cross attached to a leather thong. He smiled broadly. "I am made Christian."

"Son," Marwood said, "I can't ride clear across country because some old Indian spirit man says so. I am a U.S. Deputy Marshal. I have to have a pretty good reason before I do something like that."

The boy thought this over. "A reason of the law?"

"That would help."

"There are hunters in our country. They kill many buffalo. One day they will be gone, and so will the People."

"I'm sorry, William, but that's not good enough for the U.S. government. In fact, it's what they want."

William Red Corn thought another long while. He scratched his head and poked at the fire with a curved stick. Finally he made up his mind. He was young, but his face was solemn.

"There is a very cruel buffalo hunter," he began. "He is a white man from Illinois. He poaches on herds hunted by the People, and shoots other white buffalo hunters for their hides. He shot one buffalo hunter in the head, but the gun misfired. The ball hung in the barrel and the powder scorched the man's scalp, knocking him cold. The man he shot was my cousin, Jumping Elk Smith. But he thought my cousin was dead, so he stole the hides and sold them to a field agent."

"What is this white man's name?"

"I do not know him," William Red Corn said. "But he is called Clete Stride by those who do."

Marwood told Carlene over breakfast what he was planning to do. "Judge Creighton signed the warrant last night. I have to go get him," he said.

She watched him across the table. "Clete is not the kind of man who's easy to get," she said.

"Carlene, do you still love him?"

She looked down at her plate of food. "I told you I was your woman now," she answered. "If you have to bring him in then I guess that's the way it has to be." She looked up. "I will be here when you get back, John. I will always be here."

A month later, as the trees were beginning to leaf, Marwood and the old man and his grandson rode into the Mandan village. There were many round earthen lodges, with two-room log cabins and sun-bleached tipis on a high bluff overlooking a gunmetal river. The large earthen lodges were placed in a circle around a central plaza. In the middle of the square stood a solitary cedar post.

White Sky Heart pointed at the sacred post. "*Numank Maxana*," he said. Marwood felt a hollow pit start to form in his stomach.

They rode past old women pounding corn in stone bowls. Others used bone scapulas as gardening hoes, and deer antlers to rake and till the rich earth.

They dismounted outside a buffalo-hide tent. William Red Corn brought the horses to a corral with a snubbing post. When he returned he said his grandfather wanted Marwood to undress.

"Where is Clete Stride? He's who I came for."

"He is not here right now," William said. "He is out on the plains killing buffalo."

"Look, boy, I am not here to play games with this old man. I don't want to be incapacitated and have that killer come back on me."

"No white man will enter our village during the celebration," William Red Corn assured him. "He would be stopped, or most likely killed. Would that not also suit your purpose?"

Marwood stared at the old man. During the long ride here he had spent many an hour in conversation with the grandfather, with William acting as translator. He wasn't sure the man's motives were entirely above board, but standing here, with the sun in the sky and the people crowding around him, a sense of calm infused his soul that he had never before experienced.

Whatever was going to happen to him in this village, he knew it was the right thing. He had his whole life to study on this question and had yet to see any light in the dark. It was time to find answers to the questions that plagued him. He took a deep breath and let it out slowly. Now that he was here, he could not under any circumstance imagine walking out of the village and returning to Tomah.

"Show me what you have," he told the old man.

Inside the buffalo-hide tent was a large wicker basket shaped like a washing tub. William Red Corn built a roaring fire outside the tent. He used the fire to heat heavy round stones.

Marwood undressed. Under the grandfather's direction he stepped inside the wicker basket and sat down. His heart was beating hard. White Sky Heart crushed handfuls of sage and medicinal leaves, and tossed them into the basket with Marwood.

When the stones were hot and splintering, William Red Corn used a forked stick to roll them inside the sweat tent. His grandfather threw more crushed sage on the rocks and doused them with water. The rocks splintered. Roiling, fragrant steam filled the tent.

Marwood's pores opened. He bent his head and gasped for air. Balls of sweat dripped off his chin onto his naked chest. He thought of his life—the parts he could remember—and wondered what more he could learn.

He was honest enough to admit he was afraid what the answers might be.

Once the steam bath was complete, the old grandfather brought him outside and sluiced him with gourds full of ice-cold water. Marwood shivered like he had ague. William Red Corn handed him a wool blanket to chafe his limbs and shoulders and get his blood running through his veins.

Marwood's head spun from the extraordinary bath. Something in those leaves had stolen his senses. It was like he was drunk. He let himself be pulled through the raucous village, heard music and singing all around him. People danced. They came up to him and danced and moved away in wild gyrations that had meaning to everyone but him. There were so many things going on around him, bright colours and brighter sounds, he could not keep track of it all.

His head swimming, they brought him to a big Medicine Lodge on the north side of the village plaza. It had a square smoke hole at the top. There stood other men waiting patiently for his arrival. These were the village leaders and elders from disparate clans, here to bear witness.

Marwood was led across an extended porch into the middle of the lodge hall. Willow boughs and ceremonial bundles of crushed sage were scattered here and there on the earthen floor. Intermingled with these were buffalo skulls, horse skulls, and not a few human skulls, with their dark, empty eye sockets and bony grins. In the centre of the ring, arranged on a tree stump like the instruments of an amateur surgeon, lay bone skewers, thin wooden splints, and a sharp scalping knife.

A thick wooden beam went across the roof; it was supported by four massive wooden columns with packed earth and heavy square stones at their base. Long cords of buffalo hide hung from the central beam like the crinkled skins of dead snakes.

They were not alone in this place. Other men were waiting for them in the smoky chamber. These strangers sat around the circumference of the lodge puffing long wooden pipes, watching Marwood and talking quietly among themselves. Marwood was led to the place of honour in the ring. There he sat alone.

Outside the lodge, the Mandan people sang and danced and feasted. Sometimes Marwood heard loud shrieks and screams and people running, followed by more dancing, and more energetic music.

He did not eat or sleep for four days. He was allowed to lie on a buffalo skin when he became too weak to sit up, but never to sleep. His eyes burned in his face like embers. His mind was aflame. His tongue was so swollen with thirst he could not swallow.

He started off counting the number of times he saw the sun appear in the square smoke hole of the lodge. By the third day he lost interest in this activity. Things like sun and light and smoke didn't mean anything in this world. He knew that now. He laughed at one point because he recognized their absurdity. All that mattered was the bone and heart and blood of man living. Everything else was lies and shadow.

Several attendants entered the lodge. They were ceremonially dressed in skins and bright feathers, their bodies painted in mingled colours and mystic signs and portents. Someone stood up and called Marwood's name. But it was not the name of *John Marwood,* but that of another, in a tongue he did not recognize yet understood, as if from some ancient particle of memory that had floated to the top of his consciousness.

His head came up at the mention of this name. He blinked and pushed himself to his feet, swaying like a slender reed. His body was like cindered sticks and shirred meat loosely packed together. If he moved, or tried to walk, he would surely disassemble into separate shards, like brittle glass shattering under the impact of an axe.

White Sky Heart lifted the scalping knife to the sunlight streaming through the smoke hole. He prayed aloud, invoking his gods. When the prayer ended he pinched the muscle of Marwood's right breast and passed the knife cleanly through. Blood ran. One of the attendants pushed a wooden skewer under the dense breast muscle. Marwood's breath whistled through his gritted teeth. The incredible pain brought his senses to a pitch. His mind throbbed like a taut wire, and the world was filled with whorls of red pain.

Another attendant attached one of the ceiling cords to the skewer. White Sky Heart performed the same operation on Marwood's left breast. More wooden skewers and wide bone splints were attached below his shoulders, elbows, and knees. The last two splints entered his thighs.

Blood poured from the multiple wounds. Marwood's whole world pounded between agonized shards of flashing light and darkness.

The attendants hauled on the ends of the leather cords. Marwood was wrenched into the air. His head fell back and his eyes bulged from their sockets. The light from the square smoke hole bathed his face and naked, straining body. Blood dripped from his trembling feet, hands, and elbows.

He swung free of the ground. The attendants tied off the ends of the cords; they were not done torturing him. They attached buffalo and human skulls to the splints and skewers embedded in his jerking body.

Marwood felt himself drawn between sky and ground, air and bone. Blood and death. One of the weights, a human skull with a bullet hole in the cranium, brushed the ground. The attendants loosened one cord and pulled Marwood up until the skull swung free. They tied the cord off and carefully watched his dangling body.

There were drums beating outside the lodge. Marwood's thundering heart pounded in time to their murderous rhythm. His mind fragmented into sections, flying apart like a murder of crows.

"Hax," he said. It was but his breath trying to suck life into his torn body. Brutal exhale: "San."

White Sky Heart advanced carrying a long hickory pole.

He touched the end of the pole to Marwood's bloody back, and spun him around in the light and smoke.

"For what is man's mind but a caution of madness?"

Marwood recalled his father upon seeing the city of his childhood.

The desert city of his birth, with stone ramparts and black stone towers. He and his father hunting a lion. A sister—older than him, with children of her own. His mother, his mother.

The men of the city. Their tattooed faces, speaking in a tongue lost to time. His tongue. The Eternals themselves riding pale horses. They came to take him from the only place he called home, and sent him into a world where he was made to stand against that which must be faced.

They took him because in his heart he alone carried a wintry thing with a maw that could swallow worlds. But his strength lay in the fact it was more afraid of him than he was of it.

So he travelled through amaranthine seas. To places that might never be, or could not become until something was set right.

These were the people Eternals looked for. People destined to travel forever.

Abaddon. Bilgames. Many more lost to time and dust. Some of which could not be pronounced with the simple mechanics of a human tongue.

He was one of them. It never ended because it was the storm itself, the unending conflict that made the world a reality.

There would be one last place where he would stand, and die.

"Hax." Breath rasped inward. Final exhale. "San."

Darkness closed around him like claws.

Marwood opened his eyes. He was lying on a soft mule deer robe. The slanting rays of the afternoon sun streamed through a smoke hole.

They were in White Sky Heart's private lodge. Attending women removed the bloody skewers and splints from Marwood's body. They laved his wounds with cold water and applied medicinal salve with the tips of their slender fingers. One of the women sprinkled his body with crushed sage leaves, which she rubbed gently into his skin.

Marwood raised his aching left hand. He tried to focus his eyes. The first joint of his little finger was chopped off. He let his hand fall to his side and groaned.

That's when they knew he was awake, was alive. Would live.

William Red Corn pressed the bone nipple of a water pouch to Marwood's dry lips. He sucked the water and took a long, shuddering breath. He drank again.

White Sky Heart sat across from them, eating handfuls of jerked meat and hominy. He did not appear overly concerned with the events surrounding him, or the speed and method of Marwood's recovery. He spoke to William Red Corn and returned to his meal.

The boy crouched beside Marwood. His young face was grave, his eyes full of tears.

"Now you can sleep," he told him, "and my grandfather will die in peace."

PART VI

The Sunset of Destruction . . .

CHAPTER 26

Carlene wept when she saw his scars.

"Do you think you're an Indian?" she cried.

"I don't know what I am," he said, and it was true. He was no longer the same man. As a spear point hardened by fire, so he now was.

He had never been a warm man. But now he was more distant, more alone, than ever before. Carlene saw it right off. Everyone who knew him in Tomah did.

She shook her head in defiance. "I don't understand you," she said. "You've been gone three months. We thought you died out there on the Three Forks."

"No," Marwood said, "I did not die. But I see things that were once hidden to me, and I will not turn back to the man I was."

"You were supposed to go after Clete and bring him in," she said in an accusatory tone.

Marwood stared out their window at the tents and clapboard shacks below. "Yes," he said, "but when I got there I decided to do something for myself instead."

He left the window and faced her. "I can't go back to everything I once was," he said. "I don't know who I am, but I know who I'm not."

Later that day, Judge Creighton and he talked about his experience. They met that night over supper, in the very saloon where Marwood had killed the Ketchum twins, and Henry Pickett, for lynching a Lakota Indian chief.

"Are you all right, John?" Creighton asked halfway through the fried chicken and greens.

"Yes, sir," Marwood replied. "I think I am now."

Creighton eyed him across the table. "What happened to you out there among the Mandans?"

Marwood pressed his lips together and leaned back in his chair. "It's like what happened on the Llano Estacado," he said. "Or Sand Creek. You can't explain it to another man who wasn't there. Not because you don't want to, but because you know you yourself will never fully understand it."

"Can you work?"

"Yes, sir. I am ready for work."

Marwood lawed out most of that remaining year in Tomah, seeing Carlene sporadically. They continued to share a room at the hotel, but Carlene had taken another across town. When Marwood got word of Clete Stride once again moving through the territory, he went back to Carlene and told her how it must be.

"I am going after your husband," he said.

She let out a shuddering breath. "I guess I know what for." Her face was white as sacking flour. The only other time he saw her this upset was when he came back from the Mandans, broken and carved up.

"He will kill you," she warned.

"Or I, him." Marwood stood in the dull light of their bedroom window. Across the street were the charred timbers of a saloon. The fire had trapped twenty people inside. Sometimes, after a hard rain, their white bones were seen poking up through the black ashes.

It was not the first time Stride had visited Tomah before his warrant. In the past, before Marwood visited the Mandan village, Carlene had gone to live with Clete for the month or two he remained in town. He was, after all, her lawful husband. When Clete left again for the killing fields, she moved back to the hotel room she shared with Marwood.

In truth Marwood did not care at the time. He had no real call on Carlene, or she him. Having Stride visit his wife a few months out of the year worked no great hardship on Marwood, and he welcomed the arrangement. Carlene could be a catawhomper at times. He didn't mind the breathing space.

This time, however, it was different. Since his return Marwood had strong evidence Stride tried to murder a man on the high prairie, and had stolen his hides. As far as Judge Creighton was concerned, when Marwood first presented the case to him it was enough to hang the turd.

"I can't have him in my backbearing the rest of my life, Carlene," Marwood told her. "Not if you and I are going to be together."

Carlene had a bowl of cotton on the table in her room. She kept it there to remind her where she came from, and where she never wanted to return.

"I'm afraid what might happen to you," she told him.

"I've tracked and brought in men before."

"Not like Clete, you haven't." She stopped picking at the cotton bolls and swallowed her fear. "Is that what you want? For us to be together?"

"I think so. Don't you?"

"Yes," she said. "I do. But I'm not convinced it's what you need right now. I don't know if I am what you need right now."

"After I bring Stride in I want you to move back to my hotel room," he told her.

"All right," her voice was meek. "I'll do that, John."

That afternoon he packed his war bag and had the livery stable saddle his horse and bring it around to the hotel.

Carlene stood on the wooden boardwalk with a purple parasol. She had been crying. He kissed her.

"I will be back when I can," he promised.

"You are never coming back." She looked into his flint-grey eyes. "We both know it."

"I want you to have something." He took the locket Quillen had given him and pressed it into her gloved hand. "I picked it up a long time ago, before I did any real lawing. Been waiting to give it to the right girl."

She closed her hand tight, held it to her breast. Her nose was red from the tears. "Where can I reach you?" she asked.

"I will let you know where I land." He took the reins of his horse, a flaxen gelding with a dark mane, and mounted.

Carlene put her hand on his left arm. "Be careful. The snows fall heavily in the passes this time of year."

He squeezed her fingers. "Goodbye, Carlene."

"Goodbye, John."

He pulled out of Tomah leading a packhorse. When he got halfway down the uneven dirt lane he looked back. Carlene waved. He lifted his hand in return.

That night he made camp in the foothills of the Boulder Mountains. He crouched beside an outlaw's fire drinking black coffee. Night sounds filled the cold, frosty country. The stars were thick dust on crushed black.

He felt civilization slough off his shoulders.

In the morning he broke camp, kicked out the fire, and rode. When he reached Platte Bridge Station he learned he had missed Clete Stride by a week.

"He pushed south," one of the soldiers said. "Killed a whiskey drummer before he left. They say he's got a Mexican woman down in Nogales he cut up pretty bad. But she stays with her sister now."

Marwood sent a telegram to the sheriff in Nogales and rode off.

In Laramie he saw churches, schools, and neat painted houses. At the terminal of the Union Pacific Railroad he found another telegram waiting for him. It was from Nogales. Clete had a small *estancia* used to run cold brands on stolen Mexican cattle. The sheriff down there was keeping an eye on the woman spoken of. Marwood replied that he was on his way.

During the first week of February, 1874, he was riding along the Cache La Poudre River, watching white water spill over black rock, when he came round a wooded bend and caught three men killing Cheyennes.

He rode up on them out of a tree break. The trees were leafed out and he remained hidden. He watched as they were cutting up the last woman—she was very pregnant. One of the men ripped her swollen belly open with a hog knife. He pulled out a wobbling fetus by one leg. It was pink-purple in the high morning light. The wrinkled umbilical cord stretched to the girl lying on the ground.

She was alive—barely—and begged for her baby. The man, little more than a thirteen-year-old with bowl-cut hair and the sloe eyes of a cretin, laid the baby on the ground. He stomped its head with his hobnailed boot.

The woman screamed. Another man cut her throat to shut her up. The cretin carried the baby toward an iron spit on the campfire.

All this happened in the fifteen seconds it took Marwood to ride clear of the slender trees. He turned his horse broadside. It nickered and whisked its tail.

The men were so busy debauching and killing they hadn't seen him until he halted his horse.

"What are you boys doing?" he called.

They froze, looked at one another in confusion. One spat between his feet. "Killing these here Cheyennes for their horse."

Marwood looked at the five dead bodies in the grass, and the sleek pony staked out and grazing five rods away.

"You boys jumped them from this same break I rode out of," Marwood said.

"You take it right," the first man replied. He had long hair, and white knife scars webbed his arms. His teeth were gone; he gummed his words when he spoke. "They was so busy resting they horse, they didn't see us steal up in their shadow."

"It was a regular hog killing," the second man said. He bent down and cut away a scalp from an old dead man. The scalp dripped from his hand. "They's plenty here, if'n you want," he called.

The first man pointed a knobbed stick he used as a shillelagh at Marwood. He had a pocket revolver in a Mexican carry, tucked up front in his waistband. "Mayhap you come down off that big horse," he said. "I don't like the way you rode up on us like a bandit."

The second man squinted. "Hey, that's right. You acting all high hat like you law, or something."

"I was badged in Montana Territory."

The first man laughed. "You are out of your corral."

"I am a federal marshal, and you boys done ran out your string."

Marwood shot the leader with the knobbed stick and gun. The other two scattered like frightened quail.

Marwood lung-shot the second man through his back. The killer crawled the short grass thirty feet until blood filled his air pipe and he drowned.

At the first sign of trouble, the small cretin took off like a roadrunner across the flat prairie. He clutched the hog knife in his fist like a totem.

Marwood chucked his horse forward into a canter. The little boy was running flat out. Marwood's horse caught him, paced him.

The boy looked through his sweaty blond hair. He was smart enough to run, but too ignorant to jink under Marwood's horse and buy himself more time.

Marwood thumbed the hammer back on his pistol and shot him through the head.

He pulled up and stepped off his horse, took the boy's scalp. Then he mounted up, brought the horse around, and walked it back to where the dead Cheyenne Indians lay.

He picked up and put the family side by side. He took the baby and placed it in the dead mother's arms. Their belongings had been strewn over the prairie. He found blankets and covered them.

When he finished, he cut the scalps from the other two murderers, and hanged them, dripping, off his saddlebow.

In Pueblo he rented a room for the night. He had a hot bath, and while sitting in the soapy tub he examined the white Mandan scars on his body.

The next morning he walked from the *posada* to the town marshal's office.

"Stride? That son of a bitch is dead," the marshal said. He was a lean man with short black hair and a walrus moustache. He carried a ten-gauge shotgun and wore a purple paisley vest, blue twill jacket, rumpled trousers, and a wide-awake hat.

"Where is he?"

"Buried out on Chicken Hill, back of the sawmill."

"How did he die?"

"Smallpox. Caught it from the Pawnee while riding through Wyoming Territory. Two antelope hunters brought his body in from Fountain Creek way."

"Show me."

They walked down the long street and ducked between a row of buildings to reach a back pasture choked with scrub and bloodweed.

"Where have you been lawing, mister?" the town marshal asked.

"Tomah."

"Where?"

"Tomah. Montana Territory."

"Where the hell is Tomah?"

"It's off the Prickly Pear valley," Marwood explained.

"You mean Helena, don't you?"

"It was called Tomah while I was there," Marwood said.

"Mister, it ain't never been called Tomah."

The town marshal led him up a bare slope of loose shale. They stopped at a grave with an iron bedstead for a marker.

"There he lies."

"Dig him up," Marwood said.

The town marshal choked back a snort. "Like hell I will. He can rot."

"I am a federal officer. I order you to dig up this body so I can identify it. Otherwise, I will submit your name to Judge Creighton for blocking an official investigation."

"Judge Creighton? Judge Samuel *Buford* Creighton?"

"The same."

"I heard about that fucker. Whole back country's heard of him."

"Yes," Marwood said. "He's a bastard, and so am I."

The town marshal hired two men to dig up the grave. They lifted the body wrapped in sixteen-ounce duck canvas, choking back their vomit as green putrefaction dripped from the head and feet of the corpse.

"Unwrap him."

They did and backed away, handkerchiefs pressed to their mouths, eyes watering from the rot fumes.

Marwood knelt beside the dead man. He got back to his feet.

"Not him," he said.

"What do you mean that's not him?" the town marshal asked.

"Clete Stride has his right hand, not a stump. He pulled one over on you, Marshal. Probably paid those hunters to bring in this here beggar." He looked around the spare field. "Where is Lewis Spaw buried at?"

"Under that scrag bush, yonder."

Spaw had a wooden peg hammered into the ground for his marker. Marwood walked over and looked at it a long time. He could smell the wild sage and cilantro from the surrounding fields.

"I thank you for offering me your dun horse," he said low.

He stood another long minute, and turned away.

CHAPTER 27

Ninety-seven days after leaving Montana Territory, John Marwood rode into Nogales, Arizona, on the Feast of Saint Valentine, 1874.

A group of lawmen waited for his arrival outside a Wells Fargo bank. They sat under black walnut trees lining the main street, smoking cigarettes and eyeing Marwood with resistant stares.

"You got the warrant?" the sheriff of Santa Cruz County said.

Marwood tapped his coat pocket. "Right here."

The sheriff held out his hand. "Let's see it."

Marwood tossed it down. He waited for the sheriff to verify his legal authorization to take possession of Clete Stride.

The sheriff folded the warrant and handed it back. "I'd rather jail Stride here."

"Take that up with Judge Creighton," Marwood said. "He figures he's making enough concessions having Stride rot in Yuma territorial prison instead of hanging him in Montana Territory."

"What did Stride do in Montana Territory?"

"Shot an Indian buffalo hunter."

"Hell, is that all? Stride's been running stolen cattle across the Mexican border down here every winter. He'll steal them in Arizona, sell them in Mexico, then steal them back and sell them with a running brand to the United States Army."

Marwood stuffed the official warrant back into his rough pile coat. He folded his hands over the saddle horn and stared at the sheriff. “Not my problem,” he said.

The sheriff viewed Marwood with increasing suspicion. He had seen the scalps hanging from his saddle and they unsettled him.

“You rode damn near a thousand miles to take Stride to Yuma prison?” he asked.

“Yes, I did, Sheriff. Now are we going to bring this man in, or jerk our pizzles here in the street?”

“He’s out there,” the sheriff said. “Let’s go get him tomorrow morning.”

They went out early morning and rode abreast onto the property mentioned. It was a poor *estancia* abutting the Santa Cruz River. To the west were the cactus-encrusted flanks of the Sierrita Mountains, and farther on from that a long blue line of cordilleras.

They moved for position through thorn brush and chaparral while the sky lightened behind them. The house was mud-adobe, with a low sagging ceiling and a tin pipe for a chimney.

They burst through the front door. A Mexican woman stood bare legged in the *cocina* lighting a wood-burning *chimenea*. She turned from the clay stove with the lucifer smoking in her hand.

The sheriff shot her through the breast. She slumped against a clay comal, upsetting a water jug. Marwood had already turned at the door and moved at angle for the only other entryway in the room.

Beyond the open doorway was a small bedroom. A man’s legs were miserably tangled in the yellowed bed sheets. He was trying to get to his feet and reach a loaded gun on the dresser.

Marwood kicked Stride’s legs out from under him. The man

sat heavily on the floor in his long drawers, his hair tousled.

Marwood looked down at the man. Stride had a blunt face and heavy jowls. His eyes were brown, hair thinning.

"I have to agree with the sheriff," he told Stride. "Riding a thousand miles to kick your stumbling ass out of bed was hardly worth it."

Stride was held in *cárcel* for two weeks. This went a long way to salving the sheriff's pride while the legal paperwork was routed through official channels.

On the last day, Marwood took custody of his prisoner. He had a horse waiting for Stride.

The sheriff met him outside and the prisoner was formally exchanged.

"Do you mean to say you're not taking a stage to Yuma?" the sheriff asked incredulously.

"I'd rather ride it," Marwood said.

"It's across the Sonoran Desert."

Marwood had had enough of this punctilious government man. "I thank you for your help, Sheriff," he said. "You can get back to sitting under your walnut tree and smoking cigarettes. Let's go, Stride. You got prison chains waiting on you in Yuma."

"You are the most uncompromising sonofabitch I have ever had the displeasure to meet," the sheriff told Marwood. "I will be glad to see the back of you."

"I appreciate the compliment."

Marwood touched his hat brim with his forefinger. He and Stride rode out of the city of Nogales. The sheriff watched them leave.

Marwood had Stride manacled on a black mare outfitted with a wooden saddle hull. Stride's hands were locked tight behind his back. Iron chains ran through eyelets on the saddle to a thick iron ring around his waist.

Stride complained about the primitive saddle. “This iron gets too hot in the sun. I'm blistering up terrible.”

“Your comfort is no concern of mine,” Marwood told the prisoner. “Remember, you decide to run, I will put a ball in your back.”

“I can't run nowhere in these here iron chains.”

“That's the only thing keeping you alive,” Marwood promised him.

They camped under cottonwood trees at the Quitobaquito Springs. Stride said, “Carlene sent me a wire you was coming. I take it she wanted me to dry gulch you. Had every intention of doing so, but you were so long in showing up I figured you to give up on me.”

Marwood wasn't particularly surprised Carlene had tried to warn Stride. “Long in coming?”

Stride nodded. “That sheriff was right about you. You are hard to figure out. Most men would stage down from Montana Territory. Even out to Yuma. I got tired of waiting on you, mister.”

“I'd rather do things my way,” Marwood said.

They rode through a broad reach of Joshua trees. The land was hard and stark, and the distant crumpled-paper hills riffled in the growing heat. A *polvo diablo* blew through their path, whipping their clothes and horses. It moved across the bleak desert, an undulating spindle of whirling sand, flake rock, and cactus needles.

Ten miles out of Yuma Marwood stopped at a natural *hueco* to water the horses. He let Stride off his horse for a piss break. His hands were cuffed in front of his body.

When Stride returned from the saguaro he had visited he saw Marwood sitting his horse, a gun in his hand.

“I figured it would be like that,” Stride said.

“You figured right.” Marwood rolled the hammer back.

“Is this here about Carlene?” Stride asked.

Marwood thought. "It's a lot of things, Stride. Half of which you could never guess."

"I ain't crawling on my hands and knees for you, Marshal. You and every motherless lawman can suck a pig's tit."

Marwood levelled the gun. His finger tightened on the trigger.

Ten miles away, on the clear open desert air . . . he heard bells. Church bells peal from the town of Yuma. The tiniest toll of ringing brass. But there was no other sound in the desert clear that could have stopped him at that moment.

Marwood holstered his gun. "Get on your horse, Stride. Lock those cuffs back around your waist or I'll kneecap you with a rock."

Stride opened his mouth, closed it. He licked his dry, sun-blistered lips. "You ain't going to burn powder on me?"

Marwood looked at the bright desert and listened to the bells. "No," he said. "They've granted you a pardon."

There were three telegrams waiting for him in Yuma.

TRANSFERRED NEW MEXICO TERRITORY STOP TAKING YOU WITH ME STOP NO LONGER DEPUTY MADE FULL MARSHAL CONFIRMED U.S. WAR DEPARTMENT STOP

The wire was dated seventeen days ago. The next was more recent. It read:

EXPECT YOU STAGE YUMA HYPHEN MESILLA FOLLOWING PRISONER REMANDED YUMA PRISON STOP AWAIT INSTRUCTIONS STOP

The last wire had missed Marwood by a single day. It had come in while he was out on the desert wide, listening to the bells:

NEW POST HAXAN STOP SANGRE COUNTY STOP
MEET YOU THERE COMMA GOOD WORK STOP

Marwood sold his horse and took the Butterfield Stagecoach Line to Mesilla on the government's dime. The coach stopped outside the La Posta Compound within the week.

Marwood stepped off the stage with the other coach passengers. He strode wearily across the dusty plaza, working his way stiffly through the Camino Real freight caravans, which had shut down for the night. He walked through a massive wooden gate with his war bag.

The sky burned late fire—a waxing moon. The Organ and San Andres Mountains bracketed the bustling border town like the arms of a sleeping giant.

He followed a *zaguán* into a wide patio with green plants and dribbling water fountains. Three Mexican children husked corn in a corner of the patio. He asked for a table and was taken into the main restaurant.

A waiter brought over a chalkboard with the night's menu. Marwood ordered *porcina* and *frijoles*.

"*Qué quieres tomar,* señor?"

"*Café, por favor.*"

The waiter poured his coffee and Marwood looked up. And there, across the room's divide, sat Captain Botis, watching him with summer eyes.

PART VII

. . . the Ashes of the West

CHAPTER 28

Marwood stood beside the table. "Captain," he said. "Have a seat."

Marwood scraped a chair out, sat at the other end of the rounded table with his gun hand clear of the wall.

The waiter caught up to him and brought his meal. Botis worked on his own plate of fried turkey and greens.

"What brings you to Mesilla?" Botis asked.

"I was going to ask you the same thing," Marwood said. "We didn't get to many towns when we were riding together."

"No," Botis agreed. "We did not have the opportunity." He scrutinized Marwood's face, his clothes. "I heard you took the badge up north."

"Yes, I did."

"How far you willing to ride that river?" Botis waited.

"You are a wanted man, Captain. There is paper out on you."

"Son, you and I are beyond the simplicity of paper," Botis said.

"Yes," Marwood agreed, "I believe that is so. What are you doing here in Mesilla, Captain?"

"I had to be here. It was ordained."

Both men bent to their plates and ate. After he finished eating Botis lighted a black cigarillo. He sat with one hand on the table and the other on his knee.

"Let me ask you something," he said. The cigarillo was cocked between his fingers. "Why did you ride with me?"

Marwood's voice was thick with reflection. "Because I liked it," he said. "It was the one time I remember being truly happy. When we were killing our horses and drinking their blood on the Llano, I was content."

Botis nodded. "Yes, even then. I saw that light in you the first time we met." He plucked the pince-nez spectacles from his vest pocket, squared them on the bridge of his nose with his accustomed ease. "But, now when I look at you, I see a wholly different man. A man I do not recognize." His voice was without warmth. Not accusatory so much as evaluative.

"I suppose I have changed in ways," Marwood allowed. "I won't say they're all for the better."

A young man began to play a Spanish guitar on the far side of the restaurant. The song was "Lágrima." Men stood around him, listening to the music, keeping their thoughts to themselves. One of the men wiped his eyes.

Botis turned from the scene. "Every man's life whittles down to a point," he said. "When a man is at this crossroads he has to decide whether he goes forward or back. It is a decision every man must face at least once in his life, if he wants to be considered a man. Most men choose the easy path. It is a choice they regret when they are sitting alone in a darkened room and the weight of their decision has them by the throat."

The young man on the guitar played an arpeggiated minor chord. A woman who worked at the restaurant climbed up on a chair and began to sing a sad *corrido*. The man who had been crying was now smiling.

"Then there are those men who choose the second path," Botis said. "These are the men history remembers, or the men who write the histories themselves. But there are yet other men. Men like you and men like me. Those men who don't choose paths. Men who never turn back or go forward but stand in one place and challenge all who come before them. And it is from these challenges, and these successes, that the paths other men take are made. Without these men there are no paths to be had, no choices to make. Do you understand what I am saying?"

"I think so."

"Yes, I believe you do." Botis flicked ash and drew on his small cigar. "It's a shame we cannot ride together like we used to. They have all gone under. Did you ever notice how everyone in my company started dying when you came aboard?" He stubbed the cigarillo out. "So turns the world into kingdom night."

"You still have that horse?" Marwood asked.

Botis wiped his mouth with a napkin. He folded it, placed it aside, and rose from the table. "Yes. Acheron awaits our presence."

They walked side by side, turning the corner at the Corn Exchange Hotel. Then they followed a dirt street past the Basilica of San Albino and down a winding path edged with ocotillo, purple nopal, and sporadic clumps of wiregrass. Moonlight glittered on the quiet *acequias* while bats flitted between the stars.

At last they went through a squeaky iron gate and entered a quiet cemetery.

Cairn headstones and iron bedsteads served as markers for most of the unknown graves. They were out a ways from the central plaza of Mesilla. Someone had been burning leaves during the day; the wind had taken the ashes and scoured them all over the graveyard. It was peaceful yet somber, the way it always is in the desert wide when men are prepared to die.

"I love this land," Botis said. "My God, I love it with my life."

Acheron, blue marble carved, stood under the pale moonlight, swishing his tail back and forth. His eyes were black fathomless pits. He shook his head and the metal bits of his bridle jingled. Botis had unsaddled the horse; it rested at the foot of an unmarked headstone.

They walked up on a freshly dug grave. Botis removed his hat and threw it onto the turned mound of earth. He started to undress. Marwood did the same.

Botis stripped to his waist. His fat muscles were like stones beneath his oil-sweat skin. Marwood glimpsed the running brand scrawled across his back—a single word of lingua lost in time. A name unspeakable; an ancient power.

He saw Marwood's scars. "Ah," he said, "now I understand. So does the circle close upon two Lone Men."

Both stripped to just their trousers and boots. Botis pulled his knife. The blade gleamed. Marwood flicked out his skinning knife and locked the blade.

"Do you think you are the only man to come west, searching for something he lost?" Botis asked.

"No," Marwood answered. "But I have found it now."

"Then let us down into the killing bottle."

Botis jumped into the open grave. Marwood followed him. Their world turned into a rectangle of scarred earth, dangling cactus roots. Night-sky black, powdered with star frost.

There wasn't much room for killing, but killing was all they had left between them. Botis lunged. Marwood parried the thrust with the haft of his knife. He raked at the eyes of the man with the nails of his left hand. Botis leapt back to avoid being blinded. Loose sand and rock spilled from the sides of the grave, and choked them both.

They slammed into each other and grappled. On the desert, Marwood had watched two Gila monsters fight each other to the death—black and red beaded bodies, their limbs straining, lungs pumping, each waiting for the other combatant to tire under the grueling sun.

That's how Marwood and Botis fought. They remained

locked and intertwined at the bottom of the grave as if frozen in amber—one man lying half on top of the other, legs wrapped and straining, arms struggling to hold knives away from heart and throat. Sand spilled from the edge of the grave—a coarse rain. There was no air. Botis moved an inch, seeking an opening. Marwood counter-moved, tried to shift his weight to leverage his arm under Botis's throat. Botis used a knee to anchor himself against the grave wall, fend off the attack, and avert disaster.

They were dying for want of air, and both men knew it—they were already half-buried as it was. Primitive instinct, the great leveller of science and reason, took hold in a sudden frenzy of will. They became snarling, circling demons lying in the bottom of the black grave, with wintry things awakened full in their hearts, roaring and uncoiling in hell-flame fury. In paired nisus they fought while the window of life narrowed along twin lines of convergence.

Marwood scraped his elbow along the rough edge of the grave wall above Botis's head. Sand spilled into the captain's eyes. His grip loosed a fraction, and Marwood's knife slipped and went in, deep, went in again, and stayed.

Blood welled in Botis's mouth. "My boy . . . my boy," he said.

Marwood lurched to his feet, hands on either side of the collapsing grave. He tried to keep the walls from calving in and burying them both. He stepped on Botis's chest and jumped and grabbed the crumbling edge as earth spilled around his body with a hiss.

He was out, rolled, and gasped air into his burning lungs. He was like a thing crawled from earth, dead.

The grave finished collapsing in a depression of rock and fine sand.

Marwood sat back with his hands resting on his knees, head down. He coughed, breathed, coughed again, and drew sweet air into his wracked lungs.

He still gripped the knife. One by one, he loosened his fingers from the weapon. His arms and legs streamed blood runnels. The old Okipa scars had opened up—stigmata to mark his past and waypoint his future.

He got to his feet when he thought he could stand without falling over. Acheron watched him across the open field of buried, nameless dead. Marwood walked up to the blue roan. It shied away, shaking its head and snorting with alarm. Marwood talked to it, called its name, tried to get close to it and catch the reins.

Every time he drew near the big horse lifted its startled head and shied off.

Marwood went to the saddle. He dug through the preserved scalps and human skulls piled on top, found a coil of rope. He tied it into a *reata*.

He came back, swinging the noose in a gentle arc, and spoke to the animal again, called it by name. Acheron lifted his startled head, ears perked. Marwood threw the rope, and the lasso fell around the horse's neck. He tightened the noose and pivoted with the horse as it ran in a circle around him. He jerked up the slack and the noose crimped. Acheron's eyes were terror wild—mane flying, tail uplifted.

Marwood wrapped the rope around the unknown headstone and, using it as a snubbing post, continued to choke the horse with the noose while it ran around him in ever tightening circles. He was merciless in how he drove the animal into the ground. Eventually Acheron, out of wind, rolled onto his side, chest barely heaving, neck outstretched as an offering. Marwood took up the rest of the slack, coiling the free end of the rope, and stood on the final yard. Acheron kicked his long legs, tried to get up, failed.

When the horse was near dead Marwood loosened the rope all the way. He knelt down and placed his mouth over the horse's nostrils. He blew air into its nose.

A second time.

A third.

The horse bolted to its feet in a wild thrash of dirt. It stood, legs trembling like twanging cords, its blue coat covered with splotches of white lather.

Marwood stroked its ears and nose. He spoke to it. The horse cooled, and became gentle. He stroked its forehead and muzzle, patted its withers.

"Acheron."

The horse whickered and swished his tail.

CHAPTER 29

Marwood rode out of Mesilla. On the road past the last *acequia* he spotted a lone telegraph pole where the wires had been hacked down. A dead man hung from the pole without his boots. His neck was elongated, his face corrupted with black blood.

He hung, a motionless strawman in the gloam. Marwood looked at him a moment, chucked the horse forward.

He took the San Augustin Pass through the Organ Mountains, and when he came out the other side he saw the lights of a small town sparkling in a low, fertile valley. He was so high in the mountains the lights of the town twinkled like remote stars. Far, far away, they were the lightest dust imaginable, yellow-white pinpricks clustered in the dark.

And when he saw the lights, he knew them for the place he would live, and the place he would die.

Then, sitting Acheron, he saw Cibola for the fourth, and last time in his life.

Gold pillars climbed from black desert. Long walls of ivory staked with onyx spheres. Shimmering, like an incandescent fever dream. The madness of men, and the caution they bring to the world as they war and battle for supremacy. Eternal, until that which is wrong is set right, and a man can stand alone, free, and unfettered by time.

Marwood thought back to the lost canyon. The Llano Estacado. Bozeman Pass. Sangre Valley. In that quaternity he saw the circle travelled, and knew why he had been brought here.

He could either go forward or go back. The choice lay before him.

The city melted away, carried off by desert winds. Marwood rode another mile and came to a trading post fashioned of adobe brick and mountain stone. He tied his horse and went inside.

The storekeeper who owned the trading post glanced up from a stack of green hides he was notching. He took in Marwood's drab appearance in the weak glow of a tallow candle—one of dust and blood, and the ashes of the west.

"Help you, mister?" he asked.

"I am riding through the desert. I need beans and salt. Powder and lead, if you have it."

"Sure thing." The man gathered up the order. As he did, he cast sidelong glances at Marwood, taking in his duds, his soiled face, and his hands covered with blood and powdered with grave dirt.

The storekeeper laid the goods on the counter with care. Marwood looked it over and paid for the supplies before exiting. He packed his purchases in the saddlebags and mounted Acheron.

The trader followed him out.

"Mister," he said, "if you don't mind, what caused you to walk into my store in such a condition?"

Marwood gathered the leather reins through his hands.

"I was burying a friend," he said.

EPILOGUE

The old man stopped by the graveyard to rest. Upon doing so, he spied a basin of sand in the middle of the cemetery. He went through the open gate and walked toward it, stiff-legged, for the burden on his back was incredibly heavy and he was very, very old.

He stopped beside the strange hollow in the ground. Slowly, so he would not fall himself, he slipped the wide leather straps off his aching shoulders and put the salt barrel down.

He sank to his knees, an attitude of forlorn prayer. He took a deep breath.

Then he bent forward, and started to dig with his bare hands.

ABOUT THE AUTHOR

Kenneth Mark Hoover is a professional writer living in Dallas, TX. He has sold over sixty short stories and is a member of SFWA, HWA, and WWA. His fiction has appeared in *Beneath Ceaseless Skies*, *Ellery Queen's Mystery Magazine*, *Strange Horizons*, and others. You can read more at kennethmarkhoover.com or follow his blog at kennethmarkhoover.me or follow him on Twitter @kmarkhoover.

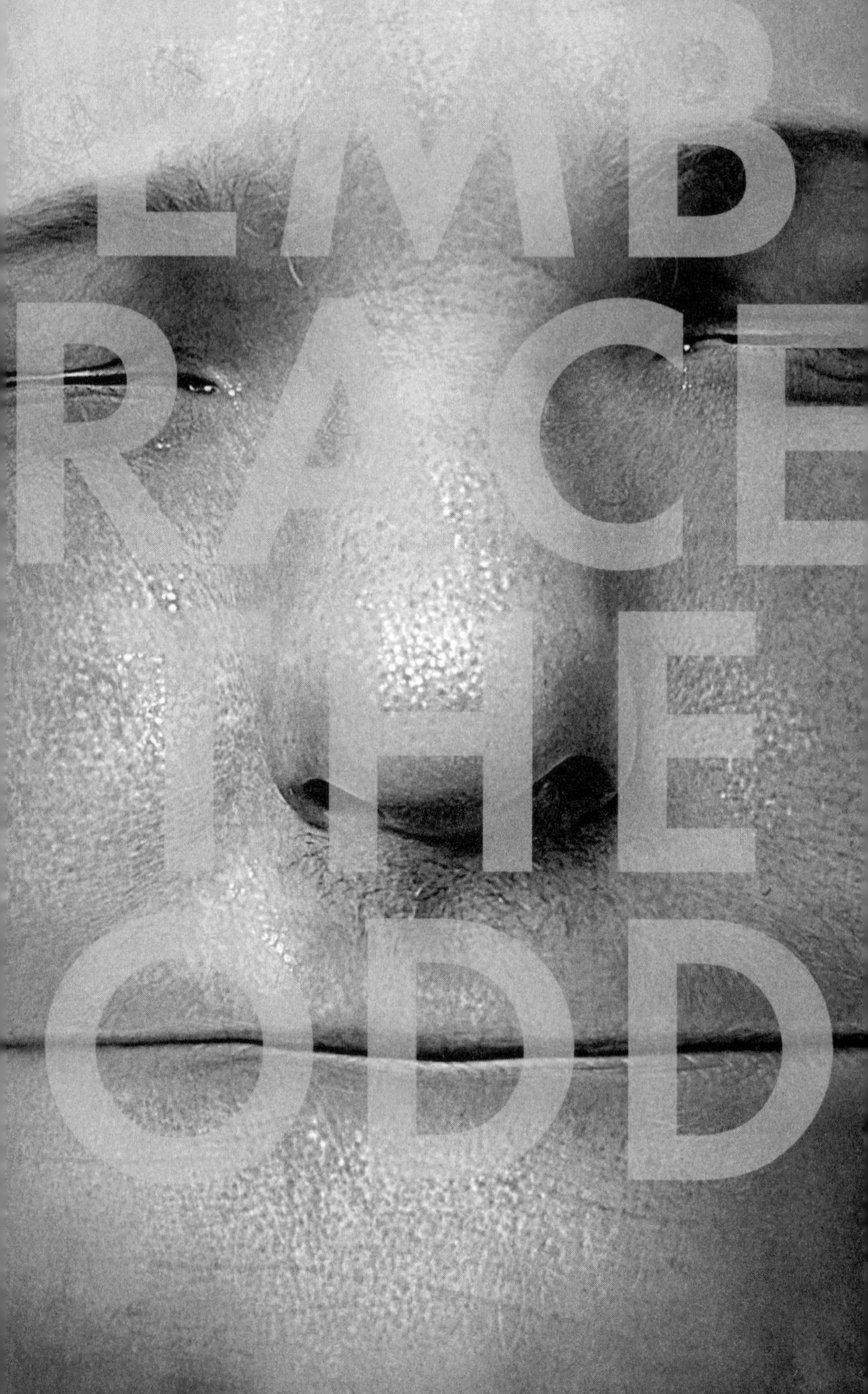
EMB
RACE
THE
ODD

HAXAN

KENNETH MARK HOOVER

Thermopylae. Masada. Agincourt. And now, Haxan, New Mexico Territory, circa 1874. Through a sea of time and dust, in places that might never be, or can't become until something is set right, there are people destined to travel. Forever. Marshal John T. Marwood is one of these men. Taken from a place he called home, he is sent to fight an eternal war. It never ends, because the storm itself, this unending conflict, makes the world we know a reality. Along with all the other worlds waiting to be born. Or were born, but died like a guttering candle in eternal night . . . *Haxan* is the first in a series of novels. "*Lonesome Dove* meets *The Punisher* . . . real, gritty, violent, and blatantly uncompromising."

AVAILABLE NOW

ISBN 978-1-77148-175-5

THE HEXSLINGER SERIES

GEMMA FILES

BOOK ONE: A BOOK OF TONGUES

ISBN 978-0-9812978-6-6

BOOK TWO: A ROPE OF THORNS

ISBN 978-1-926851-14-3

BOOK THREE: A TREE OF BONES

ISBN 978-1-926851-57-0

ALSO AVAILABLE FROM CHIZINE PUBLICATIONS

THE ACOLYTE

NICK CUTTER

Jonah Murtag is an Acolyte on the New Bethlehem police force. His job: eradicate all heretical religious faiths, their practitioners, and artefacts. Murtag's got problems—one of his partners is a zealot, and he's in love with the other one. Trouble at work, trouble at home. Murtag realizes that you can rob a citizenry of almost anything, but you can't take away its faith.

AVAILABLE NOW

ISBN 978-1-77148-328-5

AGAINST A DARKENING SKY

LAUREN B. DAVIS

A new novel from one of Canada's most acclaimed and celebrated writers, *Against a Darkening Sky* is set in 7th century Northumbria and is full of magic and mystery, Davis's new work explores what happens when one's experience and beliefs clash with those of the people in power.

AVAILABLE NOW

ISBN 978-1-77148-318-6